For: Helen and Dick Renne

Published by Lotus Press,
Moto-Azabu 2-10-10, Minato-ku, Tokyo, Japan

Cover by Akira Tsuchiya

LCC Card Number 77-185126
Manufactured in Japan

THE
DARNED NUISANCES

by Jack Seward
and Charles Beardsley

LOTUS PRESS
TOKYO

FOREWORD

With the exception of the late General Douglas A, MacArthur, the characters in this story are fictitious. Several of the happenings, however, are not.

As the American forces were landing in Japan in 1945, large numbers of young Japanese women took to the hills in fear of the lustful attentions of the conquerors. And some, like those in this story, fled for reasons more dramatic and well-founded. Later, after they were persuaded to return to their homes, many of them had occasion to meet these same American men on a more equal footing, after which it became difficult to determine which were the conquerors and which the conquered.

The Chikugo River and the resort town of Oguni are real, as are the formidable honey-tanks, eel traps, and the Japanese fondness for the taste of eel. All of the exotic foods described herein are gourmet dishes actually served in Japan, although admittedly rice and pickled vegetables comprise the bulk of the daily fare.

About one thousand Americans—like the three main characters in this tale—were trained at the Japanese language school at the University of Michigan during the war for duty in the Pacific Theater and for later assignments in Japan with MacArthur's staff sections, including the Military Government Teams. One of the authors went through this language training program and was stationed in Fukuoka shortly after the end of the war. When asked to what extent this story is autobiographical, however, he refuses to make any comment—and a distant look comes into his eyes.

As for the surgical operation around which the climax is centered, a Japanese gynecologist-turned-plastic surgeon, Dr. Kohei Matsukubo, has perfected such a technique and has by now performed many thousands of these operations successfully. The procedure is exactly as described herein.

The Buddhist clergy may not be as permissive as suggested in this story, but it cannot be denied that they are much more tolerant of man's vices—if that is the proper word—than most of their Western counterparts.

General MacArthur's indirect involvement in these events is, of course, cut from whole cloth. Nor did he have a brother who attended Annapolis. At least, not that we know of.

The Publisher

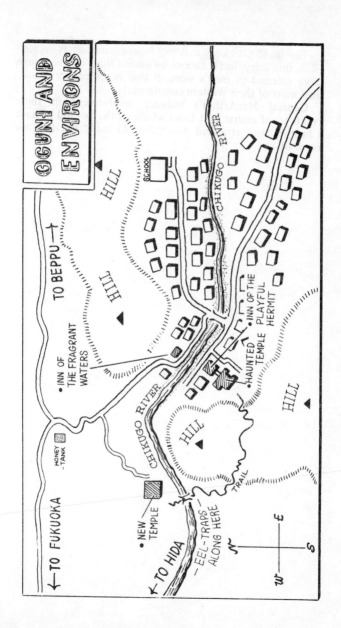

OGUNI AND ENVIRONS

TO FUKUOKA

TO BEPPU →

HILL

HILL

HILL

SCHOOL

CHIKUGO RIVER

INN OF
THE FRAGRANT
WATERS

HONEY-
TANK

CHIKUGO RIVER

INN OF
THE PLAYFUL
HERMIT

HAUNTED
TEMPLE

HILL

HILL

NEW
TEMPLE

TO HIDA →

TRAIL

EEL-TRAPS
ALONG HERE

N

S

W

E

CHAPTER ONE

"Ah swear Ah'm gonna get me one of them *geisha* gals an' sack out for a *whole* year," True vowed in a tight voice.

"You and your infernal satyriasis!" said Chauncey severely.

"Mah *what*?"

"Satyriasis," explained the scholarly Chauncey, "is a state of excessive and persistent tumescence in the phallus."

"Huh?" asked True, the awareness in his eyes fading back to another age.

"Chauncey just means that you're horny, True," explained Sam kindly.

"Uh? Oh, yeah," said True, looking reassured and somewhat pleased.

"And I agree with Chauncey that it would be better if you did have more than one level of consciousness. . . . besides sex, that it is."

"Can Ah help it if Ah. . . ."

"Never mind," Sam said. "Besides, we gotta start thinking about where to spend the night. I sure as hell don't want to have to sleep out here in the rice-paddies."

It was early September of 1945. The battered Army jeep was carrying three young American lieutenants from Beppu to Fukuoka, on Japan's southern island of Kyushu. The tallest of the three was Chauncey MacArthur, a son of grape-growers in Fresno, California. The one of medium size was Sam Bruce, who had survived a Chicago ghetto upbringing without too many permanent scars. And the shortest and most compact was Truman Foote—commonly called True—from Escambia County, Alabama.

Their long months in an Army Japanese language school and their later experiences as combat interrogation officers in the Pacific Theater had welded them, despite their wide differences in background, into a functioning—although not always harmonious—unit.

Their first assignment with the 341st Military Government Team in Fukuoka had been to cross Kyushu by jeep and contact their opposite numbers at the M.G. Team in Beppu, which they had just done. The ink was scarcely dry on the *Missouri* surrender document, Nagasaki was still in radioactive ruins, and Allied units were moving rapidly into all of defeated Japan's islands.

The three lieutenants had first driven around the northern perimeter of the island's coast to Beppu, intending to cut straight back across Kyushu to their Fukuoka base, but a few miles out of Beppu the trans-Kyushu highway was obliterated by bomb damage, so they were forced to wander off through the rice-paddies in a southwesterly direction. Three hours later they were still following a narrow road that climbed up and down low verdant hills bordering the rice plain, dipping occasionally into the lowland paddies and vegetable plots. Whenever they passed through the cultivated areas, the air became suffused with a powerful odor.

"For chrissake," growled Sam Bruce, his homely face and sharp eyes a study in magnified revulsion, "what's that godawful stench?"

"Honey-tanks, of course," said Chauncey MacArthur of the fair complexion and aristocratic features. He sat in back with his long legs wrapped around a huge Quartermaster cooking pot in which cans of beer, ice, and water sloshed to the erratic rhythm of the bouncing jeep.

"Don't smell like any honey Ah ever ate!" countered Truman Foote, whose thick Alabama accent emanated oddly from a face that would have been more at home along the Texas-Mexico border. He stoutly denied, however, his friends' repeated allegations that his paternal grandmother had been seduced by a strolling Spanish guitar player.

"You've both got sieves for minds," said Chauncey. "Don't you remember that lesson in our Yamanuma textbooks about night-soil and honey-tanks?"

Sam, who was driving, apparently did, but with regret. "Yeah, I think I do, now that you mention it. It talked about shortages of—uh, chemical fertilizers in wartime and how the Japanese save their night-soil in tanks in the fields and after it ferments, they pour it over rice-shoots and young vegetables."

"Night-soil?" repeated True blankly.

"Human feces," supplied Sam, grinning his habitual lop-sided grin. "Excrement, ordure, sewage, dung—or in a word more familiar to you, cornpone—shit."

"Oh, yeah, kinda like we raise mushmelons in cow manure back home in Alabama," said True, unfazed. He had grown accustomed to their needling insinuations, most of which were traceable, he realized, to their resentment against the ease with which things came his way, including girls. Chauncey worked hard for success, and Sam connived, while True dawdled along but got there somehow. . . .and sometimes before the others.

"There's one now!" Chauncey cried, waving his beer can toward a concrete-lined pit by the side of the road. It was filled with a scummy brown liquid on the surface of which fermentation bubbles floated in dreary shy clusters, as if ashamed of where they had allowed themselves to be found.

The jeep swerved as Sam grabbed for his hip-pocket handkerchief and clamped it to his nose. "Christ, you don't have to point," Sam's muffled voice came through his improvised gas mask. "I know where it is."

Chauncey consulted his watch as the jeep bounced on. "Three o'clock. I don't see how we can make it back to Fukuoka before dark. For all we know, we might be driving around in a circle. We could even end up back in Beppu."

"At least we'd have a bed in Beppu," Sam reasoned, "with the M.G. Team."

"Sure, with beautiful Japanese dolls and whiskey and all," said Chaucey with some cynicism, for Japan was lifeless and dreary after the long war years. Nearly all communications were out of order, gasoline shortages kept vehicles off the roads, postal service was desultory at best, restaurants, bars, and stores were closed. Most of the Japanese people huddled fearfully in their homes, expecting annihilation by the Americans at any time. A few braver ones ventured forth into the countryside at night to barter for food with farmers. Kyushu's cities like Fukuoka, Kokura, Moji—and, of course, Nagasaki—presented landscapes of bombed-out desolation. There was so little activity that the countryside appeared uninhabited as well as desolate. Downright spooky, Chauncey decided, for once agreeing with one of True's earthy observations.

Both Chauncey and Sam often wondered how True had finished the Army's Japanese Language School at the University of Michigan. Yet miraculously he had made the grade, and after graduation and commissioning, they had all spent fourteen months with the Allied Translation and Interpretation Service in the Pacific, where their job was extracting tactical intelligence from an occasional POW the American troops managed to capture. With the signing of the surrender they were detailed to new assignments with one of the M.G. Teams that would administer the defeated empire. Banished was more like it, Chauncey thought, as the jeep rolled into a crater-like pothole and then bounced out, lurching crazily for the shoulder of the road.

"Goddam!" True shouted, "there goes our friggin' wheel!"

Chauncey nudged Sam on the shoulder; Sam winked back at him in the rearview mirror. True was up to his old tricks again; he had the South's most fertile—some preferred to call it dank—imagination.

But at that same moment Chauncey happened to glance to the right and saw a lone wheel pacing them on a parallel course about three feet from the jeep. He nudged Sam again, this time with more spirit. "It's a wheel, all right," he bellowed. "Stop the jeep!"

Which was totally unnecessary; the jeep was already skidding to a stop at the side of the road, the naked end of one axle digging itself into the dirt. The wheel rolled impudently on ahead, raising a small cloud of white dust behind it.

Sam cut the ignition off and the trio sat watching in stunned fascination as the wheel followed a rut for ten yards, bounced out and onto a low dike dividing two rice-paddies, and then plunged with a plop and despairing gurgle into a honey-tank full to the brim with abominable brown liquid.

For a moment, they were speechless, but all were thinking the same thing. They had had a flat thirty minutes out of Beppu that morning and had replaced it with their only spare. Thinking that they would be able to take a good paved highway all the way back to Fukuoka and assuming that there would be repair facilities along the way, they had voted against returning to Beppu to have it fixed. Now their grim choice was between walking and retrieving the wheel floating in the honey-tank.

"Shit!" grated True, while Sam and Chauncey agreed that this was an oddly accurate comment.

Recovering his senses, Sam disgustedly climbed out of the jeep and examined the axle for damage. "True probably didn't tighten the lugs enough when we had that other flat two days ago back in Fukuoka," Sam conjectured, glaring at the Alabaman.

"*Ah* didn't have nuthin' to do with it," True vowed. "It musta been the motor pool."

"How're we going to get the wheel out of there?" asked Chauncey, glancing deviously at True.

"Shucks, it should be easy."

"I doubt that."

"Sure," said True, "all you'd have to do is. . . . . ."

"Show us," suggested Sam.

"Me?"

"Scared?"

"Hell, no!"

"Hell, yes, you are," laughed Chauncey, getting out of the jeep himself.

"All right, Ah'll just show you guys."

A bamboo pole lay on the dike leading to the honey-tank, probably left there by a farmer. Grabbing it, True set off briskly for the depository of night-soil.

"He'll never make it," Sam predicted.

"He won't come back smelling like a rose, that's for sure."

True stood on the rim of the odoriferous tank and balanced himself precariously on its narrow footing. Each time he tried to catch the elusive wheel with his pole, the wheel floated away from him. Finally, in angry disgust after several fruitless tries, he reached too far, lost his balance, and plunged headlong into the honey-tank. Wailing as he fell, he disappeared for a long moment in the vile, syrupy liquid, then surfaced filthy, gasping, and clinging to the floating wheel—too scatologically shocked to cry out for help.

Chauncey and Sam ran toward him, trying not to fall

down helpless with laughter and picking up two more bamboo poles on the way.

Gagging and coughing, they somehow fished True out of the tank without getting themselves contaminated. Then they backed away from him as he crawled up on the bank, brown, dripping, and in deep trauma.

One look at their hysterical faces brought True out of his numbness.

"You bastard sons-a-bitches!" he sputtered. "Laugh! Go on and laugh. It didn't happen to you."

"We're not laughing," said Chauncey, choking in an effort not to. "We're just chanting a prayer of thanks. Now what we want you to do is go over to that stream and wash off the wheel and yourself and then meet us back at the jeep."

"You bastards!" True repeated with a snarl. "It's all your fault."

"A little while ago you said it was the motor pool's fault," said Chauncey with restraint. "Go ahead, True, take a dip. It's the only thing you can do unless you want to remain an outcast for life."

Sullenly True stood up, shook himself like an wet dog, and rolled the wheel slowly along the dike toward the banks of the clear stream.

Sam and Chauncey watched him, not daring to even look at each other for fear they'd burst into uncontrollable laughter.

Ten minutes later a somewhat cleaner but still reeking True brought the tire back to the jeep. Lugs were borrowed from the rim of the flat spare tire and soon they were once again on their way. Before they had gone a mile, however, Chauncey complained from the back seat, "I can't sit downwind of True any longer."

Sam stopped the jeep and True dismounted to let Chauncey out. Before Chauncey could leave the vehicle, however, Sam suddenly slammed it into low and gunned off in a cloud of white dust, with True running frantically after them, screaming picturesque obscenities.

"Hold on, Sam," Chauncey said after a moment. "As much as I'd like to, we can't just leave him here."

Reluctantly Sam applied the brakes, letting True catch up with them.

"You. . . .goddam **Yankee**," he swore at Sam, panting and quivering with rage.

This was no time for explanations; they'd only make matters worse. Chauncey moved over to let True climb in back, and off they went. As the jeep bounced along the dirt road over a particularly steep hill, Chauncey said, "You know, I'm kinda worried. . . . . . ." Daylight was beginning to fade. "Even if we do find a hotel, they'll never let True in."

"Sons-a-bitches," growled True.

"You'd better pray," advised Sam, "that you can wash off that odor. Otherwise, they might refuse to let you into the States."

True grinned for the first time since his ducking and pulled at his crotch. "Goddam, that won't be no hardship. We got us a whole country full of poontang right here."

Sam and Chauncey exchanged smiles; they could hardly deny that the possibility existed, once they got the lay of the land. . . . .

It was dusk by the time they spotted a village in a valley several hundred feet below them. As they descended, a river came into view—the Chikugo, they learned later—with a number of unpainted wooden buildings lining its banks. Switching on his headlights, Sam drove the jeep slowly through the small community. Judging from the number of three and four-story inns along the main road, the village appeared to be a resort of some kind.

"Goddam," True said, "it looks plumb deserted."

"Yeah, it's eerie all right," Chauncey observed. Then he caught sight of two figures scurrying down a side street into the protective concealment of night shadows. "Guess we scared them when they saw our jeep coming."

"I'm stopping right here," Sam said, pulling up sharply in front of the first inn with a faint glimmer of light. "You're the spokesman," he told Chauncey, "so get us some rooms."

Chauncey banged on the wooden door of the inn and waited. Nothing happened, nor was there the sound of anyone moving around inside. The whole village was cloaked in ghostly silence, as if everyone had anticipated their coming and were silently cowering indoors, terrified of risking any contact with the reputedly ferocious American troops.

"Go on," Sam barked from the jeep, "knock again."

"They's got to be somebody around," said True.

Chauncey had lifted his hand to knock again when the door suddenly opened. An old man stood there, quaking and squinting fearfully at the American. Right out of one of those classic Japanese prints, Chauncey thought: baggy pants, short *happi* coat, stubby chin whiskers, and shiny bald head.

"We need rooms for the night," Chauncey said in polite Japanese.

The old man leaned forward, flared his nostrils, and sniffed inquiringly in the direction of the jeep. His features collapsing into a wreath of repugnance, he stepped back quickly and slammed the door in Chauncey's face.

"Christ!" Chauncey muttered, "the old son of a bitch almost took my nose off."

"So we'll try the next one," said Sam, gunning the jeep back to life. "Come on."

At the Inn of the Fragrant Waters, an affable middle-aged matron answered the door. Showing no external evidence of the old man's repugnance or trepidation, she agreed to accommodate them overnight.

Chauncey signalled to Sam. When the jeep was parked and chain-locked, the trio filed indoors for the formal signing of the register.

"You are the first Americans to come to Oguni since before the war," the woman told Chauncey as he signed his name, rank, and unit number.

From one side of the lobby came a round of gleeful girlish laughter. Three young hotel maids were peeking at them from behind a worn folding screen. Although he couldn't see them clearly, Chauncey heard one of them say in Japanese, "What in Buddha's name is that horrible stench? Do you think *all* Americans smell like that? I thought they were supposed to make a cult of cleanliness, as we do. . . . ."

"Silly fool!" hissed another, "You must expect such odors from hairy foreign devils who live on the flesh of animals."

"Let's wait till they come down to the public bath. Then we can see what they're really like," the third maid proposed, whereupon all three surrendered to more trilling laughter and disappeared.

CHAPTER TWO

In early August—only a few weeks before Lt. Truman Foote fell into the Kyushu honey tank—a gold-braided commander in the Imperial Japanese Navy was striding back and forth across his green-carpetted, third-floor office in the headquarters building on the Kure Naval Base. Each time he came to the east-facing windows, he halted briefly to glance out over the harbor at the few remaining sea-worthy vessels still riding at anchor there.

He was Commander Junichi Ohara, and his bailiwick was public relations for all navy activities within Kure's area of jurisdiction, which included Kyushu. Japan was on the verge of national disaster—the BOMB would fall on nearby Hiroshima within hours—but Commander Ohara was blissfully unaware of its proximity. In the best of stern navy tradition, he was barking alternate orders and questions at a navy lieutenant who stood at parade rest before the commander's desk.

"Well, Nishi-kun, are you satisfied with the arrangements?" His Japanese speech was clipped and fast, its forms those of a superior to an inferior.

"Yes, Commander." Nishi came halfway to attention as he spoke. He didn't like Ohara, but the raw voice of overbearing authority was a stimulus to his reflexes.

"All the parents are willing?"

"They are, sir."

"And the girls?"

"Their parents assured me that their daughters were wild with delight at the honor being bestowed on them."

"Hmmm." Stalwart supporter of Nippon's cause though he was, Commander Ohara had seen enough of the world to have certain private doubts about such exultant instances of super-patriotism and ultra-nationalism. Could people *really* be that wretchedly.....? He shook his head to cast off such thoughts. So what if the parents were laying it on a bit thick? The point was that they had agreed, and he had his hands on the makings of a stupendous coup in public relations. He began to mentally calculate to see if his pay as a captain would enable him to take Teruko's younger sister into his snug little home away from home. The thought of sleeping with two sisters at the same time titillated his sexual fantasy, and he thought that both of the girls would be willing.

"Sir?" Lieutenant Nishi's voice broke in on his revery.

"Eh?"

"I was saying that the fourteen bridegrooms are willing, too."

"What? Of course, they're willing, Nishi. What the devil are you talking about? We selected them for this assignment, didn't we? I don't recall even asking their opinions. They're navy officers, aren't they? A bit young, of course, and they don't get much training at the Special Attack Forces school these days, but still. . . ." Sudden suspicion glinted in Ohara's dark eyes under the oddly-arching brows. "None of them hinted at any dissatisfaction, did they?"

"No, sir. Nothing like that.Those young fellows—well, as you know, sir, they're something of a special breed. I mean, the way we culled them from schools all over the country. Excessive zeal, blind obedience to Imperial authority, willingness. . . . .no, I should say *eagerness* to die for the Emperor, and all that. What I meant was that all fourteen of them went out of their way to thank me for the assignment."

"I should think they would," the commander harrumphed. "A chance to shack up for a night with someone beside those Fukuoka whores before they take off for—uh, Nirvana." Before he installed Teruko in a Kure apartment as his mistress, Ohara had caught a dose of clap from a *baishumpu*—or 'seller of spring', as the Japanese delicately called prostitutes—in Fukuoka, and his wife still chided him for not taking the proper precautions.

"Yes, sir," Nishi agreed. It was after five o'clock and he wished the C.O. would shake the lead out. He wanted to see if he could get Lieutenant Aoki to pay him the fifty yen Aoki had lost at mahjong before train time.

"You're leaving tonight?"

"Yes, sir."

"Have a drink before you go." The lean, stiffly-erect Ohara went to his desk and dug a bottle of Toyo whiskey out of a drawer. The lieutenant fetched glasses from a cabinet behind the gold-and-black *byobu*, the three-sectioned standing screen.

"*Tenno Heika Banzai*! (May the Emperor Live Ten Thousand Years!)" Ohara slurred the words of the ritual toast to semi-incomprehensibility.

Nishi repeated the formula and downed two fingers of the one year-old whiskey.

Blinking the tears out of his eyes, the commander sputtered: "I wish I could go with you, Nishi-kun, but I have to go to Hiroshima tonight and be there for two days. No getting out of it. You're sure you can handle everything?"

"I'm sure, Commander. The girls' fathers are taking care of the mass wedding ceremony, the visit to the shrine, and the inn reservations. And the transportation, too, although I had to issue them some navy gasoline for their cars. . . ."

"I know, I know," interrupted Ohara. "I mean about the press coverage, the photographers, the. . . ."

"All taken care of, sir," the lieutenant hastened to assure him, putting his glass down suggestively within inches of the bottle of Toyo.

"Take all you want," Ohara said with a nod at the bottle. "And get yourself a good night's sleep on the train to Fukuoka. I've given you a lot of responsibility in this assignment, and I want you to be on your toes tomorrow."

"I know, sir."

"But do you really know, lieutenant, what this could mean to the Special Attack Forces?" Ohara's eyes shone with a sudden intensity.

"I think so, commander. It could inspire all our *kamikaze* pilots to. . . . ."

"What did you say, *kamikaze*?"

"Oh, didn't I tell you about that? One of the newspaper reporters in Fukuoka yesterday used the expression, and I thought we might adopt it for some of our press releases. A rather vivid expression, don't you think? We were talking about the fourteen pilots taking their brides off to the inn right after the visit to the shrine and the reporter laughed and predicted that they would sweep down on them like a *kamikaze*." Lt. Nishi essayed a half-smile.

The commander stared at the subordinate officer with no sign of understanding on his face.

"Well, you know, sir. . . ." Nishi hesitated at his own effrontery". . . . .the Mongols raided our coasts right there at Fukuoka in the thirteenth century, and it was a typhoon that broke up their ships and drove them off, so we called that typhoon a Wind from the Gods and. . . ."

"Dammit, Nishi, I don't need lessons in Japanese history from you! I know where the word *Kamikaze* came from. It's just that I don't see the connection between a God-sent Wind and some young officers taking their brides off to an inn for their wedding night!"

Nishi coughed faintly in apology. "Now that you mention it, sir, I guess there's not much connection. I suppose I was really thinking more about the idea of those same pilots sweeping down and driving the American enemy ship off our coasts. Knocking holes in them, you know, just like they're going to make holes in those girls. If you want, I'll have the word *kamikaze* erased from today's releases. They're still in Communications. . . . ."

"No, no, Nishi. Go ahead and use the word." Actually Ohara now saw that *kamikaze* was a very apt expression, and he made a mental note to himself to use it in his conversation with the admiral when he met him tomorrow in Hiroshima. Without having to say so, he could leave the impression that it was his own brain-child. "Anyway, Nishi-kun, I want to emphasize how extremely important this affair in Fukuoka could be. The news that fourteen beautiful young girls—true *Yamato nadeshiko*—from the very best Fukuoka families are giving themselves in marriage to fourteen. . . . .uh, *kamikaze* pilots. . . . ." Ohara wanted to familiarize himself with the usage ". . . .should run through the country like a shot of adrenalin. That's why I want you to get the best possible press coverage for the wedding ceremony. Enlistments in the Special Attack. . .uh, *kamikaze* forces should double, even triple the nation's will to resist. . . .what was it that confounded Englishman said? 'in the streets, in the air, on the beaches?' Anyway, the will to resist will be fanned to white-hot intensity. The Emperor himself may even deign to notice the event. Women throughout the country will give up more of the jewelry that we know they're still holding out. In fact. . . . ."

Nishi took a chance and looked rather obviously at his wrist watch.

"All right, all right, Nishi-kun. I know you have a train to catch. Be off with you. And report to me in detail as soon as you return. Understand?"

"Yes, sir." Nishi saluted, spun sharply about, and left the room. Although he had no way of knowing it, that was the last time he would ever see Commander Junichi Ohara.

CHAPTER THREE

The clear morning light awakened True shortly after dawn. Exiled with his *futon* to the large balcony outside the spacious front room the three of them had been given, True had slept well and hard, in the process finally airing himself free from the last vestiges of the honey-tank stigma.

He stretched and looked out on a charming scene. For a moment he wondered if he was in fabled Shangri-la. The small valley was lush and green before him, rising steeply from the banks of the crystal river that glittered invitingly in the warming September sun. The river banks were lined with weathered wooden inns with shops between them. In rising tiers on the slopes behind the inns stood a few private dwellings, flimsy structures built more for the warm season than for year-round habitation. Maybe there were fifty or sixty buildings altogether, True figured, which would mean a population of only a few hundred.

The walls of the valley were covered with cultivated pine trees, in dark contrast to the lighter-green bamboo groves on the lower slopes. Steam rose from tall chimney pipes atop each inn's roof, evidence of natural hot springs. The road to the west by which they had entered the valley was hidden behind their inn, invisible from the balcony, but True could see where it ran past the entrance to the inn's courtyard, crossed the bridge over the river, and then wandered up and out of the valley to the southeast.

Besides bicycles, the only modern vehicle in sight was their jeep, standing in exotic isolation. A few rickshaws stood idle and empty along the streets. Two people—one old man and a small boy—were leisurely fishing from atop a grouping of large red rocks upriver. Three women were performing their ritual of morning wash at the river's edge, slapping garments against the flat red rocks. This pastoral scene claimed True's undivided attention until he saw something else that wrung an oath of admiration from his lips and awoke Chauncey.

"Jesus in the mawning!" he cried. "Come see what Ah found!"

She stood on the fourth-floor balcony of an inn on the opposite bank of the clear, turbulent river, taking deep breaths. It was difficult to tell much about her at sixty yards, except that her abundant hair was the color of honey and that she was obviously Caucasian, not Japanese.

Rubbing sleep from his eyes, Chauncey said: "For once you made some sense with your hollering," he said, then went back into their room for his binoculars, stumbling over Sam in his eager search.

"What the hell do you want?" Sam asked thickly from the depths of his *futon*.

"True's found a good one," Chauncey said, locating the binoculars.

"A good what?" Sam asked resentfully.

"A beautiful American girl, all alone on a balcony across the river."

Sam shot out of bed as if he'd been triggered, almost bowling Chauncey over as he made for the balcony. "Where, where?" he shouted, running up beside True with Chauncey right behind him.

"How do you know she's American?" Sam demanded.

"She's sumpin' else," True said dreamily.

"European?" suggested Chauncey. "Maybe Scandinavian—or even German."

"Hey," said Sam, "being German would account for her not being in a prison camp, wouldn't it?"

"Right. Or she might be from some neutral country like Switzerland," said Chauncey, warming to the subject. "Look at *that*!"

Goggle-eyed, they all craned their necks as the object of their admiration took one final deep, bosomy breath and then turned and disappeared abruptly through the balcony door into her room. With the morning sun in her eyes and her apparent disregard of the landscape, it was probable that she had not seen the three ogling male figures across the river.

"Well," said True, "Ah'll be a dirty name. What do we do now?"

"Pack up and get going," said Chauncey. "Hanging

around here won't do us any good."

While True and Chauncey were shaving, Sam disappeared from the room and was gone for nearly an hour. When he came back, the bill was paid, their gear was loaded, and his friends were waiting for him in the jeep. As they chugged up the steep winding road out of the lovely valley, Chauncey passed out K-Rations.

"Ah hate K-rations," True said flatly. "Ah wouldn't use 'em to slop mah hawgs with back home."

"Mmmmmm," said Chauncey, turning around to face True, who was still relegated to the jeep's rear seat. "Maybe you think we should have eaten the breakfast they offered us back at the inn?"

"Ah wish we had," said True. "Anything'd be better'n this crud."

"Even cod-fish eye soup, dried seaweed, pickled giant radish, and salted trout entrails?"

"Cut it out!" Sam shouted, swerving in his nausea dangerously close to the precipitous embankment.

"Say," Chauncey said, "what were you up to back there?"

Adjusting his cap at a cockier angle, Sam grinned and said, "I couldn't leave without finding out who she was."

"How'd you do it?" True wanted to know.

"Simple. Just gave an old guy who works in the inn a pack of cigarettes and thirty minutes later he had all the dope."

"Well, don't keep us in suspense," pressed Chaucey. "What's her name, address, and telephone number?"

"And does she put out?" added True.

"So speaketh Peter Peckerstiff," grinned Sam. "Her name—he told me in Japanese—is 'Hiruda Rittah.' I guess that comes out Hilda Ritter in English. She's Swiss, all right. And she's here as teacher or chaperone or something of a group of fourteen Japanese girls."

"Now that you went to all that trouble," Chauncey asked, "what're you going to do, write her a letter?"

"I dunno," said Sam, who was then silent for a moment before adding, "Say, speaking of writing, did you mail those MacArthur letters?"

"Yes, but I'm still not convinced it's such a bright idea," replied Chauncey.

"It *is*, Chauncey, it is. Believe me. Somebody'll notice them and then word'll get around. And True and I'll drop some hints at strategic places."

"What you mothahs talkin' about?" True demanded.

"We might as well tell him," said Chauncey with a sigh.

"Okay," Sam agreed. "Now listen, True. We're going to have some letters mailed to Chauncey from Tokyo."

"Who's gonna mail them?" True asked.

"One of our former classmates who's now in GHQ, but that's besides the point. The return address on the envelopes will be 'D. MacArthur, Daiichi Building, Chiyoda-ku, Tokyo.' They'll naturally be addressed to First Loot Chauncey MacArthur, 321st Military Government Team, Nishi Nakasu, Fukuoka-shi, Fukuoka-ken."

"And all that jazz, yeah," added True. Then it dawned on him. "Daiichi Building! My cotton-pickin' balls, that's *General* MacArthur's headquarters!"

"As I have said often before," Chauncey remarked, "you are a true genius."

"As soon as the Japanese mail service is regular again, Chauncey'll be receiving one of those letters every five days or so."

"Why not A.P.O.?" True asked. "It's faster. . . . ."

"It would involve risks we don't want to take," said Sam. "Matters like fraud and stuff."

"But you know Chauncey's no kin to the General. What're you tryin' to do?"

"The letters are for Colonel Dawgleish's eyes. We want him to *think* that Chauncey's related to Douglas. That's where you come in, and you better not screw it up, buddy. The mail clerk or somebody's bound to notice the return address on the letters sooner or later. He'll ask you or me some questions, like if Chauncey's really related to the General. So we begin to talk about the General's brother, the one he refuses to recognize because he chose Annapolis instead of West Point. Sibling rivalry, you know. But he's so fond of his brother's son that he keeps up a private correspondence with him, and so forth, far into the night."

"But it ain't true," True said emphatically.

"Your name's True and you're not for real either," Sam snapped.

"What's the C.O. gonna think when he hears 'bout this

nephew bullshit?" said True, still bewildered.

"You wait and see," Sam said. "Dawgleish is so goddam eager to trade his eagle for a star he'll kiss the ass of the first likely ladder to success. He'd do almost anything to make Regular Army. Maybe he'll even lick Chauncey's cruddy boots to get him to put in a good word with Uncle Doug. After all, if Chauncey receives personal letters from the King of Kings. . . . ."

"You bastards!" True rasped admiringly when the light shone through.

Sam stepped on the gas as they sped down the grade, leaving Oguni behind them, locked in its verdant, somnolent valley. "We got work to do, men! Fish to fry and female lives to enrich."

CHAPTER FOUR

Although the first reports of the atomic bombing of
Hiroshima reached Fukuoka in the early afternnon of the
same day, it was not until evening that a glimmering of its
full significance began to seep through.

Tsutako Sugimura, seventeen-year-old daughter of the
managing editor of the *Nishi Nippon* newspaper, heard it
first from her stunned father just as she was leaving her
home for an informal meeting of the fourteen brides-to-be
at the nearby residence of Mieko Shimizu.

She was the second to arrive at Mieko's, Sachie Iki
already being there. Breathless with excitement and a
dimly-perceived dread, she could hardly wait until the maid
left the spacious *tatami*-floored room to tell what she had
heard.

"Something terrible has happened in Hiroshima!"

"I don't know what could be any worse than what's
about to happen right here in Fukuoka," Sachie said drily.

"What on earth do you mean, Satchan?" Tsutako asked,
shocked and distracted momentarily from her own por-
tentous news.

"You know what I mean, Little Miss Oh-So-Innocent,"
Sachie said, looking up at the still-standing Tsutako from
under lashes abnormally long for Oriental eyes. "This is just
like dealing in human flesh! It's a despicable idea: forcing
us into marriages that can't possibly last but a day or two."

"Sometime the Special Attack pilots do come back,"
Mieko interposed gently. A quiet, thoughtful girl, she
seldom spoke, but the others listened when she did.

"All right, so a few of them come back from their first
raid," Sachie argued angrily. "They'll just send them out
again in a few days, won't they?"

"If you object so strongly," Tsutako asked, "why didn't
you protest?"

"*Protest*? Why, I screamed for two hours and then cried

all night when my father told me. *Of course*, I protested. What the hell good do you think it did! None. NONE AT ALL! Not with an old fool like my father. Oh, no! The glory of Japan! *Yamato damashii* and all that crap....."

"Maybe it won't be so bad," the gentle Mieko suggested. "They might let us get married again later."

"You know better than that," Sachie flashed back at her. "They'd say we weren't being faithful to the memory of our dead husbands."

"Well, if the Americans do to Fukuoka what they did to Hiroshima this morning, we won't have anything to worry about at all," Tsutako said, remembering her momentous news.

"What do you mean?" Mieko asked.

"The Americans bombed Hiroshima this morning."

"We heard that. . . ."

"But Daddy says it wasn't just an ordinary air raid," Tsutako said, pulling her *zabuton* up closer to the other two girls. "Just one or two planes—and only *one* bomb."

"One bomb?"

Tsutako nodded, her neckline-length hair bouncing with the excitement of her movements. "Only one. And it destroyed the entire city."

"But. . . ."

"Hiroshima simply doesn't exist anymore," Tsutako said, driving home her lesson.

The soft-spoken Mieko saw the implications before Sachie. "If the Americans have a weapon like that, we don't have a chance against them, do we?" She addressed her question to the garden beyond the veranda on one side of the room.

"Daddy says this will mean the end of the war, probably in just a few days," Tsutako commented, rearranging the lower folds of her chic white-and-green summer weight kimono.

"Unless those old fools in Tokyo get stubborn."

"Satchan, you shouldn't say. . . . ."

"Why not? Let's all be truthful for a change. Why the hell should we ruin our lives for a lost cause? None of us really want to go through with this stupidity, do we?"

Sachie could tell from the quickly-averted glances that her thrust had struck home. "Let's all just be honest with each other," she urged, her voice taking on a pleading note. "If we act together, maybe we can think of a way to get out of this."

"But the ceremony takes place tomorrow," Tsutako pointed out.

"It won't take place if we're not here," Sachie said, standing up in her determination.

Both Tsutako and Mieko were clearly horrified.

"My father would skin me alive," murmured Mieko, aghast at the mere thought of such rebellion.

"Not if we're not here," Sachie repeated.

"I know that look on your face, Satchan," Tsutako said. "You've got something devious in mind."

"Let's wait till the rest of the girls get here. Then I'll tell you."

An hour latter fourteen lovely young girls, all dressed in expensive, multi-hued *kimono*, were seated in a circle in the same room, drinking weak green tea with demure gestures and composing their thoughts while steeling their wills to go through with what they had just voted to do.

Sachie, the leader of the rebellion, asked, "Is there anything else we need to discuss?"

"Yes," said Mieko.

"What?"

"We've forgotten one thing, Satchan. We're all minors and if we try to go anywhere in Kyushu, someone is sure to ask questions. I mean, fourteen young girls without any adults. . . ."

"She's right," Tsutako seconded.

"If only we had one of our teachers with us," Mameko Endo said, "we'd look just like any other group of girls on a school excursion."

"Teachers!" Sachiko scoffed. "They're worse than our parents. They're *always* raving about dying for the Emperor."

"Not Miss Ritter," Sujiko Honekawa said. "She's not like that."

"Because she's Swiss, of course."

The girls were referring to Miss Hilda Ritter, who taught French at the exclusive girls' school they all attended in Nishi Koen in Fukuoka.

"But would she go?"

"She might," said Tsutako. "She just might."

"All right then," said Sachie, rising to her feet gracefully, "let's three of us go ask her. The rest of you go on home. If you don't hear anything from us tonight, just assume that we'll leave tomorrow morning, after the banks open."

"And don't forget to bring your bank books," Tsutako added. "Without the money in our savings accounts, we won't get very far."

CHAPTER FIVE

"The last item I'm going to take up today," declared Major-General Vandel, stars gleaming brightly on his starched collar, "may well be the most vital and sensitive issue of the entire occupation thus far on Kyushu. Now I don't have to tell you gentlemen—" those present included the A-2 and his assistant from Itazuke Air Base, a Hakata Port Authority Navy captain, a dignified British Navy commander representing His Majesty's several vessels now moored in Hakata Bay, and variously graded Army officers attached to the CIC, CCD, RTO, and 341st Military Government Team "—and I don't have to emphasize how important the moral aspects of our Occupation are at this early and critical moment."

Chauncey stifled a prodigious yawn, thinking that the whole meeting had been one enormous mountain of bullshit. What really concerned him at the moment certainly wasn't this stupid conference but another one he and his two buddies had been summoned to attend yesterday. Right after their return from Beppu, his C.O.—Colonel Dawgleish (pronounced Dog Leash, how else?)—had called them in his office, appointed them as Liaison Officer, True as Arms Disposal Officer, and Sam as Assistant Supply Officer with the additional titillating responsibility of P.X. Officer, if and when such coveted merchandise ever reached the Team.

Major-General Vandel paused effectively before saying, "Fourteen Japanese girls are missing."

The singularity of his statement, far afield from anything the assembly had expected, caught the flagging attention of even those officers who were accustomed to catching five minutes' sleep during staff conferences.

"The fathers of those girls called on me in a body yesterday," Vandel continued, more confident now that he saw the alert gleam in the assembly's collective eye, "to report their daughters missing and to request our official assistance in finding them."

The general turned to a Marine major on his left and ordered, "Tom, read that list of names and affiliations."

The major fumbled through his dispatch case and produced a sheet of onion skin.

"Mr. Hachiro Honekawa—" he read "—president of the Tamayo Department Store. Mr. Tomoji Endo, senior partner in the largest legal firm in the prefecture. Mr. Saburo Chino, director of the Sekijuji Hospital. Mr. Shigenori Iki, director of the company that handles all Fukuoka's night-soil. Mr. Namiji Shimizu, writer of eleven popular novels. . . ."

The general held up his hand. "That's enough, Tom. That'll give you officers some idea of their potential influence. And just so we won't misunderstand each other, I know as well as you do that we've just knocked the tar out of these people in a bloody war of *their* own making. I don't intend to mollycoddle them, not even if Hirohito himself came crawling through that door right now, begging for favors."

The general was a tall, weather-beaten Marine who talked from the side of his mouth in a stentorian voice. He meant what he said, and Chauncey, for one, believed him. But what was he trying to say? Famous for coming right to the point, today he seemed unusually garrulous and round-about.

"However—" the general frowned at one and all "—if we can get the full cooperation of all the distinguished local citizens of Tom's list, we're going to have a much easier job of running this island. They'll be invaluable to a smooth administration, because the list reads like a 1945 edition of *Who's Who in Fukuoka*. And remember that cooperation's the key to a successful Occupation. So far, it appears that the man on the street will work with us, anyway—what can he lose?—but we want the upper echelon, too. And that's why I'm making a campaign issue of helping these men locate their missing daughters."

Next to Chauncey, Colonel Dawgleish cleared his throat, and when the colonel cleared his throat, as Chauncey knew only too well, some kind of crap always filled the air about him.

"Sir," the colonel spoke up, "I'm afraid I still don't understand. You say the daughters of these men are missing. But when—and how? If I'm not being too inquisitive. . . . "

The major laid aside his sheet of onion skin. "It seems that the girls all disappeared the day after we bombed Hiroshima, so there may be some justification for the explanation that they thought that Fukuoka might be next and simply decided to get out before it was too late. But on the other hand the fathers tell us that the girls were going to be married that day to. . . . . "

"*All* of them?"

"Affirmative. All of them, in a mass ceremony to a bunch of pilots. Some PR genius up in Kure is supposed to have dreamed it up to. . . . "

". . . . .bolster morale," supplied the general.

"Yes, sir," the major nodded. "The fathers apparently can't quite bring themselves to believe that their daughters were running out on the wedding. . . .it was supposed to have been a tremendous honor for them. . . .but the point is that they did disappear, and it looks to us as if they knew what they were doing."

"Why?" asked Dawgleish.

"Because they took all the money out of their savings accounts that morning," the major said, then added, "It came to a considerable amount."

"Fourteen Japanese girls among millions on the island," mused Captain Jim Nicholson, a tough infantry officer on detached duty with the RTO in Fukuoka.

General Vandel nodded his understanding of the captain's point. "We've got just one thing working for us. The police think that the girls took one of their teachers with them, a woman who teaches French at their school."

"So we look for fifteen Japanese women instead of fourteen."

"No, Captain, not quite," the general rasped. "We looked for fourteen Japanese girls and one *Swiss* woman with light brown hair."

"Swiss?"

"Affirmative," said the major. "And there're not many of *those* on Kyushu."

Chauncey sat bolt upright, experiencing an instant of

– 32 –

pure *deja vu*. He must have lived through just such a scene in a previous existence.

The general was saying, ". . . .the breakdown in Japanese communications and transportation has made it practically impossible for them to mount any kind of a thorough search. We've got the radios and vehicles with gasoline and what not, so they came to us."

"But sir," said Dawgleish, eager to keep himself prominent in the eyes of a superior officer, "what could have happened to them? Fifteen women don't just vanish."

"Who knows?" said the general. "That's what we've got to find out."

Chauncey smiled to himself, believing he could answer that question. But he didn't, wanting time to think about a vague plan that was building up in his consciousness.

"Anyway," said General Vandel, rising to his feet, "we're committed to a quick solution. All units under my command will be on watch from now on for these young girls and their Swiss chaperone. That's all for today, gentlemen. Thank you. See you next week. Meeting dismissed."

Chauncey drove Colonel Dawgleish back to their billet—the *Koki-kan* or Inn of Ultimate Delights—through rubble-strewn streets.

"What do you plan to do about the girls, sir?" he asked the colonel en route.

Dawgleish tugged at one of his jug ears, then pinched his bulbous nose. "Christ, Lieutenant, I guess I'll just have to order everyone in the Team to keep his eyes peeled for them. . . . By the way, General Vandel overlooked an important point."

"What's that, sir?"

"The Swiss woman's name. It wasn't mentioned."

"Hilda Ritter, sir," Chauncey said brightly, without thinking.

Dawgleish turned and stared at him. "Hilda Ritter, eh? How the hell do you know? No one mentioned it at the meeting."

Quickly Chauncey crawfished: "Well—uh, I just happened to get a glimpse of it in that report the major had as I was waiting for you."

"Oh yes, while I was talking with Vandel, of course. . . ."

"That was close," thought Chauncey.

"We've got to put our backs into this one, Lieutenant," said Dawgleish heartily as they pulled up in front of the billet. "Think what a trophy those fourteen girls would make!"

"Yes, sir, they sure would," Chauncey agreed, inwardly growing more excited as his earlier idea grew in scope, glory, and sheer audacity.

That evening in their quarters, Chauncey told Sam and True what had happened at General Vandel's staff conference. The account was interrupted now and then by Mabel, who divided her time between wrapping her arms around True's neck and cadging sips from the handiest drink.

Mabel was a large female monkey that had been left in the Inn of Ultimate Delights by an American major in transit from Indo-China to the U.S. Their maid Sumiko—a jolly, round-faced country girl—had taken pity on the lonely creature and had tried to take care of her, which wasn't easy in that time of extreme shortages.

Mabel's affair with Truman Foote had been a case of love at first sight, at least on one side. She had taken a single look at him, leaped to his shoulders, and kissed him soundly on the neck. From then on, True didn't have a chance, and Sumiko had been more than willing to relinquish her guardianship. True had named the monkey Mabel because of what he said was an amazing similarity between her neck-nuzzling and ear-kissing proclivities and those of a girl he had known back in Escambia County, Alabama.

"You idiot," Sam growled at Chauncey, when they had heard all the details of the disappearance of the fourteen girls, "what's wrong with you? Are you tongue-tied or something?"

"What do you mean?" said Chauncey.

"Aw, come on," said True, unwrapping Mabel and pushing her firmly away, "we *know* where those girls are, don't we? Who could forget that gorgeous dish we saw doin' the breathin' exercises back theah in Oguni? You should've told ole Dawgleish."

"More to the point," Sam said, "why didn't you just stand up and give Vandel the information yourself? To hell with giving Dawgleish the lead, that prick. Let's take the credit for *ourselves*."

"Calm down," Chauncey told them, "and give me a chance to explain. If you guys will go along with me on this, I think I know how we can get ourselves an all-expenses-paid vacation and maybe even a promotion or some medals."

"Screw the medals," say True. "Ah'll take the vacation."

"I don't follow you, Chauncey," Sam told him, "but I'm damned if you don't come up with original ideas now and then. Like that whorehouse in Manila that you got declared off-limits so that we could have the girls all to ourselves for a week."

"Then he went and charged those gals twice what our bill came to just to get their place put back on-limits again," True remembered with a laugh. "Sure, Ah'll go along with your idea, Chauncey, whatever the hell it is."

For once, they were all in agreement.

CHAPTER SIX

"I still wonder if we did the right thing," Hilda Ritter was saying to Tsutako Sugimura and Sachie Iki in her room of an inn in Kurume.

"I'm sure we did, *Sensei*," Sachie said, addressing the Swiss woman with the Japanese word for teacher and using very polite forms of speech. Sachie was a girl of strong likes and dislikes, and their teacher of French fell into the former category with her. Without reservations she liked and admired Miss Ritter. She admired her non-Japanese independence of spirit, her qualifications as a teacher, her more-than-adequate ability in Japanese (which Sachie knew that so very few foreigners ever mastered), her identification with the girls she taught, and her wholesome good looks. Not true beauty, perhaps, but certainly in close accord with all that Switzerland stood for in Sachie's imagination: invigorating mountain air, high mountains and virgin snow and picture-book valleys, milk chocolate, precision watches, wholesome dairy products, and orderly living. Because of this fond respect, Sachie accorded their teacher and chaperone a degree of politeness in her speech that she gave to few others.

"And besides, *Sensei*," Tsutako was saying, "we'll keep our promise. We'll remind our fathers that we had already decided to go when we first talked to you. And that you tried your best to persuade us not to, but when you saw that we had really made up our minds, you felt you had to come along to protect and watch over us."

"I wonder if your fathers will ever speak to you again, or to me for that matter," Hilda mused. She sat between the two young girls at the low table on the *tatami* matting, turning a delicate tea cup round and round in her hands. It was late afternoon in Kurume, where Hilda and the fourteen girls were staying in a small inn two blocks from the railroad station. They had been there since fleeing from

Fukuoka ten days earlier.

Much had happened during those ten days. The second atom bomb had been dropped on Nagasaki, and the Emperor had announced by radio—it was the first time that most of the people had heard his voice—that the Japanese Empire had no choice but to surrender. He had called on his people to "endure the unendurable," and many of them had wept in the streets. Through it all, the girls and their chaperone had stayed mostly in their rooms in the inn, fearing that at any moment their fathers or the police or Imperial Navy officers would find them and cart them back to Fukuoka for some unimaginable punishment.

"But it's working out just as we thought, *Sensei*," Sachie said, her pert features intent on convincing Miss Ritter that she had not been wrong in taking flight with them. "We've lost the war, and those pilots. . . ." Sachie steadfeastly refused to call the men their fiances ". . . .were all killed."

"We don't know that for certain, Sachie-san," Hilda Ritter said, pouring more tea for both her pupils. "All we know is. . . . ."

". . . .that the squadron took off on a mission the day after we left Fukuoka," Tsutako concluded, bowing slightly as she accepted the offering of tea, "and that they are never given enough fuel to get back on these days."

"Which serves to fortify their resolve," Hilda noted drily.

"They *must* be dead, *Sensei*, and now that the war's really over, don't you think it's time for us to go home?"

"I guess so," the Swiss woman said reluctantly. "But I've been thinking that the longer we stay away, the more time your fathers will have to calm down. They could have me fired from the school, you know."

"Oh, no," Tsutako protested, her concern showing clearly. "We wouldn't let them. Besides, they should be grateful to you for seeing that no harm came to us."

"Perhaps," Hilda replied with a slow nod, but she had certain reservations. In retrospect, what she had done now struck her as an awesomely foolhardy and ill-advised thing: Running away with the daughters of fourteen of the most influential families in Fukuoka Prefecture—fiercely-proud, old-line familites who had solemnly agreed to give their daughters in marriage to fourteen pilots of the idolized

Special Attack Forces, leaving these same young men, who had been touted as the Last Hope of the Nation, waiting at the Shinto Shrine, with swarms of newspaper reporters and photographers standing all around to witness their shame.

Still, these girls were her pupils and she felt a strong responsibility for their welfare. Besides, she privately sympathized with their position: What normal women—and especially beautiful, privileged girls like these—would want to marry one day and be widowed the next, even to soothe the Emperor's doubtless fevered brow?

That night fate caught up with the fifteen fugitives.

They were finishing dinner at a long, low table formed by lining up six of the individual tables from that many rooms. Two sets of *fusuma* or sliding wood-and-paper doors had been removed to create one large room from three smaller ones. The serving maids had brought tea and fruit for dessert and had cleared away the other dishes. Hilda Ritter raised her hands for silence.

"I know that some of you think that it's time for us to go back to Fukuoka," the teacher began. "I'm not so sure myself, but I think I should respect your wishes in this matter. So let's take a vote on whether to stay away longer or return. All those who. . . ."

She never finished the sentence. A door from the outside corridor slid open and into the room stepped two men in the uniforms of officers in the Imperial Japanese Navy. Both were young, slender, and crew-cut. One was tall for a Japanese, the other about five inches shorter. Seeing Hilda Ritter, both bowed briefly in her direction, stepped farther into the room, and knelt on the *tatami* matting with hands on knees. The shorter of the two spoke in a low, taut voice.

"We have found you. At last."

"Why, you're Nemoto-san," said Sujiko Honekawa in a frightened, bewildered voice against a background of gasps and whispers.

"No, it can't be!" Mameko Endo's face paled and her mouth refused to close. "Yoshikita-san? But you're dead! I mean. . . ."

Ensign Yattaro Yoshikita—the taller officer—accorded Mameko only the briefest of glances. "We are nearer death than life," he said cryptically.

The surprise and fright were too much for the fourteen

girls to contain any longer. The room filled with mounting movement, exclamations, questions, protests, pleas, and cries of consternation. Hilda Ritter saw that she had to control the incipient hysteria.

"Be silent, girls! There is no reason for you to carry on like this. I told you that we were not certain that all the men in the squadron had gone to. . . .a glorious death." Her hazel eyes flickered at this unaccustomed expression of nonsense. "If two of your fiances are still alive, let us rejoice." A particular fear had taken form in Hilda's ready mind as soon as the two ensigns had entered the room, and she was already working out a counter-strategy.

"For a foreign devil, this woman has some slight wisdom," Ensign Nemoto observed to his comrade. He turned to Sujiko. "Who is she?"

"She is our French teacher," Sujiko answered. "We met her by accident here in Kurume yesterday."

"Oh, do you speak French?" Nemoto asked the Swiss woman, who had a way to answer such a stupid question.

Addressing the girls in French, Hilda said, "Listen carefully and do exactly as I say. I am not certain, but I suspect that these men may have some form of revenge in mind. Revenge on you for running away. If so, we must pretend to humor them and look for an opportunity to escape. Watch me carefully and take your leads from me, no matter how strange they may sound." To herself, Hilda added a silent prayer that neither Nemoto nor Yoshikita understood French.

"Hmmmm. I guess perhaps you *do* speak French," Yoshikita said grudgingly, "but there was no need to say so much to prove it. Are you a French citizen?"

"No, sir, I am Swiss. As you know, Switzerland was neutral in this war, but I myself have been a strong supporter of your grand Greater East Asia Co-Prosperity Sphere and your principle of the Eight Corners of the World Under One Roof." In humble Japanese, Hilda was practising a degree of guile that tasted like gall to her tongue.

Gratified by this arrant sycophancy, some of the apparent tenseness left the two ensigns.

"Perhaps you are hungry from your travels? Hilda asked. "Girls, make room for the honorable officers at the table.

Sujiko, you call the kitchen and tell them to bring their best dinners for two more guests. And hurry!"

With proper *samurai* disdain for food ("Even though he has not eaten for days, the *samurai* wields his toothpick with a flourish") Nemoto and Yoshikita allowed themselves to be seated at the end of the long table with their backs to the *tokonoma* alcove, the place of honor.

"And Sujiko," Hilda called to that girl, "tell them to bring *sake* first. Insist on the best!"

In the true Japanese tradition, the thirteen remaining girls sat silently around the table, eyes downcast at hands folded in laps. It was just as well, Hilda thought. She didn't want the navy officers to be aware of the fear that they all felt.

"While we are waiting, perhaps you would be good enough to tell us what happened to you and the others," Hilda suggested, while arranging *zabuton* and ash trays for the convenience of the two men.

Anger flashed in Yoshikita's heavy-lidded eyes. "These girls. . . ." he said contemptuously ". . . .failed to appear at the place where the mass wedding ceremony was to take place, thereby shaming all of us, as well as the Imperial Japanese Navy. There can be no excuse for such conduct! These creatures. . . ." his voice had risen to a half-shout ". . . .were supposed to be the Flowers of Japanese Womanhood, and yet they. . . ."

Improvising quickly, Hilda interrupted, "But I understand that they were *told* not to go. Isn't that right, girls?"

Fourteen heads nodded as one.

"Who gave such an order?" Nemoto demanded suspiciously.

"Why, Tsutako Sugimura's father—you know, the managing editor of the *Nishi Nippon* newspaper—called and said that he had heard it from Navy Headquarters, I believe. Isn't that right?"

Again fourteen heads of raven-black hair inclined three inches. "Tsutako's father told them that another bomb like the one that fell on Hiroshima might be dropped on a city in Kyushu and that the wedding was postponed and that the girls should leave immediately for Kurume." Hilda held her breath, wondering if these lies would pass muster.

Yoshikita looked at Nemoto for a long moment, then

said. "Do you think it's possible?"

Nemoto shrugged.

"Did you see Mr. Sugimura that day?" Yoshikita pursued.

"No, he wasn't there," Nemoto replied. "We thought that the news of the Hiroshima bomb was keeping him at his desk."

"Hmmm."

"But Yoshikita-kun," said Nemoto, "it doesn't really matter, does it? It doesn't change our plan, does it?"

"Not in the least," Yoshikita admitted.

Hilda Ritter felt a chill. There was something implacable in the pale faces of those two dedicated young men. She knew the precepts of *Bushido*, the Code of the Warrior: "Life is but a preparation for Death." "The *samurai*'s life is likened to a cherry blossom; it is brief and glorious and its demise is beautiful." "He who shirks death defiles the tombstones of his ancestors." "Between death and life, death is the better, for it is a *samurai*'s prime opportunity to test his soul."

Two serving maids bowed and entered the room carrying trays of *sake* and food. They arranged the dishes while Mameko and Sujiko—at Hilda's insistence—served their fiances, who drank with calm deliberation as if it were a duty and not a pleasure.

As she watched them drink and then eat, Hilda remembered the most famous tale in all Japanese literature: *THE TREASURY OF THE FORTY-SEVEN LOYAL RETAINERS*. Briefly, it was the story of a certain *daimyo* or lord who was shamed by another *daimyo* at court. In drawing his sword to avenge his honor he violated a strict prohibition of the Shogun and was sentenced to commit *hara-kiri*. Forty-seven of his faithful *samurai* vassals took an oath to avenge him and underwent privation and ignominy for years to achieve their goal. When at last they had succeeded in decapitating the offending lord, they all gathered at a shrine in the Takanawa district of what is now Tokyo and disembowelled themselves.

Hilda Ritter knew that the pilots of the Special Attack Forces considered themselves to be modern *samurai* and she wondered. . . .

When they had finished their food and drink, Nemoto

nodded at Yoshikita and both of them pushed themselves away from the table and rose to the more formal kneeling position. They bowed their heads in a moment of silent contemplation. Yoshikita spoke.

"There is no longer any reason to delay what we have come to do."

None of the girls spoke, and even Hilda Ritter felt fright clutch at her throat.

"On the day after the marriage was supposed to take place, our squadron took off from Gannosu Air Base with orders to attack the American fleet between Kagoshima and Okinawa," Ensign Yoshikita said quietly, as if relating an event in the distant past. "My plane developed engine trouble over Kumamoto and I had to land at an emergency field near there. Due to defective parts, Nemoto-kun's engine failed completely within sight of Kagoshima, and he had to ditch in the bay."

Ensign Nemoto's mouth tightened in grim recollection and there was a suspicious wetness in his eyes.

"Our twelve comrades flew on to glory!"

"*Banzai*!" seconded Nemoto in a choked voice.

"None of them returned, and we feel certain that each one took an American battleship or aircraft carrier to the bottom with him."

"We have but two regrets," said Nemoto, "One is that we were not with them."

Everyone waited in tense silence for the voicing of the second regret. When it did not come, Hilda steeled herself and asked what it was.

"Our other regret," said Nemoto, his eyes taking in all fourteen of the colorfully-clad maidens, "is that our comrades were not able to marry before they died for His Imperial Majesty the Emperor."

"We have, however, thought of a way to relieve ourselves of both of these regrets," explained Yoshikita, an inspired light coming into his eyes.

Here it comes, Hilda thought.

"We are going to join our comrades so that we can apologize to them in person," Yoshikita said, unable to control the exultant joy in his voice.

"And we are going to take these fourteen girls with us," added Nemoto triumphantly, "so that they can be wedded to us throughout Eternity."

Hilda saw a shudder run through fourteen female bodies, but the navy officers were too engrossed in the prospects of a glorious demise to notice.

If she were to save them, Hilda knew that she would have to act now, with the utmost cunning and deception.

"Although I am only a lowly foreigner, I fully realize how thrilled my students must be. Aren't you, girls?"

Fourteen heads nodded—almost imperceptibly.

"I presume," Hilda plunged on, "that while you two gentlemen commit *hara-kiri* with your daggers, you will expect the girls—the brides, that is—to cut their throats in the true tradition?"

Nemoto and Yoshikita nodded, obviously pleased at finding enthusiastic and understanding support for their plan, even from a foreign woman.

"Then I suppose you have brought the fourteen knives?" Hilda asked.

Nemoto and Yoshikita were momentarily nonplussed. "Well, no, we haven't," Nemoto said. "You see, we didn't know we would find the girls here and. . . ."

"Well, then," said Hilda, all business, "why don't you run out and get them? In the meantime, I'll have the girls bathe and change into their ceremonial *kimono* and be ready by the time you return."

Doubt appeared on both the ensigns' faces, so Hilda said quickly in French, "For God's sake, girls, pretend to be eager!"

As they caught on, heads began to nod and faces brighten. Sujiko said, "Let's hurry," while Mameko added, "It wouldn't do to keep them waiting." In a clear voice, Fukako Okuyuki spoke up, "I'm so glad they found us," and joyfully Michiko Chino chirped, "Just think, we will be with the others soon."

Satisfaction slowly replaced doubt in the faces of the navy officers. Rising to their feet, they prepared to leave.

"Now don't forget," Hilda cautioned, "to get knives of the proper size. Just any old butcher knife won't do, you know. Not if we are going to do this thing right, for the sake of the Emperor."

At the mention of the Emperor, the spines of the navy pilots stiffened and they marched out of the room, promising to return as soon as possible.

Motioning the girls to be quiet, Hilda tiptoed to the door and listened as the footsteps faded down the corridor and stairs. Then she hurried across the room to the windows and watched as Nemoto and Yoshikita left the inn to find a store where they could buy knives of the correct length.

Behind her several of the girls broke into tears while others jumped to their feet and began to scurry wildly about.

Furiously, Hilda turned on them and snapped, "Stop it! STOP IT! Now listen to me: You've only got one chance, and that's to get away from here as quickly and as quietly as possible. Throw a few things in your bags and meet me at the rear entrance to the inn in five minutes."

"But where are you going, *Sensei*?" quavered Mieko Shimizu.

"I'm going down to the front desk to pay our bill and bribe the clerk to say that we all disappeared in the direction of the railroad station."

CHAPTER SEVEN

The first letter from "D. MacArthur" in Tokyo arrived Friday afternoon, evidence that the Japanese postal service was at least partially restored.

Sam—a dedicated, stalwart, and masterful liar—put his heart and soul into the project of preparing the Team for Chauncey's precarious nephewship to the Supreme Commander. He picked up the MacArthur letter to Chauncey in the mailroom but did not bring it to his friend's desk in HQ until the close of shop that day. That way, he figured, it would sit all weekend in plain view on Chauncey's desk, so that Colonel Dawgleish and Captain Ruby Whacker, the mountainous WAC adjutant, might notice it, since they both had to pass Chauncey's desk to reach their own offices.

Sam also hung a framed photograph of General Douglas MacArthur wearing sunglasses and with a corncob pipe in his mouth in the *tokonoma*, the Japanese place of honor, in Chauncey's room. Over Chauncey's protestations—that was going pretty damned far, he argued—Sam signed the picture, "To Chauncey with Great Affection, from Uncle Douglas." Then he studied the photo for a moment and crossed out the Uncle—but lightly, so that it could still be made out—and added the surname MacArthur.

That evening Sam paid a casual visit to the Fukuoka Area Officers' Club. The paint was scarcely dry on the refurbished club, but already the whisky was flowing. It was hard to get a tube of toothpaste anywhere, but all the liquor you could drink was selling for around $5.00 a case, and very few club members were sober much beyond the first hour of the drinking day.

Grateful for the fact that it had at last become that kind of war, Sam sat down at the bar next to a gullible second lieutenant from the Team's Education Section.

"Hi, Sammy, ole boy," Milton Potter greeted him. "You

look down. Whassa matter?"

Sam shock his head, picked up his drink, and stared into it dolefully, letting his despondency sink in.

"Whassa matter, I said—?"

"It's my roommate," Sam sighed.

"Which one? You got two."

"Chauncey MacArthur."

"Whassa matter with ole Chauncey?"

Sam turned a pitying gaze on Potter, hoping it would make the intended impression. "You mean you don't *know*?"

"About what?"

"About Chauncey's relationship to the Supreme Commander."

Potter chuckled. "Oh yeah, sure. What is he? Lackey, father-confessor, butt-boy, striker, batman. . . . ."

"Of course not!" Sam growled. "He's the General's *nephew*, that's what! Just take a look at that autographed picture in his room."

"The nephew of *Douglas* MacArthur?" Potter cried, nearly falling off his bar stool. "You serious?"

"No," said Sam sourly, "I just like to lie like this. I get my kicks this way. Listen, Chauncey's tight as a virgin hummingbird about it, but True and me, we know what's cooking. Chauncey asked to be stationed out here in the sticks because he doesn't want to trade on his uncle's name. Why, he could be sitting in his own mansion in Tokyo with a dozen broads bathing his balls for him if he wanted it. But no, he's down here in the sticks, and he's modest as hell. He doesn't want any publicity, he's like that. But it's getting us down, he's so *paranoid* about it. Sometimes we can't even call him by his last name, he's that sensitive."

"Holy Mother!" breathed Potter. "Royalty right here in Fukuoka and I didn't even know it! Wait'll I tell Jimson."

Captain Jimson was the worst gossip Sam had ever known. He couldn't have hit it luckier.

"You tell anybody," Sam said ominously, shaking a finger in Potter's face, "and I'll put the P.X. off-limits to you! We got enough troubles without publicity like that. I'm only telling you, because I just can't stand all this secrecy any longer."

"Okay, okay, I won't tell anybody. I promise!"

"One word about this, and I confiscate your PX ration card, Potter," Sam said, slurping down the rest of his martini and slipping off the stool. "I gotta go now," he said, "See you later."

He turned and walked briskly away from the bar, suppressing a smile. He was absolutely certain that within an hour Potter would be bending Jimson's ear.

While Sam was out spreading lies, True and Chauncey were taking it easy back at the *Koki-kan.*

"If Ah knew as much Japanese as you do, Chauncey," True said, cradling Mabel's head in his lap, "Ah wouldn't give a damn whether the general was my uncle or not."

"He's not, but I admit you do need some help with the language, True. Hey, let's have a quick review right now."

"Screw that. Ah'll get by somehow."

"But you usually get the sentences backwards, and if that doesn't happen, you use the wrong words at the wrong time."

"What do you mean?"

"Like yesterday, for example, when Sumiko came in and told you the bath was ready, you said *'Kono densha wa Hibiya ni ikimasu ka?*"

"So what's wrong with that?"

"Nothing really, except it means, 'Does this streetcar go to Hibiya?' "

True cackled at his own blunder. "Ah'll be an egg-suckin' mule! I wondered how come she sashayed outta the room laughing like a plain fool."

"That what's I mean. And then this morning at breakfast in the mess-hall when the Japanese waiter asked you how you wanted your eggs, you told him, *'Koe wo agetara utsu zo.*' "

"Don't that mean 'sunny side up'?"

"No, True, it means, 'If you call for help, I'll shoot you.' You're still back in the jungle warfare book."

"So that's why Ah didn't get mah eggs done right," True muttered resentfully. "Maybe you better teach me some new ones, Chauncey. Somethin' like 'My friend is Douglas MacArthur's nephew.' That ought-a set mighty sharp with ole Dawgleish."

"You'll have a chance to find out tomorrow morning."

"You mean I can talk to the C.O. in Japanese? I didn't

know he knew any of them heathen tongues."

"He doesn't, but I bet he'd talk in Mandarin Chinese if Doug's nephew asked him to."

The trio trooped over to Dawgleish's office the next morning, as per their master plan. Captain Ruby Whacker was posted outside the colonel's office, brusque and formidable. She was habitually surly to most of the officers in the M.G. Team, except True. It was probably a question of the affinity of behemoth women for compact little men, for True was small, though well put together; and maybe Ruby had a thing about almost impenetrable southern accents or curly hair. Whatever it was, True was generally used as an entrance wedge whenever Sam or Chauncey wanted an audience with the C.O.

True was pushed forward so that he would head the committee. Ruby looked up from some letters she was sorting at her desk and said in the sweetest tones her hoarse voice could muster, "Good morning, True Foote, and how are. . . ." Then, glancing beyond him at Chauncey on the right flank and Sam on the left, she scowled and added, "You sure do keep randy company, I must say. That monkey's bad enough, but these guys. . . ."

Sam and Chauncey knew there was little they could do about Ruby's searing tongue; she outranked them.

"Well, speak up," Ruby said loudly, "what's the game this morning?"

"We want to see the colonel about our new assignments, Captain." Chauncey adopted a humble posture. A woman of Ruby's size wasn't to be trifled with. Her coarse voice, corseted torso, protuberant bosom, and flashing eyes made him think of one of those ancient Greek machines of war that rumbled along belching flame and flinging boulders.

"Ha, two more minutes and you'd have to hunt me down in the crapper," Ruby said without embarrassment, "and then you'd have to wait indefinitely. Just so happens you can go right in. The C.O.'s free." She rendered True a lewd wink; he squirmed beneath its intensity. "And so'm I, dumplin', and don't you forget it. I cook a great mess of greens, you know, just like your mammy."

Ruby rose to her full six feet, stretched a powerful arm around her desk and gripped True's thigh so hard that he paled. "Save a little for Ruby, honey," she said throatily, then thudded off for the john.

"Well, kiss old rusty!" exclaimed Sam, lost in the wonder of what they had just seen.

True shook his head and rubbed his throbbing thigh. "Ah sweah, a man'd have to be mighty hard up to piddle around with a woman like that."

Chauncey started for the door to the colonel's office. "Come on, men. Here we go."

The colonel sat huddled over a portable phonograph with his back to them. It was playing a scratchy disc so softly that they couldn't make it out.

"Sir," Chauncey began tentatively.

The colonel whirled around and scowled at all three of them, seeing them as a triptych. Then, editing out Sam and True and zooming in on Chauncey, he said in a merry, cordial voice, "Well, well, well, if it isn't the *young* MacArthur! Chauncey, my boy, how are you? Have a chair. . . . Here, you two, get this man a chair and be quick about it! Haven't seen you since Friday, Chauncey." At that point the record ran down, so he shut off the phonograph and turned back to the junior officers. It would be the letter, of course, that made all this difference, thought Chauncey.

"So—how can I serve you this morning, lad?" Dawgleish said in unctuous tones, totally unlike his usual fang-revealing bark.

"Well, Colonel Dawgleish, I'd like to talk to you about our assignments and what you and I heard at the staff meeting on Friday."

"I'm only too eager to help you, my boy. Anything, anything at all."

"Well, sir, it's like this: Me being Liaison Officer and Lieutenant Foote being Arms Disposal Officer calls for a lot of travel around Kyushu. And while Lieutenant Bruce's two jobs—Assistant Supply Officer and P.X. Officer—don't call for any travel, he doesn't have any work right now either, so. . . ."

The colonel's smile was still slightly patronizing. "Mmmmh, you've got it all figured out, haven't you?"

"Well, sir, I thought we might all three kill two birds with one stone."

"And how do you propose to go about performing that

— 49 —

bit of legendary legerdemain?"

"We're going scouting for those fourteen missing girls, sir, while carrying on our other duties, or most of them, anyway."

"What a great idea, Chauncey!" the colonel cried, slapping the top of his desk delightedly. "My boy, you've got brains in your head, where they belong!"

"Then you don't mind?"

"Mind? Why should I mind, my boy? Forget your Team responsibilities! These men can, too. You three are my Japan experts, my cunning oriental linguists. You're the logical ones to go out looking for those innocent little girls. And, Chauncey, you'll be in charge. After all, you're a genuine bona fide MacArthur, born to leadership. Wait!"

He rang for Ruby Whacker who came gallumphing in, jugs jouncing, fresh from the crapper, and darting a syrupy sidewise smile at True.

"Captain, cut these men some travel orders."

"Travel orders?" Ruby looked discomfited. "Where to, sir?"

"Make them open so they can go anywhere in Kyushu on official business and can requisition food and lodging from any indigenous source they wish to use. Also, call the Supply Officer and the Mess Officer and inform them that Lieutenant MacArthur here—" Chauncey received a warm avuncular smile "—can draw on them for *anything* he wants. *Any* time."

"Yes, sir," Ruby said, trying hard to suppress her surprise as she went out. Chauncey could understand her bewilderment. The colonel almost never did any favors like that for anybody. As tight with them as with his money.

"Thank you, sir," said Chauncey. "I really appreciate...."

Dawgleish rose and strode around his desk to throw a friendly arm around Chauncey's shoulders. "No, no! *I* should be the one to thank *you* for this magnificent plan to comb Kyushu for the girls. I only wish I wore a star on my shoulder right now, so I'd rate a full-time aide-de-camp with brains like you instead of that female Gargantua I'm stuck with. You'd be superlative, my boy, and what a knockout team we'd make, eh?"

Now it was a dig in the ribs and a close-up leer.

Dawgleish had the breath to neutralize a honey-tank, thought Chauncey.

"It's a very pleasant idea, sir. Sort of a marriage of brain and brawn."

"It's brilliant," Dawgleish admitted, missing Chauncey's point. "Maturity and experience mated with youthful vigor and initiative. Yessiree, if only your uncle. . . . Heh, heh, what I was about to say was, we'd show this country a thing or two together. *And* those goddam Marines, too." Both hands on Chauncey's shoulders, he looked him squarely in the eye. "I'm going to miss you around here, Chauncey, but the Team'll muddle through somehow. You're free to take off just as soon as Captain Whacker cuts your orders. Of course, I'll worry about you, so perhaps you'd better get in touch with me every few days, sort of keep me abreast. I'd like to know you're all right. Someone—in Tokyo or somewhere—might want to know where you are. I think you know what I mean."

"Oh yes," Chauncey replied, soberly straight-faced, "I know exactly what you mean, sir."

"Well, then, good luck." The colonel clasped Chauncey's hand warmly with both of his. "And God go with you, my boy."

Chauncey turned quickly to hide his grin of triumph and strode from the room, Sam and True trailing in mock meekness, hoping they wouldn't fall down outside and have hysterics right in front of Ruby Whacker. She would never understand.

CHAPTER EIGHT

"Why, that raddled old bitch!" Chauncey exploded as
Sam maneuvered the jeep skillfully around potholes on the
drive from Hida to Oguni.

In the rear seat, True and Mabel clutched each other
fearfully amid the chaos of Army rations, beer cases, hard
liquor, and a bare minimum of personal gear. Even Sam's
expert driving could not afford the passengers much
comfort or security on such roads.

"Talk about your prurient eye, that horny broad's sure
got one!" Chauncey's reference point was the carton of
magazines he held in his lap. He had snitched it from
beneath Captain Ruby Whacker's desk while she was on one
of her ritual safaris to the crapper. Deceived by the erudite
camouflage of the top magazine, *The Journal of The Asiatic
Society*, Chauncey had scooped up the entire carton
and took off without bothering to glance under the top
copy. And now, safely out of Fukuoka and beyond the
range of Ruby's volcanic wrath, he was shuffling through
the magazines and discovering that he had stolen nine back
copies of *Torrid Screen Stories*, fourteen of *Cute Cinema
Cut-Ups*, seven of *Hollywood in Bed*—with the one *Journal
of the Asiatic Society*.

"Wouldn't you know it!" Chauncey moaned. "She's got
the intelligence level of a pre-adolescent sex fiend!"

True and Mabel peered curiously over his shoulder.
"Hey, Chauncey," True cried gleefully, "we got us some
pin-ups!"

Chauncey started to repack the carton, preparatory to
jettisoning it. "Out it goes," he said grimly, and both Sam
and True had to restrain him, Sam almost losing control of
the jeep in the process.

"Damn fool!" Sam growled. "We can use the paper to
stoke our fires."

"Yours don't need any stoking," Chauncey declared.

"You two degenerates are already bogged down in lust and depravity."

"That depraved part ain't exactly a nice accusation," said True sullenly. "Ah once had an uncle that was arrested for that in Georgia. He was seventy-six at the time. They caught him grossly exposing himself to a neighbor's favorite ewe. He finally got the charges squashed but had to get outta the state forever or be tar-'n'feathered."

"Anyway, keep the magazines," Sam said. "Maybe that picture of Betty Grable on the cover there will help you forget about eels." Sam was referring to Chauncey's new-found fondness for that popular Japanese dish.

"Yeah," True grunted. "Ah don't see how Chauncey can eat the slimy things."

"I am a gourmet," Chauncey replied stiffly. "Something you hamburger and hot dog buffs will never understand. At least *I* can be absorbed into the cultural delights of Japan, whereas you bums. . . ."

"Culture?" Sam growled. "Is charcoal-broiled eel culture? And then that vile purple pastry you're grown so fond of. The one that's so nauseating that I've got a mental block about its name."

"Daketsu anko."

"Ah kind of like it," True confessed. "Not as mouth-waterin' as hawg casings in vinegar or stewed squirrel heads, but it's passable good, all the same."

"I may just vomit all over you two," Sam threatened. "Keep it up, and I will."

"Daketsu anko," True murmured from the back seat, flipping pages in his Japanese pocket dictionary. "That's somethin' Ah shouldn't forget! Sweet motha! It says it's sugared soybean jelly laced with snake-blood."

"Even worse than I thought," said Sam, gagging.

At that moment, they were passing the fatal spot where their wheel had parted company with the jeep on their previous run.

"Yep, this is the place," said True. "Maybe Ah can find it if you stop and lemme look."

"Find what?"

"Mah lil' ole rabbit's foot Ah've had since Ah was practically a pup."

"Sometimes you're tiresome as hell," said Sam, braking

to a neat stop parallel to the infamous honey-tank site. "Go ahead, look around. It's a waste of time, but I've learned from experience that once you get an idea into that thick head of yours, there's no shaking it loose until you've had your way."

"Okay," True cried excitedly. "Here, you hold Mabel," he told Chauncey and climbed out of the jeep.

But in the transfer, Mabel slipped out of Chauncey's grasp, jumped to the ground, and went scrambling and screeching across the field toward the honey-tank and its adjacent bamboo grove, True in hot pursuit.

"Mabel, honey! Come back heah!" True yelled. "Wait for ole True! Stop!"

Sam and Chauncey joined in the chase. It was easy to see that Mabel didn't know what she might be letting herself in for. Sam grunted in despair as he watched her skid to a sudden stop and inspect the tall stand of graceful bamboo on the far side of the tank. Something instinctive was sending her signals, so with a squeak of joy she scurried around the tank's perimeter and scrambled up a slim bamboo trunk only a couple of feet from the edge. Her raucous rapture filled the air as she neared the top of the bamboo, which had begun to sag dangerously under her weight.

"Come on down, Mabel!" Chauncey bellowed.

True stopped at the foot of the bamboo as the others closed in. "She don't know come-here from sick-'em." True said in disgust, looking around for a clod to chunk at her. Reaching down, he saw he'd almost stepped on his rabbit's foot with its tarnished golden chain, as good as the day he had lost it.

As he picked it up, the bamboo top broke, and Mabel fell with the scream of a lost soul into the honey-tank, sinking from sight a good eight feet from shore.

"Oh, Christ, we gotta save her!" True said frantically, motioning for Chauncey to pick up one end of a long piece of fallen bamboo and hold it while he ran around the cesspit with the other end, thus making a solid handhold for Mabel. They lowered the bamboo pole until it was only a few inches above the tank's surface. Meanwhile Mabel had shot up out of the slimy depths and was floundering around, gasping, spluttering, and trying not to make waves.

When she saw the bamboo lifeline, she grasped it with prehensile fervor. Slowly they lifted her out of the muck. She looked exactly as if she'd been dipped in tar and was fearfully awaiting the application of feathers.

Shaking herself, she lost no time in running along the slender bamboo toward her adored master, recognizing him as her true savior. When she was close enough to the bank that True could throw down his end of the bamboo pole without dropping her back into the sludge, he did so instantly and began to sprint in the opposite direction from the jeep. Mabel paused on the bank only long enough to dash slime from her eyes, then bounced off after True, chattering out her thanks and adoration.

Chauncey and Sam watched in fascination as Mabel flew over the ground with the swiftness of a turpentined road-runner.

"I've never seen monkeys run before," Sam noted calmly. "They're just awfully damned fast, aren't they."

"But look at that True Foote go!" Chauncey said admiringly. "He's no slouch, either."

"Let's hope they both keep right on going. Forever and ever. . . ."

"Uh-óh, they're changing course," said Chauncey apprehensively. And sure enough, True was beginning to circle and gradually heading back toward the jeep.

Sam and Chauncey stared at each other for a few seconds, then without another word turned and raced for the jeep. They leapt in, gunned it to life, and stood ready, just in case.

Chauncey trained his binoculars on the chase. "True's just jumped the goddam stream," he narrated. "That must be a world's record for the broad jump! Sweet shades of Jesse Owens, I'll bet it's eight yards wide!"

With her shorter legs, Mabel couldn't make such a prodigous leap, so she skipped nimbly down the bank to a narrower point, only three yards across, and managed it easily there. She was hard on True's heels now.

"She's almost got him!" Chauncey groaned, offering the binoculars to Sam.

"I can't bear to look," Sam said.

At that instant, Mabel caught up with her master and sprang lightly to his shoulder, nuzzling him passionately.

That was the final ignominy for True. With Mabel aboard, he threw himself into the clear stream in a racing dive. Mabel, her master, and the odoriferous cloak of ordure that now clung to both of them vanished from sight and, even better, from smell.

Sam shook his head, while Chauncey howled with laughter.

"This time the Oguni folk are really going to believe that's his life-style," Sam observed.

"We could just drive off and leave him," Chauncey suggested only half in jest.

"I'm sorely tempted," Sam replied as they watched True surface and heard Mabel's plaintive wail floating clearly to them across the rice-paddies. "But we couldn't. The poor bastard's accident-prone. Besides, if Mabel's his mascot, he's ours. We'll just have to bathe him and drench him in Old Spice and then maybe he won't drive those fourteen Japanese girls away."

"Fourteen girls, fourteen targets," mused Chauncey.

They sat in silence and thought about the intriguing possibilities of what lay ahead in Oguni while True and Mabel drearily climbed whimpering out of the stream, shook themselves, and headed slowly back toward the jeep.

CHAPTER NINE

Ensigns Nemoto and Yoshikita plodded down the dirt road, smallish puffs of dust erratically marking their weary passage. In the two weeks that had passed since they caught up with their fleeing brides-to-be, certain distinct changes had been made in their appearance. While there was still a degree of determination in the set of their shoulders, the observer could not fail to mark the dirt and grime on their uniforms, which came from sleeping in fields more often than not. And the looseness of the uniforms' fit, which came from subsisting on handouts, reluctantly given but gratefully received. The worn shoes. The lengthening of head and face hair. And the crescive wildness of eye.

The two navy officers had trudged from Kurume, where they had found the fourteen girls and their chaperone, back to Fukuoka, thinking that their elusive quarry might have returned to the presumed safety of their homes. In Fukuoka they had surveilled the fourteen homes—all of which were in the upperclass residential district south of Nishi Park—for three nights, ready to take action. Finding no trace of the girls, Nemoto and Yoshikita left the city and headed north for Kokura, asking questions of the dazed, often uncomprehending survivors of the war all along the way. Then south again, through Kurume, to Kumamoto. To Dazaifu. And to Karatsu. To Tosu, Iizuka, and then to Saga.

Sometimes they rode trains. If the trains were running. Although they had little money, conductors were letting all men in uniform ride free, assuming that they were newly discharged and on their way home. But unrepaired air raid damage rendered most train service non-existent or, at best, whimsically intermittent.

Travel by automobile was out of the question. All gasoline had been reserved for aircraft use, while even the cars of the police and high government officials ran only if their engines had been converted to power derived from the burning of charcoal.

So mostly they walked. Nor did they stand out on foot. Homeward-bound men in uniform were no rarity on Japan's roads. Like the others, Nemoto and Yoshikita shouldered knapsacks into which were crammed the remnants of military life and—in their case at least—fourteen new, sharp knives with one-edged blades a standard eight-and-a-half inches long.

Before bedding down each night—on bundles of last year's rice-straw when they could find it, the two palely dedicated *kamikaze* pilots performed the same ritual. They divided the knives into two piles of seven each. One by one, almost reverently, they removed the balsa-wood scabbards and wiped the blades free of largely imagined grit and dust. Before replacing the knives in the knapsacks, they gripped them firmly in their hands and contemplated the reddest depth of their campfire for a long moment. They thought of their comrades whose skeletons had by now been picked clean by conger eels on the bottom of the sea south of Kagoshima. They looked down in distaste at their living bodies as if resenting the flesh that still clung to their own bones. They flushed at the thought that they were still among the quick when they should have been with the gloriously dead. They ground their teeth at the recollection of the fourteen maidens who had stupidly shamed their betters by fleeing from marriage with themselves and twelve other Stout Hearts of the Realm.

"Yoshikita-kun, when we find them," Nemoto was asking, "what shall we do with the barbaric Swiss female?"

"Let her go, I suppose."

"But she tricked us, didn't she?"

"We cannot be certain of that, can we? Perhaps those shameless hussies tricked *her* and then she went after them to bring them back."

"Hmmmm."

"Either way, it is of little consequence," stated Yoshikita with cool deliberation. "Should she thwart us this time, we will. . . . .dispose of her."

"When will 'this time' be?"

"Sooner or later."

"We should be meeting American troops any day now."

Nemoto spat away from Yoshikita. "Perhaps it would be better if we gave up this tiresome marching and flung ourselves upon them in a magnificent two-man *Banzai* charge."

"No, Nemoto-kun, our course is clear. You must not falter or doubt. Our twelve comrades will be lonely without their rightful brides, and since those wenches do not have the good sense to go to their masters of their own free will, then it behooves us to light a small fire beneath them."

"A fire," Nemoto said, grinning, "in the form of a razor-sharp, highly-tempered blade?"

"Precisely." Yoshikita too smiled in grim pleasure, but he found the action awkward for seldom-used facial muscles.

"I wonder if the Americans will stop us on the roads?"

"Why should they? We are only two among hundreds, even thousands of others."

"We have no military orders," Nemoto pointed out.

"Nor do many of the others."

After five more minutes of heat and dust, Nemoto glanced shyly at his companion, then sighed and shook his head as if in regret.

"What is it now?"

"I was just thinking. . . ."

"You're not. . . .reconsidering, are you?"

"No, not that," Nemoto denied stoutly, stiffening his shoulders. "It's just that. . . .well, I wish I could get a little of that first."

"A little of what?" Yoshikita asked grumpily. "Sometimes I don't understand you at all, Nemoto-kun. What in Nirvana are you babbling about?"

"A little of. . . .Sujiko," Nemoto answered sheepishly. "You know, a piece of tail. . . ."

"Nemoto-kun!"

"What's wrong with that?"

"You're an officer in the Special Attack Forces, aren't you? Don't forget you've dedicated your life to the Emperor!"

"Why should the Emperor care if I get a little before I sacrifice my life? Why, he never even heard of me."

Yoshikita was near apoplexy. He sputtered and hissed in extreme indignation. "That's sacrilege! How dare you mention His Imperial Majesty and.... sex in the same breath."

Sulkily Nemoto replied, "I've read the Imperial Rescript on Education and the Imperial Rescript on Filial Piety and the Imperial Rescript on Good Form While Viewing Cherry Blossoms and. . . . " he paused to catch his breath "....all the other Imperial Rescripts and I don't remember anywhere that the Emperor says, 'Thou Shalt Not Get Thyself a Little Now and Then.' "

"Be silent!" Yoshikita ordered sternly. "Get a grip on your 'monkey-and-horse' passions. Obviously the heat and our long journey have unseated you. If you can't control yourself any better than this, Nemoto-kun, I shall have to consider leaving you behind when the brides and I go off yonder to meet our more fortunate comrades."

Ensign Nemoto hung his head so that Yoshikita would not see the unbidden light in his eyes.

CHAPTER TEN

"We'd better not go barging right into Oguni this evening," Sam said later when they sighted the hill that cut off the town and its charming valley from the rest of the world.

"That's right," agreed Chauncey, who was riding in the front with Sam. "If word gets around that we're in town, it might drive Hilda Ritter and her girls deeper into the hills."

"Ah still don't get it," complained True, who was sitting, shivering and depressed, in the back seat with Mabel. "We know Hilda Ritter's in Oh-Gooney, so those gals are bound to be with her. All we gotta do is nose 'em out and latch onto 'em, ain't it?"

"Listen, True," Chauncey began patiently, "and this time try to understand: First of all, we don't have the *authority* to 'latch onto 'em', as you put it. We don't have police powers, get it? We have to either persuade them to return of their own free will or call in the Marine MP's."

"So what's wrong with that?"

"That's my next point: We don't want the girls to go back to Fukuoka yet. When they go, we go—and that means back to work for us, doesn't it? Which we don't want, right?"

True nodded his enthusiastic agreement with that point.

"In a nutshell," Chauncey continued, "our problem is to keep the girls here in Oguni and cut them off from communication with the outside world as long as we can."

"While we do what?" True wanted to know.

"While we watch them. Make sure they stay where they are."

"But where we gonna sleep?" True asked querulously.

"In the woods, if necessary. Or maybe we'll find an abandoned shack on that hill behind the town. Anywhere we can keep our eyes on the girls without being seen."

"But *then* what're we gonna do?" True was in the mood

to bitch about everything.

"Nothing."

"Nothin'?"

"That's exactly right: nothing," said Chauncey. "Nothing—except sleep and eat and sleep some more."

"If I slept for a solid month," said Sam, "I'd still be behind."

"Nothin' but sleep an' eat?" Dawn was beginning to break for True. "Say now, that's not such a bad. . . . Yeah, I see. Then every foah or five days or so, we'll scoot back to Fukuoka, stock up on hooch and rations, and tell ole Dawgleish we still ain't found 'em. . . ."

"If we're not going to stay in Oguni tonight," interrupted Sam, worry edging his voice, "then we'd better start looking for some other place."

A short distance farther on, the road divided. The fork to the left led up over the hill and into Oguni. The right fork was narrower and looked less often used. They went to the right.

Three hundred yards later, the road came to the Chikugo River, then turned right again. Up ahead, in the gathering dusk, they saw the partial profile of a structure half-screened by trees. As Sam pulled up to a stop in front of it, they realized that it was a recently-constructed Buddhist temple.

"Maybe the priest has a room or two to spare," said Sam, getting out of the jeep. "True, you stay here and keep Mabel company. She's been in enough trouble for one day."

"Shit, Ah always miss the action," True grumbled.

"But not the shit," said Chauncey, laughing with Sam.

Sam and Chauncey approached the temple along the brief, tree-lined path. The place appeared deserted, yet from the interior issued the steady rhythm of a drum and a monochromatic, stupor-laden chanting. Skirting the large central room with its ten-foot replica of the Gautama Buddha, the pair walked softly along polished wooden corridors toward the source of the sutra singing.

They came at last to an open door; inside was a twelve-*tatami* room, spacious and high-ceilinged. A shaven-headed priest in a dark *kimono* sat chanting a sutra with closed eyes, swaying slightly from side to side. Behind him crouched two young acolytes vigorously thumping hand drums gripped between their knees. Their erratic rhythms, which countered rather than supported the priest's chanting, were nonetheless eerily effective accompaniment.

So as not to disrupt the ceremony, Sam and Chauncey remained discreetly and silently observant outside the door until the chant ended in dying drum beats, the priest's voice fading away on the still air. Then Chauncey entered with a respectful look on his face, with Sam behind him, and addressed the priest in the formal, stilted Japanese they had learned at language school.

"We are sorry to intrude, but do you have lodging for three weary and humble travellers?"

The priest's mouth dropped open; the acolytes' eyes popped open and remained that way. No one immediately answered Chauncey.

Finally Sam repeated the question in a slightly different form, and this too was greeted with silence.

"Come, come," said Chauncey, "we are no longer the enemy. We are your new American friends, come to bring you greetings and peace."

At last the priest exhaled sharply, bowed to them and said, "We shall be honored, gentlemen, if you will make use of our poor abode."

In no time the three lieutenants and Mable were settled in an eight-*tatami* mat room and unpacked for the night. While True changed into dry clothes and Mabel gobbled a cold can of C-rations, Sam and Chauncey explored the temple corridors. The room on the north side of the building opposite theirs was done in Western style: wooden floors without *tatami* or reed mats. It was evidently the library. Its wide window faced the west and the Chikugo River, now barely visible in the near-dark. Sam lit two of the several large candles in the room and with Chauncey proceeded to inspect the bookshelves.

"Sam, look! A Buddhist priest who reads Spenser, John Donne, Shakespeare, Lovelace, Dryden, and John Milton! Incredible!"

"Yeah, fantastic. Look here." Sam was across the room now, looking at other books. "Here's *A History of European Ghouls,* by G.C. Neely, and Robert Herrick's *To The Virgins, To Make Much of Time*. And here's Marlowe's

Doctor Faustus and Ben Jonson's *Comedy of Humors* for God's sake!"

At that point True walked in. "What yah all doin'?" he asked.

"What does it look like?" Sam said. "We're cataloging books."

True reached for a volume, opened it at random and started to read. "'Od's Bodkins,' quoth the King, 'but it bodes ill for yon dastardly varlet—after a fortnight of swinish lusting after drink and harlots in London town—to bestow a poulterer's pinch on the Queen's fair nates!' Then spake the Count, 'Yessiree. . . .'"

Sam grabbed the book from him. "Where does it say 'Yessiree'?"

True pointed to the line he'd been reading. "Right theah."

"You oaf, that's 'Yes, *sire!*'"

Just then a hooded nun entered the room, introducing herself with a deep bow.

"I am Daijini," she said in a soft melodious voice, "or the Nun of Great Mercy. You are welcome to use our priest's personal library. He often comes here for navel contemplation." She used the formal Japanese expression, *zazen wo kumu*, Chauncey noted. "Gentleman, I came to tell you that dinner is now ready."

"Dinner?" Chauncey echoed. "But we didn't come to impose upon your hospitality, Daijini. We have plenty of Army rations to sustain us."

"Nevertheless, the priest requests that you join us. Dinner is already prepared and will go to waste unless you consent to eat with us."

"In that case, of course," said Chauncey, and they followed Daijini along the corridor and down one flight of stairs to a spacious banquet room where the head priest and several other bonzes and nuns were assembled to greet them.

"Your host is Seido-san," said Daijini as she presented the three travellers to a venerable man in a dark robe.

"What's that mean?" True whispered over Chauncey's shoulder.

Out of the corner of his mouth Sam said, "Mr. Correct Path."

When the travellers were seated on *zabuton* on the *tatami* mats around the low, rectangular table, the head priest, Mr. Correct Path, addressed them in accented, archaic English:

"You are most welcome, honorable officers of the victorious American Army. We are made most distinguished by your graceful presence."

Chauncey wondered immediately if the old boy was putting them on. The scene had an air of Gilbert and Sullivan about it, imparting a story-book quality. But Mr. Correct Path's voice was high and clear, his smooth face innocent of intrigue. His ears were large-lobed, as were the classic Buddha statues, and his head as shiny as an amber egg. He could be fifty, thought Chauncey, or even seventy; it was impossible to tell. Anyway, he appeared to be doing his utmost to make his guests comfortable.

Chauncey replied in English, "Mr. Correct Path, please forgive our rude intrusion."

The head priest smiled. "Say no more about it. I am honored that you remember my name, May I know yours?"

Sam grinned and became toastmaster: "He's Lieutenant Chauncey MacArthur, sir."

Correct Path's heavy-lidded eyes widened in awe. "Ah, can it possibly be?" he asked, sucking in his breath. "You are related to that most renowned general and master strategist who now stands beside the August Presence of our Emperor in Edo?"

The reference to Edo, Tokyo's name until 1868, was not wasted on Chauncey. Here is a man, he thought, who lives in the glorious past.

"The truth is, sir, that I am not. . . ." Chauncey began, but Sam interrupted.

"Not General MacArthur's *son*, sir, but rather his illustrious *nephew*." Sam smiled approvingly at his own glib lie.

Correct Path rose to his knees and then launched himself into a series of three deep bows of the *koto* variety in which the forehead must touch the floor or ground covering. Sensing an importance to the conversation that they did not yet understand, the circumambient nuns and bonzes immediately began to imitate their leader.

When this obeisance was accomplished, Correct Path

spoke rapidly in the local dialect to the others and the effect was profound. They backed five or six feet away from the table and averted their eyes, as if the presence of such a close relative of the distinguished general was too incandescent a radiance to gaze upon directly.

"Of course," Sam continued nonchalantly, rising with relish to the occasion, "Lieutenant MacArthur insists that everyone treat him as—ha, ha—an equal. Why, just the other day his Uncle Doug offered to bring him to Tokyo and make him a full colonel by special decree. But you know what Chauncey MacArthur said? He said no; he was afraid of the adverse effect such favoritism would have upon our troops' morale. So you see, Mr. Correct Path, how singular a man my colleague here is. Of course, he talks almost daily by telephone with his uncle to advise him what must be done here in Kyushu."

Correct Path looked surprised. "Ah, then the telephone lines between Kyushu and Honshu have been restored? My, my, your forces are most efficient."

Chauncey covered his mouth with one hand and whispered just loud enough for Sam to hear, "You bastard, I'll get even with you yet!"

"Not exactly," Sam went on, unperturbed by Chauncey's threat, "Chauncey's uncle has strung a special emergency line just so he can communicate with his favorite nephew."

Chauncey began to wonder why Sam had not joined the U.S. diplomatic corps, where he could bring his talent for falsehood to fullest flower.

"Sir," Sam went on, "you are now in the presence of Chauncey MacArthur, soldier and peacemaker. . . ."

Chauncey stepped reluctantly forward, and in turn introduced True and Sam to Correct Path, briefly explaining that True was an agronomist and that Sam had attended pre-med school. Then he inquired, "What's for chow?"

"Chow?" Correct Path puzzled over this for a second. "Chow. . . . Ah yes, of course! You mean dinner. A thousand pardons, Your Excellency—uh, I mean Colonel—no, Lieutenant. Have patience, I shall eventually get it right. This momentous news is so unexpected."

"For me, too," Chauncey said, as Correct Path turned away to give an order.

"We are indeed fortunate tonight, gentlemen," Correct Path said, turning back to his guests, "to be able to offer you the prime delicacy of this illustrious and beguiling region of Kyushu."

"Ah'd be grateful for crumbs," said True. "Mah stummick's talkin' loud and clear."

"Since your comrade in arms, Lieutenant Bruce, has had medical training," Correct Path continued, ignoring True's remark, "I have just taken the liberty of inviting my friend and neighbor, Dr. Ino, to join us at dinner. The doctor and I share cultural delights in this benighted backwater where we are forced to reside. We hold a high mutual interest in literature, religion, and philosophy. We also play *Go*, a game similar to your chess, and toast each other's health. Or, alas, we used to," Correct Path added wistfully, "until some months ago when our precious liquor supply expired. In your Christian era year of 1940 we saw the Chinese characters on the *shoji*, so we laid by a great stock of highland nectar, hopeful that it would see us through these terrible times. However, it did not."

"Strange," Sam commented, "I didn't know you priests drank at all. Matter of fact, I've got a virgin bottle of Old Parr Scotch in my room. I'll go get it." He started to get up, but Correct Path said, "No, allow me to send a menial," then clapped his hands and ordered an acolyte to fetch the whisky bottle from the guests' room.

Chauncey said, "The reason Lieutenant Bruce is so devoted to Old Parr is that it's named after his maternal grandfather, William Parr, who was convicted of multiple rape at the age of eighty-three."

"My, oh my," murmured Correct Path, eyes twinkling, and Chauncey was relieved to see that he was regarding Sam with what amounted to an entirely new and glowing respect.

Sam blushed appropriately. "Runs in the family," he said. "My father sired a whole French village during World War One."

"Ah'm not about to believe—"True began but was interrupted by the timely arrival of the Old Parr.

"You open it, sir," Sam said deferentially. "We would be pleased. . . ."

"Such an honor!"

Correct Path snatched the bottle from his acolyte, decorked it with trembling hands, and with exceeding self-control first courteously filled his guests' glasses, then his own.

"Ah, good news from Scotland!" he cried, holding his glass of amber nectar aloft.

"To Bonnie Prince Charlie!" Sam seconded.

"Up Scotland!" said Chauncey.

"Here's to pussy!" True chimed in.

Correct Path downed his portion in one ferocious gulp, then sat back to allow the whisky to pursue its fiery course homeward.

"Sweet Nirvana," Correct Path breathed reverently, "How long I've waited for that!"

"But don't you drink *sake*, Mr. Right Road?" True asked.

"It's *Correct Path*, dumbhead," Sam hissed in his ear.

The head priest appeared not to have noticed this interplay, fondly stroking his glass and explaining that rice wine was merely a plebian drink. "A weak and characterless potion, good sirs, and fit more for the two-toed sloth, not for sophisticates and gourmets." He poured himself a generous second drink, savoring this one in tiny measured sips. As he was drinking, a procession of nuns and bonzes began to file into the spacious room bearing trays laden with covered lacquer and porcelain dishes of assorted sizes and colors.

"Ah yes, gentlemen, allow me to describe the dishes. First we offer you *unagi no nyuman*, eel-and-noodle soup. Next is *unagi natane*, scrambled eggs with eel. After that is *umaki*, egg roll stuffed with eel. Then the *piece de resistance*, called *uzusui*, a kind of eel and vegetable stew."

Chauncey looked at Sam, Sam looked at Chauncey, and True scratched his genitals. There was no doubt what the prime delicacy of the region was: their old friend, the eel.

"Later," Correct Path continued, his face slightly flushed from the effects of Old Parr, "if your hunger is not appeased, we will serve rashers of *kabayaki*—plain broiled eel marinated in soy sauce. Like the other dishes, it is superb."

"Where do you get the eels, sir? Chauncey said.

"Why, the temple itself is the local eel-ery, Lieutenant

MacArthur. That is to say, we raise eels here for profit. In these stringent times, you understand, many Japanese temples have been forced to descend—and may the Almighty Buddha forgive us!—to mundane commercial enterprise in order to exist. At our old temple across the hill in Oguni itself, we had our museum of ancient *samurai* armor and weapons with which to eke out a meager income. But when we had to abandon it and build our new temple here, we knew that few visitors would come to this even more remote spot. So we decided to turn commercial and raise eels in the Chikugo River which flows by the temple." Here Correct Path smiled modestly. "And I must admit, thanks to Buddha's blessings, we have been fairly successful. In fact, the annual festival that celebrates the prime eel season will soon begin. Despite troublous times we anticipate a brisk business in barter with the rural countryside."

Sam edged forward, a glitter of interest in his eyes. "Mr. Correct Path, is the temple you abandoned the one we saw just behind and a little above one of the Oguni inns?"

"Why, indeed it is, Lieutenant Bruce. How observant you are!"

"We saw it on our first trip. What made you move away?"

"Oguni is a snakepit," said the head priest succinctly. "Those ignorant villagers are nothing more than a pack of licentious infidels. A pox take them all! They actually came to believe that our sacred temple was *haunted*. Can you imagine?"

"And was it?" Chauncey asked innocently.

Correct Path poured himself another scotch with solemn dignity. "Of course not! We men of Buddha take no stock in such ridiculous nonsense. It so happened that one of our nuns—who shall be nameless—took too great a degree of mercy on the impoverished sexual life of a local swain and began a spirited congress with him at a secret forest rendezvous on the slopes above the temple. When she became pregnant, as women have a way of doing, she refused to name the child's father. She feared for his loss of face in the village. So she borrowed an idea from your Christian mythology—for that is what it amounts to, like some of ours—and claimed that a holy spirit had paid nightly visits to her lonely *futon*. Naturally, this set up a chain reaction of a highly controversial biological character and led to what was presumably to be Japan's first virgin birth."

"But how did this make the Oguni villagers believe your temple was haunted?" Sam asked.

"At first," Correct Path explained, "the people of Oguni doubted her tale. So, with the aid of several acolytes and novices, the nun initiated a campaign to convince the villagers that the temple actually was haunted by spirits, both holy and unholy. Without my permission, books on voodoo and the occult sciences were purloined from my library and information was gleaned from them concerning the habits of swamphaunts and boggarts, of hexes and shees, of poltergeists and leprechauns. They memorized the appearance and dress of warlocks and maras, of conjure men and pythonesses, of djins and banshees. And they practiced until they could mimic to perfection the eerie cries and sighs and moans and groans of trolls and uturuncus, ghouls and undines, of bogles, bogies, and boogey men. In fact, they all became spectral adepts in the science of loup-garous and barghests, of incubi and succubi, of gargoyles and gorgons, of nyctophiles and lupino-maniacs, of spooks and phantoms. . . ."

"Mister Path, what about plain, ole-fashioned ghosts?" True asked, swamped by the head priest's pedantry.

"Ah, thank you for reminding me, young man," Correct Path said earnestly. "Yea, verily, I forgot all about them. And also the maenads and spectres, double-gangers and vampires, lamias and *kyuketsuki*, and, of course, wraiths and werewolves. And in the same were-family come were-pigs, were-wolverines, were-dogs, were-goats, and so forth."

Correct Path sank back on his well padded buttocks and sighed from the weight of his list. Fortunately at that moment, Dr. Nagataka Ino (it meant Eternal Filial Piety Boar's Tail, he explained later) was ushered into the banquet room by an obsequious and bowing nun.

Dr. Ino was about forty, quite tall for a Japanese, yet thin and wiry. Behind Harold Lloyd glasses, his eyes gave the impression of keen, though aloof intelligence and an indifference to his surroundings.

When everyone had been properly introduced, the doctor avidly began to eat eel in various shapes and forms. As he ate, Correct Path explained that Dr. Ino was a plastic surgeon who had given up his Hida practice some years before the war in order to retire quietly in the country and devote himself to research in new surgical techniques.

"Someday—" the head priest addressed himself now exclusively to Sam, "—you must get Dr. Ino to explain to you the revolutionary new surgical technique he has developed. With your medical background, I am sure this would interest you deeply."

Sam nodded politely. "But what about the haunting of the temple, sir? That interests me more for the moment."

"Oh, that! Well, my nuns and acolytes put all they had learned into practice. They haunted the temple and its environs whenever I was not around. They even went so far as to devise ill-natured jokes that struck terror into the simple hearts of the village dolts. To make a long story short, they at last succeeded in saving the reputation of the nun. She was able to have her child in peace, since the superstitious villagers were uncertain as to the identity of the father or what world he actually came from. But of course this ruined our temple as a commercially successful religious enterprise. Oguni people shunned the place and even warned out-of-town visitors to stay away. At last we were forced to abandon it and move here."

"Who stays there now?" Sam asked, and Chauncey suddenly saw the plot clearly.

"No one," Correct Path said. "And that's a pity. It's such an attractive place, although empty of furnishings. Except, of course, for the statue of Buddha that has always been there. It is very bad luck to move a temple Buddha. We left the *samurai* armor and weapons there, too. They're safe enough. The place is considered taboo."

"And so," said Sam, "it wouldn't matter who stayed there, since the place is no longer sacred."

"Except for the Buddha, it is no longer sacred. That is right. Come, come, gentlemen, have some more eel," urged Correct Path as Dr. Ino kept eating away. "As I said earlier, if you're still hungry, we can easily prepare some *kabayaki* or broiled eel marinated in soy sauce."

A horrible gasping sound issued from True; all heads

turned in his direction. He rose to his feet, swayed unsteadily, chalk white, hands over his mouth.

"What's wrong with you? Sam demanded.

"Mah stummick. Ah gotta go! Ah ain't eatin' no eel that's urinated in soy sauce. . . ."

"What's that he's saying? Correct Path asked, leaning forward anxiously. "Is anything wrong?"

Sam smiled benignly at the head priest, rose, and placed a helping arm around True's waist. "Nothing at all, sir, nothing at all. A delicate digestive system, that's all. He's still suffering from a disorder he picked up in the Philippines. Soldiers call it Manila stomach or the GIs. Dysentery."

"Buddha bless us," said Correct Path benignly. "I hope it's not catching. We're a very healthy community, you know, thanks to eel."

True said under his breath, "Get me outta here quick!"

And with that, Sam half-carried True out of the dining room toward fresher air and away from the spicy aroma of the eel banquet.

CHAPTER ELEVEN

The three lieutenants awakened early and dressed quietly, departing the temple on foot to make a survey of Oguni's small valley from the vantage point of its surrounding hills.

As they reached the summit of the hill above the temple, the rising sun was cresting the range across the valley and sending long golden shafts of light into the violet-shadowed town. The air was pure and clear, the vista magnificent.

"Looks like an eight thousand-foot aerial view," Sam said in awe.

The precise Chauncey checked their map. "Only eight hundred."

From this elevation they could see the silvery ribbon of the Chikugo River as it meandered into view from the southeast and flowed into the Oguni valley below and slightly to their right. After enriching the meager lives of the townspeople, the Chikugo reluctantly left the gentle valley to pass by Correct Path's new temple on their left.

"Gimme the binocs, Chauncey," Sam said. "Gotta study the land."

Sam adjusted the glasses. "Well, I see the jeep, anyway." It was parked in a bamboo grove on temple property. They had given Correct Path—whom they had summarily dubbed C.P.—a fresh bottle of Old Parr Scotch to insure the vehicle's safekeeping, out of the townspeople's sight. C.P. had accepted their gift with almost tearful gratitude.

"Wonder if the old boy's smashed yet," Chauncey mused, thinking about the emotion on the head priest's face as he had bowed them up the trail.

"And there's the Inn of the Fragrant Waters, where we stayed the first night," pointed out Sam. "I think that other building over there is the Inn of the Playful Hermit, where we saw Hilda Ritter breathing on the balcony. And behind it, yeah, that's it! That building with the pagoda-like roof! That's got to be C.P.'s old temple."

"Any signs of life?" Chauncey asked.

"None. Not even any action on the bridge crossing the Chikugo."

"Gimme," said Chauncey. "It's my turn."

Chauncey surveyed the abandoned temple below. "I see the covered passageway. . . ."

C.P. had told them the passageway led from the temple to the rear of the inn where they hoped that Hilda Ritter and her charges were still staying. "The management gave us permission to use the inn's communal bath," C.P. had told them. It was situated in a large, glassed-in room at the rear of the inn. The covered passageway was built so that the head priest and his retinue could pass the short distance from the side entrance of the temple to the back door of the bath in modest comfort, regardless of the weather. It had the effect of joining the temple to the inn.

"It's just barely discernible, however," Chauncey went on, "and you wouldn't even see it unless you knew what to look for."

"The Almighty Buddha is good to us," Sam declared, not insincerely. "I think we got us a new abode, men."

True sighed. "Well, at least it's a roof ovah our heads."

"Let's go move in," said Chauncey. "It's getting hot." And indeed, the sun was already growing uncomfortably warm on their backs.

They picked their way cautiously down the verdant slope toward the deserted temple and the inns below. By this time a few Oguni-ites were moving about outside the several river-bank inns, but none showed any inclination to approach the temple compound which fortunately abutted against the foot of the hill. Although the general area was heavily forested, the slope was rather open, with low undergrowth and lush meadows. The Americans descended slowly, moving in shadow wherever they could, so as not to attract attention from below.

They reached the temple in a few minutes, without difficulty or detection. In the shadowy forested area around it an eerie silence held sway. True hung back as Chauncey and Sam stepped briskly forward and pushed one of the massive temple doors slowly open to admit the warm early autumn air into the musty interior.

When True continued to linger outside, Sam said impatiently, "For Christ's sake, True, come on. What's the matter with you?"

"Ah'm just a tiny bit worried," True said. "All them spooky things C.P. told us about. . . ."

"Well, whistle a march or an operatic aria or something," Chauncey advised.

In the infinite variety of his ignorance, Truman F. Foote possessed one redeeming grace—one ability so remarkable it amounted to a divine gift: He could recall in toto any piece of music he'd ever heard. Not only could he remember it note for note, he could reproduce it either by melodious whistling or on his trusty harmonica—his "French harp," as he called it. Oddly enough, however, he had no special love for music, certainly no connoissur's passion. One piece was like any other; Beethoven and Lead Belly were much the same to him. So because there was no purposeful editor of his musical tastes, he might come up with *"Sweet Georgia Brown"* one moment and Puccini's *Mi Chiamano Mimi!"* the next.

Follow me," Chauncey said, whereupon True at last screwed up his courage, puckered his lips, and began to tremulously whistle *"In Questa Tomba"* in his best operatic fashion, thus entering the compound in a state of advanced trepidation.

The temple was not large, but its central chamber with the large benign Buddha and high-ceilinged corridors gave the three lieutenants the impression of spaciousness and security. Apart from the worship chamber, it appeared that the temple could become for them a comfortable lodge. Pillars and rafters throughout were of massive, rough-hewn wood, and where not lacquered a dark red, were silvery with the patina of age and dust.

Passing along the outer corridors, they broke through gossamer veils of giant cobwebs that hung from the overhead beams and left their clear bootprints in the powdery dust that had long since settled on the flooring. At the rear of the temple they found a number of small cells, all six to eight-*tatami* rooms, separated by sliding *shoji* screens.

"Perfect!" Sam enthused, slapping his hands together. "We can sleep solo. Let's choose rooms and clean up a bit."

"Ah'm ready," True volunteered brightly, but he kept looking over his shoulder apprehensively whenever he thought Sam and Chauncey weren't watching.

"I want you to go right back to C.P.'s new temple and organize a safari," Sam said.

"Sure," responded True with surprising willingness. The long-unused temple upset him. In a moment, he was on his eager way, with Mabel riding his left shoulder.

Chauncey and Sam spent half an hour cleaning out three contiguous rooms, then went to survey the side of the temple nearest the Inn of the Playful Hermit. Without trouble they located the entrance to the covered passageway and followed it cautiously to the point where it issued, through half-glass doors, into the communal bath. Peering carefully through the glass, they observed what might more accurately be called an indoor swimming pool. It was square-shaped and filled with steaming water, fed from a pair of continuously flowing rusty-nozzled pipes. At a higher level on the wall, where they were less likely to be observed, were more windows affording a view of the interior pool, so they moved up a flight of four steps cut from the earth and peered through the glass apertures.

Since many similar baths in Japan were coeducational in the truest sense of the word, no attempt was ever made to thwart Peeping-Toms, like themselves. Any man or boy in Oguni could have walked buck-ass naked into the bath to join the ladies. Indeed, they would have been considered eccentric if they showed the slightest hesitation in doing so.

Unfortunately, however, the bath was now empty.

"Come on," said Chauncey, "we'll try again later."

Further exploration led them into a fourteen-mat room on the far side of the central chamber which housed the temple's collection of historical paraphernalia, the *samurai* armor and weaponry that Correct Path had mentioned. Eight glass showcases exhibited swords, bows and arrows, and halberds. There were lances, suits of armor, helmets, antique masks, and *tanto*, the shorter of the two swords carried by *samurai*. There were even some exquisite miniature *samurai* outfits, perfect in every detail, probably the playthings of the children of some famous warrior or feudal lord.

"All in all, pretty fantastic," Chauncey said when they

had finished their inspection, and Sam agreed.

They were napping when True returned with a procession of five acolytes bearing the awaited supplies. In addition to what had been in their jeep, C.P. had most thoughtfully sent along a generous supply of *futon*, candles, slippers, lunchboxes packed with dishes of cold rice—and eel.

They paid the young acolytes in American cigarettes, which were most happily received, and sent them back with a written message advising the head priest that they would come back "out" in four or five days.

Over their first drink of the day in Chauncey's quarters toward the close of the afternoon, Sam proposed to Chauncey that they set up the surveillance procedure on Hilda Ritter and her fourteen charges.

"First thing is to find them," Chauncey said.

"We face the back of the inn," Sam pointed out, "and their rooms are probably in front, facing the river."

"I know," said Chauncey. "That's why the bath is the best point of surveillance—if they're in that inn."

CHAPTER TWELVE

When it came time to make the evening survey of the bath, Sam and Chauncey opted against taking True—he might give away the show—so they decided to postpone the reconnaissance until he was asleep.

Then, dressed in their *yukata* robes, they crept cautiously into True's room to filch his flashlight, but in rummaging around in the dark they awakened Mabel, whose chattering in turn aroused True. Mumbling, he rubbed his eyes, then realized what they were doing. He bristled and became adamant.

"Ah'm puttin' on a *yukata* and comin' along," he insisted, "and you ain't stoppin' me. If mah flashlight goes, Ah do, too."

"Now, now, True," Sam said, "You need your sleep."

"Ah know what Ah need and what Ah don't need," True insisted. "And what's moah, *Ah'm* carryin' the flashlight. Cause it's mine!"

So saying, he slipped into his robe and went down the corridor ahead of them. In a few seconds, however, the pool of light abruptly disappeared, and they heard a shriek of pure terror.

"That moron," Sam grated in a disgusted voice.

"Do you think something got him?" asked Chauncey, moving closer to Sam in the clammy dark. There was no denying that an eerie uncertainty, like an unseen presence, pervaded the temple's atmosphere, whether he and Sam would admit it to one another or not.

"Maybe some of those creeps were real after all," Sam said. "Maybe they decided they liked this old joint and are still hanging around."

"I wouldn't expect that kind of talk from you, not with your big brave lip."

"Pal, in this dark hole you can expect damned near anything from me," Sam said.

"We'd better rescue True, anyway."

"If you say so," said Sam reluctantly.

But at that moment True and his flashlight burst back into the corridor and raced toward them.

"Spooks!" True yelled, waving the flashlight. "Ah stuck my nose into that room and the damned place is full o' monsters!" His voice quavered in traumatic intensity.

"I knew we shouldn't have let him come with us," Sam said.

"You were right," said Chauncey.

"Honest-to-God monsters! You all just take a peek for yourselves. Go on! Heah's the flashlight."

"Calm down, sonny boy. We saw it all this afternoon," Sam said loftily. "It's the armor and weapons museum that Correct Path told us about—in case you've forgotten."

"Oh, so that's it, huh?" said True, his voice slowly returning to normal. "Well, next time you bastards let me in on it, heah?" He handed the flashlight to Sam. "I thought Chauncey was the leader, but since you know so damn much, you take the lead. . . ."

"Don't mind if I do," Sam said, stepping to the fore. "Now, gentlemen, we'll take a little look-see at the bath."

Flashlight extinguished, the three of them crept up to the windows looking in on the pool-sized bath. The space within was well-lighted and filled with activity. What they saw petrified them into silent amazement.

The large pool was filled with young girls, all naked as peeled grapes. Some were chin-deep in the bath, others sat on the tiled rim of the pool, dangling their shapely legs in the water, splashing and churning its surface. Still others crouched on tiny wooden stools around the perimeter, soaping themselves luxuriously and ladling small pails of water over each other's shoulders and torsos.

"My God," Sam said with reverence, completely enchanted, "all it needs is a satyr or two prancing around to be right out of a Greek bacchanale."

"Heathen fertility rites," breathed Chauncey. "Perfect, absolutely perfect."

"Ah gotta a hard-on," True said uncomfortably.

"Treat it gently," advised Sam, "and you can take it back to your room as a souvenir."

"Too many girls to count," Chauncey said, slightly dizzy

at the wondrous exposure.

"Ah wasn't worrying none 'bout countin' 'em," True leered.

"Fourteen," said Sam briskly. "Fourteen Japanese and one European. A veritable treasure trove, gentlemen. Perhaps unique in the annals of Peeping-Toms."

"That theah Hilda Ritter," True pointed out, "she'd make a preacher burn his Bible."

And indeed she would, thought Chauncey. Tall, statuesque, dignified in bearing—even while naked. Somewhere in the middle twenties, he judged, with fine upright breasts, rosy-nippled, and full curvy hips. Her honey—colored hair hung to her shoulders and swung back and forth, rich as cream taffy, while she scrubbed herself. No great beauty, admittedly, but her face was attractive enough with good strong features: character, that was it; blue eyes, a wide expressive mouth, and high, slightly freckled cheekbones.

A small windowpane on True's side was broken out, and through it they could hear Hilda's voice chattering in good Japanese to a pair of young girls seated on stools close to her. There was no way of distinguishing what she said above the general hubbub, but that wasn't important.

"The cream of female Fukuoka," said Sam dreamily.

"Don't that beat all!" True declared, fingering himself.

"How old would you say Hilda Ritter is?" Chauncey asked Sam.

"Maybe twenty-four, twenty-five. . . ."

"And the girls?"

"About fifteen to eighteen, no older."

"They's old 'nuff, all right," volunteered True. "Don't worry none 'bout that."

"Amazing," Sam said. "They're all beauties, yet each one is distinctly different."

"Each one healthy and—"

"Hey, look at that!" Sam whispered.

A Japanese man, in his fifties and clad only in a loin cloth, came walking calmly into the bath from the inn's entrance. He was obviously uninterested in the girls; very casually he laid out fresh soap and rearranged pails and stools not in use.

"The bath attendant," Chauncey said.

"Jesus Christ on a raft," said True indignantly, "he ain't

payin' no more mind to them cute lil' ole things than a nanny-goat would! "

"My sainted virgin aunt," Sam said, "did you ever see such a variety of knockers in all your life?"

"Every size and shape," Chauncey agreed, "pear shape to bowling ball. And I wouldn't turn down a single chance. . . ."

"Neither would I. Hey, I'll bet old Dawgleish would go mad with lust and depravity in a place like this."

"Let's worry about ourselves," suggested Chauncey.

Hilda Ritter chose that moment to rise gracefully to her feet, the dark triangle of her crotch gleaming wetly under the overhead lights, and walk in unconcerned nudity from the bath through a door marked *Joshi*, the female dressing room. Separated from it by about fifteen feet, Chauncey noticed, was the entrance to another dressing room for men. Apparently it was quite permissible in Japan for men and women to bathe together stark naked but not proper to dress or undress together. Vulgarity enveloped only the half-draped figure, not the totally nude. It was a concept Chauncey found deliciously refreshing. Another strange aspect was that instead of revealing the deep cleavage of the bosom, Japanese women bent on provocative display lowered their *kimono* a few inches in the back to expose the heavily powdered nape of the neck. And even the most fleeting glimpse of the teeth or tongue was verboten. Discreet women covered their mouths with hands or fans while chewing or laughing.

Once Hilda Ritter had departed, the girls came to life, abandoning themselves to the nymphet pastimes of splashing water on one another, scuffling, shrieking, pinching, and giggling hysterically. Chauncey figured that this must be their daily release period in which Hilda Ritter thoughtfully allowed them to work off their youthful heads of steam.

"Goddam!" True grunted. "Ah sho' can't stand much moah of this!"

After five minutes of wild exuberance, the girls gradually calmed down. They finished their bathing and began to dry themselves, gather up their wash cloths, combs, and bottles of hair oil and then pass out of the bathing room in once again demure groups of twos and threes.

The last girl to leave—a small, voluptuous creature with wide eyes and a firm, full-breasted figure—reached up and switched off the lights, plunging the room into inky darkness, thus ending the tableau for the voyeurs.

"Ah can't get up," complained True.

"Then just pole vault back to your room," said Sam.

"That was more fun than a barrel of money," Chauncey remarked, glassy-eyed with surfeit.

"Which reminds me," said True, "Ah wonder if Mabel's all right?"

"He didn't say anything about monkeys, dumbhead."

"Ah know that, but Ah want to know how she is, anyhow. Ah'm goin'. . . . ."

"So go," said Sam, "and take the flashlight with you."

True hurried away back into the temple toward their rooms.

"Hey, Sam," said Chauncey in the darkness. "Wouldn't a nice hot bath feel great right now?"

"Nothing but pussy could feel better," Sam agreed. 'And seeing as how they turned off the lights, I guess maybe that means the bath is closed for the night."

"Obviously that's the general idea, chum. Let us descend to warmth and comfort."

They crept down to the bath doors, unlatched them, and quietly entered the bath, feeling their way carefully through the darkness to the edge of the pool. There they removed their *yukata* and slippers. Squatting on a pair of small wooden stools they began to soap and wash themselves as they'd seen "their girls" do, filling the pails from the hot and cold water faucets along the wall.

"Mmmmmmh," Chauncey groaned pleasurably to Sam, "sure as hell beats washing in cold water on an Okinawan beach, doesn't it?"

"Only one thing could beat this. . . ."

"Don't tell me, I think I know."

"Having all fourteen of those lovelies doing it for me," said Sam, anyway.

'Hey, gimme a drag on that before you throw it away," Chauncey said, chuckling.

"You know, we ought to make this a daily feature of our routine. After dinner every night we'll sneak down here and catch the girlie show and then, zip, after they leave, zip-zip, we'll sneak in, shuck down, and loll around. What say?"

"Sure, then slink back to our temple suite for a gentle night's sleep," Chauncey agreed.

"Sheer heaven," Sam murmured. "And all day we'll sleep, too. You know, I figure that on Okinawa alone I lost six hundred and seventy-one hours of sleep."

"You wanted to be on your toes in case they started shelling us again. I know."

"Let's not joke about such matters," said Sam, with a shudder, "not even in retrospect."

At that instant and without any warning the overhead lights flashed on.

Sam jumped even higher than Chauncey had seen him jump one day on Okinawa when a 155-mm howitzer shell burst not ten yards from their dugout.

"Christ, Sam!"

"Jesus, Chauncey!"

The door marked *Joshi* opened and a *yukata*-clad girl walked nonchalantly in.

Sam leaped into the pool, Chauncey an inch or two behind him, both soaped to the ears.

The bath water was only a few degrees beneath the boiling point. With howls of agony they catapulted out instantly, this time Chauncey in the lead by a foot. Plunging in white and soapy, they emerged slick-clean and an angry shade of boiled lobster red.

In desperate confusion they scurried around wildly looking for their *yukata*. Chauncey struggled into his backwards; Sam ran around crazily with his over an arm while he illogically searched for his slippers.

The girl who had illuminated their ablutions was only vaguely conscious at first of their presence, but by the time they had jumped in and out of the pool, she had staggered backwards in growing fear and opened her mouth for a lusty scream. But somehow their absurd embarrassment and their frantic, foolish attempts to make themselves presentable struck her as hilarious. Instead of screaming she started to giggle, clapped her hands over her mouth, and by the time both Sam and Chauncey were decently clad in their *yukata*, she was doubled over in hysterical laughter that echoed through the vaulted bathing room.

"*Do shimashita ka?*" Chauncey demanded when he could muster his voice, trying to give the question a measure of dignity.

"Nothing's the matter except *you two*," gasped the girl between giggles. "Who on earth are you and where did you come from?"

Reasonable response was beyond Chauncey for the moment; Sam took over. "We're Americans. We've come to this town on an important secret mission," he said in pontifical Japanese.

"But you're speaking my language," the girl said, incredulous. "And you're not so bad at it, either."

Sam favored her with a lemony smile. "Young lady, we've studied your tongue in school for many long months. My name is Lieutenant Sam Bruce and my friend here is Lieutenant Chauncey *MacArthur*."

The girl's eyes widened at Sam's underscored pronunciation of the great surname.

"Ah, yes," Sam rushed on, "I see that you recognize my friend's name. Confidentially, he's the General's favorite nephew."

"*Tashika desu ka?*" She asked, wanting to believe him but still unable to quite accept the truth of his statement.

"Of course, I'm sure," Sam said. "And you're not to breathe this fact to a living soul. As I said, our mission in Oguni is top secret, a special assignment from the General *himself*, so it's most imperative that you keep quiet about seeing us."

The girl pouted. "Can't I even tell my best girl-friend?"

"Well," Sam drawled, "maybe it'd be all right to confide in one or two of your bosom friends. But you've got to give me your solemn promise to swear them to secrecy before you tell them."

"Oh, of course, Sam," she agreed breathlessly. "May I call you Sam?"

"Anything, anything at all, dear girl."

"Very well then. I cross my heart I shall never tell more than two friends your secret."

"Good," Sam said. "Say, who was that foreign woman in the bath with all of you a few minutes ago?"

The girl giggled again. "You saw—*everything*?"

"Almost."

Undismayed by the knowledge that her new friends had been watching the communal ablutions, the girl replied, "She's our teacher and chaperone, Miss Ritter. She's Swiss. Very nice, but also very strict."

So there it was at least, thought Chauncey with relief. Out in the open, confirmed.

"We have another friend," Sam explained, "who came on the mission with us. He's asleep now in the temple."

The girl's eyes widened again. "You're sleeping *there*?"

Sam shrugged. "It's a roof over our heads. Besides, our buddy's got a pet monkey. We couldn't take the monkey to an inn; we'd attract too much attention," Sam lied.

Chauncey had been studying the girl as she studied Sam. He had always thought of the average Japanese girl as shy, retiring, bashful, reticent, and demure. Yet this charming, vital creature was just the opposite. Only about seventeen, she was conducting herself with perfect poise and girl-of-the-worldliness.

"And what's your name, miss?" Sam said. "We should know yours, now that you know ours."

"Tsutako Sugimura. I am most anxious to learn English and study everything about America."

There was no anger or resentment toward her conquerors that Chauncey could see as she talked. Evidently she did not hate them. Later Chauncey would learn that there's nothing the Japanese admire as much as a winner, even if their role happens to be that of the loser.

"I must go now," Tsutako said suddenly. "If I don't, someone will miss me and come here looking."

"And that would never do," agreed Sam, "although we'll miss your charming presence."

This time Tsutako reversed her field and reacted in typically Japanese fashion, smiling with demure composure, her eyes directed to the floor.

"Thank you, gentlemen. We'll meet again," she said, and started to go, then turned back. "I almost forgot my comb. That's why I came back. . . ."

Tsutako scooped up a comb lying near one of the faucets and murmured, "Goodbye, Sam. Goodbye, Chauncey MacArthur." At the door leading into the *Joshi* room she paused and turned back toward them: "Will you return tomorrow night?"

Eagerly, they both nodded yes.

"And will your friend—True?—be with you?"

Sam paused, then said, "Yes, I suppose so."

"Without the monkey," Chauncey added.

"In that case," said Tsutako, "I may bring two of my friends with me, the ones I shall swear to secrecy."

"Thumbs up, Tsutako-san," Sam said in his most ingratiating manner. "Hey, one more question: What brought all of you to Oguni?"

A worried furtive look came into Tsutako's eyes and she hesitated before answering, "Oh, there was an....uh, unpleasant situation back in Fukuoka and we thought it would be better if we stayed away for a little while. Well, goodnight."

Then Tsutako was gone, the lights went off abruptly, and Sam and Chauncey stood facing each other in total darkness as Tsutako's dainty footsteps gradually died away.

"Fancy that!" Sam said out of the gloom.

"Yeah, just imagine—" Chauncey replied. "Hey, you're some kind of warped genius."

"I'm sheer magic," Sam agreed flatly. "I'm gonna have to be—to lead us back to our rooms."

"Poor True."

"Poor True, my aching balls!" Sam exclaimed. "We do the work and that flathead'll get in on the goodies."

"None of those girls are his *or* ours yet, you dreamer."

"No, but they will be, baby, they will be," Sam said confidently as he grabbed Chauncey's arm and led him around the perimeter of the pool in the dark.

CHAPTER THIRTEEN

"How the hell can they stand all that heat?" Sam mused over his cup of tea next morning, referring to last night's bath. "At that temperature, the water should have been bubbling and boiling."

"Serves yo' all right," said True, still in a pet because he hadn't been there when Tsutako Sugimura came back to look for her comb. "Ah need music to console me." He groped in his musette bag for his battered harmonica, blew tentatively into it, and then began to play Jacques Hotteterre's *Sonata in D for Coloratura Bassoon*.

Chauncey had opened the sliding *shoji* doors that separated their rooms, and the trio were lounging about a low table in the center space. The shreds and hulls of three boxes of K-rations that had served as breakfast were strewn on the table top. Mabel, the fourth member of the breakfast party, had picked up a twig True had used as a toothpick and was demonstrating her own talents at cleaning her teeth in imitation of her master.

"Don't think I can stand a concert right now," said Chauncey. "What say we scram?"

Sam made a pillow of a barracks bag and stretched out on the soft *tatami* matting. "Not me. This body just wants to lie here for a couple of days and think about how wonderful it is not to have to do *anything*."

"I need some action," Chauncey declared.

"There's a small, orange-backed Army publication in your musette bag entitled *Spoken Japanese*," said Sam sleepily, "which may just open up the stopcocks of your memory."

"You two could use some practice yourselves."

True abruptly stopped playing. "Ah get by on mah soulful look," he said. "Don't need anything more."

"And I get by on my fabled beaty," said Sam. "We'll let you be the intellectual, Chauncey, if that's what you want."

"All I want is to be proficient in the language," Chauncey replied stiffly. "After all, isn't that why we're in Japan?"

Late afternoon found all three of the Americans snoozing peacefully in preparation for the evening's gala sortie.

After they had awakened, downed a few drinks, and supped on their rations, True announced that he was ready to lead the party to their private belvedere for bath-viewing.

When this suggestion was greeted by a stony silence, he said stubbornly, "After all, it *is* mah flashlight!" and refused to surrender it to either Sam or Chauncey. "At times like this, Ah like to be first hawg at the trough."

"Okay," said Sam, "lead, kindly light but stay outta the armory. We don't want to hear any more of your piercing screams."

Once they arrived at their destination by the windows to the bath, there followed some shoving and shouldering for prime position, but all done with quiet intensity.

They had timed their arrival beautifully. Already in progress was the same gasp-fetching scene that had enthralled and invigorated them the night before.

True was staggered. "Dog bite mah pecker!" he breathed in awe, dropping to his knees.

"Acres and acres of lovely young flesh," Chauncey groaned, "and it's ours, all ours!"

"That Hilda Ritter," True drooled. "Boy, she'd sho' make a dawg break his chain!"

Sam peered through the binoculars. "Shit!" he exploded. "How far is it to those three girls on the other side, Chauncey?"

Chauncey saw which trio he meant, all bosomy heart-breakers. The center one was right out of *Esquire* by Petty, with long slim legs and pert breasts.

"About thirty feet, I'd say. Why?"

"Goddam glasses," Sam growled. "They haven't got a range setting for under one hundred feet."

"Use your eyes, boy," Chauncey said, "like the good

Buddha intended."

At that moment Hilda Ritter rose gracefully to her feet and strolled out of the bath, that being the general signal for the season of license and revelry to start among the girls. For five rapturous minutes the lieutenants watched while fourteen maidens gamboled and frolicked around the pool's perimeter.

One tall, toothsome lass, somewhat darker than the others, was inspired to perform one of those posturing, contortionistic dances that the Japanese like so much. This elicited warm applause and cries of approval from her comrades. A second girl closed her eyes in response to imaginary music and waltzed slowly round and round a wooden stool. Then the fever spread. All the girls were climbing out of the bath and performing exotic dances they'd seen in the movies or on some stage. The range of gestures was incredible, some quite subtle, others almost vulgar. It was a wild and frantic scene, the kind of vision conjured up by listening to Orff's *Carmina Burana*.

When the orgy finally wore itself out, the three Peeping Toms were drenched in their own sweat and gulping fresh air. As the girls began to file out of the bath, they saw Tsutako Sugimura, the one who lost her comb, whisper something furtively to two companions.

"See that?" Sam asked excitedly, nudging Chauncey.

"I'm not blind."

"If Ah can't have Hilda," said True, "Ah get dibbies on that li'l one with Shuchako."

"Can't you say Tsutako?"

"Yeah, Shuchako."

"Well," said Sam, "what do you think, Chauncey?"

"I don't think he'll get any of them if he can't even pronounce their names."

"Ah need a bath," said True. "Let's go."

The last of the girls had departed, and abruptly the bathing room was plunged into darkness. The men trooped down through the bath house doors. In the dark True said in a stage whisper, "Wheah do we shuck down?"

"Leave your slippers here and hang your *yukata* on a wall hook. Feel around, boy, use your Braille."

"Ah lost mah slippers coming down," said True. "Damn things keep slipping off mah feet."

Sam and Chauncey groped their way to the buckets and soap and faucets. But True had his own ideas on how to take a Japanese bath. Instead of preparing himself gradually with a scrubdown, he simply stripped and jumped into the steamy pool.

His whimpering cry of pain was loud and clear, but by some miracle it brought no curious investigators, only Sam and Chauncey to his rescue. They hauled him gasping from the scalding pool, ran him quickly under a stream of cold water, then explained in basic GI language what he had done wrong.

"Just because you do everything else backwards," Sam said, "is no reason why you have to apply that principle to the Japanese bath."

"Ah feel like a steamed shrimp," True gasped.

"Come on, you two," said Chauncey. "Let's finish bathing, so we'll be ready for the three little maids from school."

Sam started humming the Gilbert and Sullivan air off-key. True chimed in and whistled it on-key for him. Then they were scrubbed, sluiced down, and safely into their *yukatas* by the time they heard a door open to feminine giggles and saw the lights go on overhead.

CHAPTER FOURTEEN

It was close to noon when Chauncey opened the *shoji* doors that formed the two opposite walls of his room and looked in on Mabel and True on one side and Sam on the other. True was snoring; Sam was breathing less raucously. True's snoring, legendary in the Pacific Theater, caused Mabel to twitch fitfully with each crescendo. This talent—or detriment, depending on how you viewed it—had often been compared to the derailment of a demented locomotive and had frequently intruded on True's love life. He had not known many girls who could endure it all night, even in the deep sleep that follows prolonged sexual abandonment.

In fact, it was True's prodigious nasal arpeggios that had kept not only True's girl friend awake half the night but Chauncey's as well. And it probably accounted for all three girls leaving before the night was half over to sneak back into the Inn of the Playful Hermit.

Chauncey stretched and smiled to himself. It was all but incredible, when you stopped to consider it carefully. The girl who had shared his *futon* was one of the loveliest of all fourteen and bore, in fact, a striking resemblance to movie actress Ann Blyth, for whom Chauncey had conceived a hopeless passion the previous summer. He had actually called Tsutako "Ann" in a climactic moment of pounding abandon. She had stopped him in mid-stroke.

"Who is this 'Ann'?" she demanded, softly, yet with firm insistence. "Your wife?"

"I don't have one," Chauncey explained in rather breathless Japanese. "Ann Blyth makes . . . . . American movies."

"Are you sure?"

"Sure."

"Prove it!"

"Right *now*?"

"Right now."

So Chauncey had been forced to disengage himself, rummage through the box of Ruby Whacker's movie junk with the aid of True's flashlight until he came up with a picture of Ann Blyth.

Tsutako snatched away the magazine and flashlight and spent the next ten minutes totally absorbed in Ann Blyth and the other cinema lovelies pictured therein, blithely ignoring his pressing needs. It was not without some expert wheedling and coaxing that he was able to mount and proceed again, enjoying the firm, warm, once-again-eager flesh at his disposal.

Tsutako Sugimura and her two friends—Sam's date, pretty but not stunning, and True's pint-size charmer—had appeared in the bath as anticipated. With no preliminary maneuvering, the girls had come right to the point.

"We would like to spend some time in your temple rooms," Tsutako had stated, heading the delegation, "so that we can become more intimately acquainted with you."

The directness of their approach threw the Americans off their stride. They hesitated, stammered, looked at each other, and in general dragged their feet.

"We are wasting time," Tsutako informed them severely.

Chauncey thereupon shrugged his shoulders and led the procession quietly through the temple to their adjoining rooms. True couldn't pronounce the name of his partner correctly, so he tried to make amends by saying to her, "*Ona ga suki da*." She responded by backing off several steps and eyeing him like a leper.

"Oaf," said Sam, not unkindly, "you've done it now."

"Ah done what?"

"Same old mistake," Sam said, "you managed to say 'I like vegetables', mixing up *ona* and *onna* again."

Ona was the word for vegetables and *onna* the word for girls.

When all six of them were settled in the center room, the Ann Blyth-like Tsutako asked Chauncey the vital question: "Are you *really* General MacArthur's nephew?"

In response to his hesitant though affirmative nod, she had pressed herself against him and suggested that perhaps it was time they divided into teams of two and closed the *shoji* between the rooms. She found no one in disagreement with her proposal.

Chauncey walked over to Sam and nudged him awake with his toe. "Rise, Casanova, and tell me all. How'd you make out?"

Sam rolled over on his back and grinned his lopsided grin, wet the tip of his right forefinger with his tongue, and chalked up "Score One" on an imaginary blackboard. "Any better and I'd be dead," he confessed. "How about yourself?"

Chauncey nodded happily, then said,. "Let's go check out Alabama's gift to Japanese womanhood."

Interrupting True's snoring always gave them keen pleasure, having suffered from its effects on many occasions, even though they had grown able—except for the very worst attacks—to sleep right on through it, impervious to the bombardment.

"Hey," Sam asked, "did you score, cornpone?"

"Naw." True yawned and scratched his groin.

"Aw, come on, boy, quit stalling. The suspense is killing us."

"Honest, Sam, Ah didn't make out. Mabel came between us."

"You mean you let that silly simian mess it up for you?"

"That's about it," True admitted, crestfallen. "The minute we got ourselves all settled, Mabel commenced baring her fangs. She didn't make noise or anything like that, but she just wouldn't let me to touch Saseko-san. So mah girl said that Mabel would hafta sleep outside."

"And you said no to that, I suppose?" Chauncey interjected.

"Ah said, '*Mabel wo koi shimasu kara* . . . . .'"

Sam smote himself on the forehead. "Oh, for God's sake! What then?"

"She turned and walked out and left me suckin' mah teeth."

"You dolt," said Chauncey, "don't you realize what you said to her?"

"Sure, Ah said Ah liked Mabel too much to put her out in the cold—or words to that general effect."

"Words to that general effect, he says," muttered Sam.

"In using the verb *koi shimasu*," Chauncey explained, "you implied that you liked Mabel in a *sexual* way. No wonder she walked out. I'm surprised she didn't smack you silly and start screaming for help."

True shrugged indifferently. "Makes me no nevah mind. If Ah had mah druthers, Ah'd druther have Hilda, anyway."

Chauncey was about to wither True with a well-aimed retort when they heard footsteps approaching along the corridor. All of them froze, including Mabel, who had been capering about playfully and wrestling with True's *futon*. If they had been exposed by True's insulted ex-partner, the game was up, their vacation idyll over.

Then they heard Correct Path's voice calling them softly, and the head priest appeared in the doorway of Chauncey's room, with Dr. Ino on his heels. Both Japanese bore packages in their arms.

"We have come laden with modest offerings," said C.P.

All three of the Americans smiled bravely, and Chauncey, thinking of eel in a dozen different gourmet forms, said, "In turn, as an expresion of our profound thanks, we would like to introduce you both to the delights of K-Rations." He pointed with magnanimous generosity toward the cartons of GI supplies in one corner of the toom. But the good doctor and C.P. did not follow his vectoring finger. Their four eyes settled as one on a bottle of scotch beside the *futon*.

Sam brought out canteen cups, True opened some rations, anyway, and after several drinks and considerable small talk about the Americans' accommodations and creature comforts, C.P. sucked in his breath respectfully and came at last to the point of his visit.

"Lieutenant MacArthur," he said in his archaic English, "I have arrived to petition you to intercede on our behalf with your illustrious uncle."

"We're listening, sir," said Sam, to allow Chauncey time to mask his features.

"Thank you for your undivided attention, all three friends," said C.P. "The truth of the matter is that my temple is in dire need of financial assistance. It is quite difficult these days to solicit funds from the farm-folk in this area without some official outside pressure. Therefore, if you could see your way clear to beg your uncle to draw up an edict which would oblige our constituents—to put it loosely—to contribute to our support, I—we—all of us—would be indebted to you and your family throughout eternity. And besides, "C.P. added, "you will gain much merit in your next stage of existence, which is what we all want, of course."

Chauncey chewed this one over. "Well, sir," he said at length, "I really don't know when I'll see my Uncle Douglas again, and. . . ."

"Lieutenant MacArthur will have to telephone the General in response to your request," Sam interpolated suavely. "And of course the General will give the matter favorable consideration. But you must understand, Correct Path, that such matters take an inordinate length of time. Red tape, we call it. The Army of Occupation is only beginning to function. The chain of command and the assignment of areas of responsibility and liaison channels with various branches of your government have not yet been firmed up to the point of efficiency. Therefore, while I don't want to sound pessimistic, it might take a month—even two—before your request filters down from the General's desk to the level of everyday action. Am I making myself clear?"

"You are, indeed," C.P. said, disappointed.

"But of course," Sam rushed on quickly, "there may be something you can do in the meantime to ease the situation."

C.P. downed the last of this scotch and reached for a refill. "And what is that, pray tell?"

"Don't you realize that you're sitting on a gold mine?"

C.P. squirmed uncomfortably and frowned.

"Oh, not literally, of course. I was referring to the lucrative possibility of your eels."

Chauncey shuddered inwardly; sitting on a mess of eels was an even less welcome thought.

"But Lieutenant Bruce," C.P. protested, "we are already engaged in raising eels for commercial purposes."

"Sure, but you're not using modern methods to get your product before the general public. What you need is someone to give you expert advice on American promotional methods."

"And how does one go about promoting such a product?" asked C.P., already showing considerable interest.

"That's simple," said Sam easily. "I can toss out a few gimmicks and gambits to start you off. I'll do it gratis, in appreciation of your generosity."

C.P. beamed happily. "Yes, yes, go on."

"Well, take your location, for example. It's lousy. I mean poor. No through traffic at all: remote, isolated. And since you can't very well move, you've got to find some way of bringing the customer to your doorstep." Sam turned to Chauncey. "You tell him. . . ."

"What Lieutenant Bruce means," Chauncey explained, relieved that Sam was about to discuss better mouse traps and not his relationship to the Supreme Commander in Tokyo, "is that your eel industry needs extensive exploitation through visual advertising. It's not enough that the business exists. People must know about it from Kyushu to Hokkaido."

"Right!" Sam plunged in again. "Like putting up a huge red and blue neon sign you can see a mile away, one that blinks on and off. Saying something like 'The Oguni Eel-ery, Where the Elite Meet to Eat—Elegant Eels.' And on all approach roads leading to the eel-ery, signs should read: 'This is the Right Road to Correct Path's Famous Oguni Eel-ery.'"

Pretty primitive, thought Chauncey, but it seemed to be working. C.P. was leaning forward, listening with rapt attention to Sam's fantasy.

"Then there's the matter of menus," Sam continued his improvisation, "You gotta hire an expert to dream up new ways of cooking and serving eel. Think of the possibilities! Eel Brown Betty, Eel Surprise, Eel Slubberdegullion, and Eel Rockefeller! Then there's the minority market—like Eel Blintzes, Eel and Bagels, Devilled Eel, Stuffed Eel. And don't forget Sweet and Sour Eel, Eel Kebab and Eel Pan Dowdy! Oh yes, you should also put free recipes in all eel containers sold through food markets. This'll really stimulate trade."

C.P. was busily scratching away in a small black notebook as Sam coursed on through an infinite variety of eel cuisine.

"Later on you can build up the eel image and tradition. Blanket the nation, then the world. Like 'An Eel on Every Plate.' How's that for a starting slogan? Run newspaper ads that read 'You Deserve the Best! Accept Nothing but Genuine Oguni Eel.' And it might not be such a bad idea to print your picture on all packaging, C.P., with a caption underneath it that reads: 'Bishop Correct Path's Genuine Southern-Fried Kyushu Eel.' How does that grab you? You gotta push the potential, see? After all, Kyushu's your southernmost island, isn't it? Hey, you could even create a National Eel Day. We do it for turkeys and call it Thanksgiving. Or you could arrange to hold a festival and elect Miss National Eel every year. And the ramifications of the export market are absolutely unlimited. I think from these ideas you'll begin to see what I mean."

"I do, I do!" cried C.P. excitedly. "The possibilities are almost infinite. Lieutenant Bruce, your astuteness and sagacity amount to genius."

"Well, thanks," said Sam nonchalantly. "And I haven't even touched on consumer trainees."

"What are they, Lieutenant?"

"Children. Children who grow up to become big eel eaters, thoroughly brainwashed with subliminal propaganda. Also, there's mucho money in a line of eel toys, soap, cookies, enema kits, fishing poles, douche bags, trusses, and possibly even contraceptive devices imprinted with squirming eels. Capitalize on the phallic symbol aspect. Now *that's* bound to be a hot-selling novelty."

Dr. Ino coughed politely at this point, probably feeling neglected with all the English flying about the room.

Chauncey smiled at him patronizingly and said in Japanese, "You're very quiet today, doctor."

"I am not acquainted with your language to the same extent as my friend," Dr. Ino said. "And besides, I have my surgical technique very much on my mind these days. I am sure you understand the demands of research and the desire to find a sympathetic audience for it."

"Dr. Ino's work is vitally important," C.P. told Chauncey. "He's extremely modest. He seldom talks about himself, so I must tell you that this new operation of his is a revolutionary one. He has already performed it successfully on a member of his own family."

"Oh?" said Sam, without much interest.

C.P. smiled mysteriously. "He has not yet been able to persuade any others to serve as guinea pigs, however, and this is extremely frustrating, especially since the operation is not really dangerous, being more restorative in nature. He often broods about this lack of interest. One day you ought to let him explain the details of the surgery."

"Of course," said Chauncey deferentially, "later on when we have more time and I've had the opportunity to acquire a certain fluency in medical terminology."

The scotch was gone. C.P. stood up, bowed, and the doctor joined him. "We must leave, gentlemen. I have much to think about in terms of the marvelous ideas you have sketched out for the eel business. And Dr. Ino must return to his laboratory, I know."

Sam dug out an unopened bottle of scotch. "Sometimes," he said as he handed the bottle to C.P., "good whisky clears the head."

CHAPTER FIFTEEN

The MP's of the Second Marine Division had set up a check point just east of Hida on the Trans-Kyushu highway, which was now in a state of tenuous repair following a week of back-breaking labor by Ceebees attached to the same division.

Ensigns Nemoto and Yoshikita had spotted the two MP jeeps and the white road barriers from a distance of more than a mile and had debated trying to bypass it. Nemoto, however, carried his point:

"No, Yoshikita-kun, we'll never find the girls if we take off into the hills every time we see an American soldier. They'll be all over the place from now on. Let's try our luck. Maybe we can fool them with the old orders assigning us to our squadron. You've still got yours, haven't you?"

Yoshikita nodded, then agreed to the trial passage reluctantly.

From a distance of forty yards they could see the MP's clearly: one sergeant, one corporal, and two privates. Then they saw another man in Marine uniform emerge from behind one of the jeeps. To their surprise, he had Japanese features.

Staunchly the two ensigns marched up to the barrier and came to attention. The Marine private laughed.

"All right, all right," the sergeant said, walking around from behind the barrier. "We got two more customers. Let's see your orders, boys."

Nemoto and Yoshikita looked at each other in incomprehension.

Evidently the sergeant was accustomed to this reaction. He spat tobacco juice on the ground and beckoned for the Nisei Marine.

"Hey, Horatius, c'mon over here."

The private laughed again, his face a freckled study in rural prejudices.

"Sarge," the stocky Nisei was saying in what was obviously native English, "how many times I gotta ask you to call me Poker?"

"You mean you like being called Poker more'n Horatius?" the sergeant asked slyly.

"Shit, yes! Like I told you before, my old man barely knew English and he just shut his eyes and picked my name outta th' phone book."

"I never heard tell a' nobody named Horatius," the private smirked.

"Shut up," the sergeant ordered, then turned back to the waiting ensigns.

"Ask 'em to show us their discharge papers or travel orders."

Poker repeated the order in Japanese. It was fluent enough but marred by a Wakayama accent, which was doubtless the prefecture from which his father had emigrated.

Silently Nemoto and Yoshikita withdrew the orders assigning them to the Special Attack Forces unit at Gannosu Air Base. The Nisei's presence had taken them by surprise; they had not expected to find an American of Japanese ancestry with the MP patrol.

Poker Shibata took the two sets of orders and began to peruse them, while the ensigns' hearts sank lower and lower.

After a long moment, Poker abruptly handed the orders back to the ensigns and told the sergeant, "They're okay."

"Pass 'em through," the sergeant ordered, spitting more tobacco juice expansively downwind.

Dazed but relieved, the two ensigns marched through the narrow space between the two road barriers and on toward Hida.

"What happened?" Nemoto asked later, perplexed.

"What splendid luck!" Yoshikita exulted, striking his right fist into the palm of his other hand. "This is a good omen, Nemoto-kun. Now I know we'll find those wenches. . . .and accompany them to glory."

Nemoto turned his face aside to conceal the expression on his face, then went on, "But why did that Nisei pass us through on these old orders?"

"Obviously he can't read Japanese," Yoshikita surmised,

pleasure still heavy in his voice.

"But he's Japanese, isn't he? I mean, he has Japanese blood, Japanese features, he even speaks Japanese. Waka-yama dialect, of course, but still. . . ."

"Many Nisei can speak but can't read or write Japanese."

"But," Nemoto persisted, "the American Marines are using him as an interpreter and translator. If he can't read the language, why would he. . . .?"

"There are Nisei and then there are Nisei," Yoshikita lectured. "Some can't read our language but pretend that they can. Others can but pretend they can't. They've got their reasons, I suppose."

"Hmmmm."

In silence the two ensigns walked on until they crossed the first hill and then were out of sight of the check point. They were more bedraggled than ever. The light of dedication shone as brightly as before in Yoshikita's eyes, but there was now a sullen set to Nemoto's mouth.

"What was that brown liquid that the sergeant kept spitting out?" Nemoto asked the more worldly-wise Yoshikita.

"Tobacco."

"Tobacco? Why should he put tobacco in his mouth?"

"In the southern and more barbaric sections of America," Yoshikita began, again mounting his lecture platform, "the farming folk use the juice of tobacco to kill insects, blind snakes and frogs, and stun and repulse hostile dogs. They fall into the habit of putting a bite of tobacco—which they quaintly call a 'chaw'—in their cheek pouches and eventually they become addicted to the tobacco so they continue to chew and expectorate it even when there is no need."

"Where did you learn that?" Nemoto asked suspiciously.

"In college, of course, in my studies of Western civilization," Yoshikita replied a trifle smugly. It gave him a distinct pleasure to parade his "knowledge" of the Western world—with embellishments—before the less learned Nemoto. Yoshikita was not himself aware of his own ambivalence: he professed to hate Americans and would gladly die fighting them, but he felt superior to other Japanese because of his knowledge of their culture.

They walked five more minutes in weary silence before Nemoto said, half to himself, "I wonder what Sujiko is doing now?"

Yoshikita sniffed. "What can it possibly matter what she's doing? What does matter is *where* she is."

"She sure has got a sweet little ass," Nemoto said irrelevantly.

"Sweet little ass, sweet little ass," Yoshikita mimicked. "Is that all you can think about?"

"When it's the last piece of ass I may ever get." Nemoto snarled resentfully, "you're damned right it's all I can think about."

Abruptly Yoshikita stopped and roared: "Nemoto-kun! Remember your duty! We're both modern-day *samurai*, aren't we? Would *samurai* think about sex when they could be purifying their souls with thoughts of mountain cherry blossoms glowing in the morning sun?"

"I'm thinking of cherries, too," muttered Nemoto. "Besides, the *samurai* fathered their share of children, didn't they?"

"You are profane!" Yoshikita expostulated. "Those things they did only as their duty, to bring forth future *samurai* for their liege lords and the Emperor."

Nemoto scoffed in open disbelief.

"Well," Yoshikita said, resuming the march, "maybe sometimes they gave in to the ardent supplications of our passionate Japanese women." He mused in silence for a minute, then added, "Women, bah! They are the root of much of our trouble. . . ."

"I'd like to have my root in a little of that trouble."

Yoshikita gave Nemoto a contempt-heavy glance. "It may be that the very devotion of Japanese men to the Emperor is exactly why our women are so very. . . .uh, eager in such matters."

"If they weren't, they might never get any," Nemoto said, agreeing for once.

Taking the lead again, Yoshikita shaded his eyes and looked to the west. "I believe that must be the town of Hida ahead."

"Where do we go from there?" Nemoto asked wearily.

"I think we should turn south and then east toward Oguni. We haven't searched that area at all."

"Oguni?"

"I was there once as a boy   It's just a little resort town on the banks of the Chikugo River, but it would be an ideal hiding place."

Inwardly Nemoto groaned at the prospect of the many long miles before them.

CHAPTER SIXTEEN

Although they had not made specific dates for another rendezvous with Tsutako and her two friends, the three lieutenants were hopeful that they would come, anyway.

When the burlesque show ended and the lights went out, they crept down into the bath, as always, to wash themselves in the dark. This time, however, they had decided to practice staying in the hot water longer, and they learned that their biggest mistake previously had been getting into the bath too suddenly. The trick was to inch one's way in, letting the body adjust itself to the extreme change in temperature.

They were still soaking in the steamy water when the lights flashed on, the door from the *Joshi* dressing room opened, and out stepped three maidens in blue-and-white flowered *yukata*.

Which was fine, except that they were not the same three as the night before.

"Dawg bite it!" exclaimed True, delighted at the prospect of possibly having better luck with a different girl. Who knew? He might even be able to pronounce her name.

"Shades of Sodomy and Gonorrhea!" exulted Sam, who valued variety in his venery above all else.

Chancey alone was not too pleased. He had been looking forward to seeing Tsutako or Ann Blyth again. But there was no help for it. He'd simply have to bear up.

The three new maidens knelt gracefully at the side of the pool to introduce themselves, sparkling with an eagerness that bespoke an interesting evening ahead.

Chauncey's new flame addressed him in Japanese, saying, "My name is Mieko Shimizu." Then, after a moment of hesitation, she added, "But perhaps you would rather call me Lana?"

"Lana?"

"You know, Lana Turner."

"Well, I know Lana Turner all right, but why should I. . . ."

"Last night you deigned to honor your *futon* partner with the name of 'Ann Blyth', didn't you?"

"Deigned to honor?" Chauncey mumbled. "Ann Blyth? Well, yes, I guess I did."

"And your friend there can't pronounce our names correctly in Japanese, can he?"

"You've got that part right," Chauncey said, knowing she meant True.

"So," she rushed on firmly, "we have all decided to adopt American names to simplify our association with you."

"That's a good idea, but you don't *look* like Lana Turner—even though you *are* just as pretty, of course," he hastened to add.

To which compliment the girl responded with a dazzling smile. "Oh, we did not choose the names because of any physical resemblance. We just took the names of the American actresses whom we admire most and think are the most beautiful. We realize that most of us, except possibly Ann, who, of course, is a great beauty—might not look much like our heroines. But we do admire them so much. . . ."

"But where did you get the names?"

"From the movie magazines you sent over."

"*I* sent over?"

"Of course."

Chauncey was mystified until he recalled that he had given Ann/Tsutako a sheaf of them the night before.

"So," he said at last with amusement, admiring his new partner, "you're Lana Turner. . . ."

"Oh yes," she replied proudly, "and Fukako Okuyuki over their is Carole Landis," pointing to True's date. "And Sujiko Honekawa with your friend Sam is Katharine Hepburn. Now, if you will please step out of the bath, I will service your needs."

Chauncey glanced quickly at Sam and True, who had been receiving similar indoctrinations from their new dates.

"Well, I don't know about that," Chauncey stalled, but Lana Turner stamped her dainty foot in mock anger at his reluctance.

"You will do as Lana Turner says," she commanded him, and so, taking a grip on his modesty, he rose dripping from the pool to be immediately enveloped in a towel and expertly rubbed dry. A very sensuous experience, he had to admit.

Seeing that Chauncey had survived, Sam and True followed suit.

As Lana finished towelling Chauncey, she remarked, "Oh, by the way, your three dates for tomorrow night will be Veronica Lake, Rita Hayworth, and Dorothy Lamour. Veronica is Michiko Chino, Rita is Kusako Fukadani, and Dorothy is Mameko Endo."

Chauncey had his *yukata* on before Lana's statement fully registered.

"Wha-aat?" he stammered. "What's this about three other girls tomorrow night?"

Lana appeared unable to understand his consternation.

"But that's the only fair way," she explained, turning to her colleagues for support. They smiled and nodded at her in emphatic agreement. "You see, Lieutenant MacArthur, we drew chopsticks today to decide who would have the incomparable honor of coming to visit you tonight and tomorrow night. I was fortunate enough to win for tonight. Rita Hayworth drew you for tomorrow night. We just couldn't be fair to everyone if we did it haphazardly. And we couldn't let one girl be so honored more than once. Well, at least not until after all fourteen of us have been through the honor line once."

My God, thought Chauncey, they're making it sound like they're going to be awarded the Congressional Medal of Honor or the Japanese Order of The Golden Kite.

Sam and True also heard Lana's remarks.

"Hey, I don't believe it!" Sam said. "You gotta be putting us on!"

Lana Turner delivered him an icy glance. "I have no reason to lie to you, Lieutenant. I happen to have very high principles."

"Well, do tell!" said True.

"You keep mentioning honor, Lana," Chauncey pointed out, anxious to know what lay behind this highly unusual philosophical system the girls had devised.

Suspicion glinted for a second in Lana's dark eyes; she

inspected him shrewdly. "You *are* Lieutenant Chauncey MacArthur, aren't you?"

Admitting as much, Chauncey saw it all, like a sudden revelation.

"Then you *are* the nephew of that illustrious personage who has deigned—" that word again, he thought "—to come to the Land of the Ripe Rice-Ears. . . ." she used the words *Mizuho no Kuni*, one of the more formal names for Japan ". . . .to guide His Imperial Majesty, the Emperor, through these troubled times, aren't you?"

Lies, lies, lies! The words ran through his head like the refrain of a popular song. Sick up to his Adam's apple with intrigue, he was on the verge of telling the truth when Sam jumped in.

"Lana, *of course* he's the General's nephew," Sam lied with unctuous smoothness. "But like all heirs of distinguished blood, he has that inherent lack of ostentation that makes such lines great. He is modest, Lana, earnest and sincere—but, most of all, *modest*."

"Thank you, Lieutenant Bruce. We all understand that reticence is a hall-mark of character and strength," said Lana with what appeared to be enormous relief. "For a moment there I thought—But never mind. We all talked it over very seriously when Miss Ritter was not present, thinking she might not understand our Japanese feelings in a delicate matter of this sort, and we decided we would be remiss in our duty if we failed to do everything. . . ."

". . . .everything possible to make General MacArthur's nephew's stay in Kyushu as pleasant as you can," supplemented Sam.

Lana favored him with a smile of genuine respect.

"How well you understand us," she told him, then turned back to Chauncey. "This applies to both of your comrades in arms as well. Your presence on our island does us great honor, Lieutenant MacArthur, and the longer you stay, the greater will be our face. If you are happy and content here—and we shall do anything, just anything at all to make you so—we hope that you will make your feelings known to your renowned uncle. And I beg you to tell him that the citizens of Kyushu respect him and are doing their best to honor and serve his nephew."

It was quite a speech, and one that Chauncey could

hardly credit as sincere. Some monstrous joke was afoot and being played on him; a nightmare of entrapment was in progress; very shortly he would awaken in his own bed. . . .or handcuffed to the bars of a prison cell.

Chancey was still staring at Lana Turner in awed consternation mingled with astonishment when the door to the *Joshi* dressing room opened again.

And there stood none other than Hilda Ritter, arms akimbo and eyes flashing.

In a trice, True shed his towel and jumped into the steaming pool. Sam, in his *yukata*, grinned like a younger version of Groucho Marx minus specs and moustache and stood his ground. Chauncey simply turned crimson, wondering how they were going to get out of his one alive, for Hilda Ritter exuded as much authority in her own way as did his false uncle, the General.

As Hilda Ritter continued to breathe militance and outrage, Chauncey noticed that the three girls had simply vanished. Where or how he didn't know. But disappear they had.

As True surfaced, Hilda Ritter reached the end of her control and let out a prolonged, high-pitched scream of distress.

Then she turned and ran.

"Get her, Sam!" yelled Chauncey, for Sam was nearest the Swiss chaperone.

But it was True who emerged lightning-swift from the pool in hot pursuit, while Sam stood and stared, glued to the tiles.

Chauncey had previously decided that nobody could ever move as fast as True had run after saving Mabel from drowning in the honey-tank, but this evening he was even swifter. In one continuous movement of unparalleled speed, he hurtled out of the bath, snatched his *yukata* from its wall hook and threw it on without missing a single stride. Then, braying with lustful delight, he flew through the *Joshi* door after his dream-girl. He had met her in the flesh at last; this was no time to hang back or stand on ceremony.

"Oh, Christ," Sam prayed, "I hope he catches her. Somehow we gotta keep her from screwing up our vacation!"

At that moment the three girls materialized again. The third one, Carole Landis, was now without a partner and promptly burst into tears. She would have to return to her room, forsaken and unloved.

"I don't know what's happening, and it won't do any good to care," shrugged Sam. "Let's go, girls."

As the quartet headed out of the bathing house for their temple rooms Chauncey stopped and held up his hand. "Wait, I thought I heard something." It had sounded very much like a high, shrill cry for help: He had visions of Hilda Ritter being ravished by an insatiably lustful Alabaman.

"I didn't hear anything," Sam said, poker-faced. "Now move your ass, we haven't got all night."

"The world's most practical guy," Chancey replied. After all, Sam's motivation was right. Why worry about True when there were fun festivals awaiting them? It wasn't every night that one had a chance to loll about on a *futon* with Lana Turner and Katharine Hepburn.

CHAPTER SEVENTEEN

True loped into the temple the next morning with a smug grin on his face, scratching his left ear with his right hand and whistling snatches from the overture to Wagner's *Die Meistersinger*.

"Well?" said Sam.

"Well what?" asked True.

"What happened?" said Chauncey.

"Don't trifle with us, man!" Sam exploded. "Spill it!"

"Simmer down, city boy," True said archly. "Jest simmer down. Ole True's got everything under *control* . . . ." He removed his *yukata*. "Soon as Ah feed Mabel, Ah'm goin' back to bed."

"I've already fed Mabel," Chauncey announced, "and we're due back in Fukuoka today to report to Dawgleish."

"Well, ain't that nice! You all jest go right ahead without me. Tell ole Dawgleish Ah'm busy roundin' up a whole museum full of *samurai* swords—or somethin' like that."

"Listen, True. Just what the hell happened between you and Hilda Ritter?"

"Don't you go worryin' none 'bout me and Hilda. We come to an understanding. She's not gonna tell anybody about us being heah. And she's not gonna move those gals anywhere."

"But where did you spend the night?" asked Chauncey patiently. "Come on, what happened?"

"Ah sure as hell didn't sleep out under no trees," True said, lowering himself to the *futon* and making room for Mabel, who was sniffing him all over with a clearly suspicious expression on her simian countenance.

True yawned and lay back on the *futon*. "Ah'm so tired Ah couldn't holler sooey if the hawgs had me down. You all get outta here and lemme get some rest."

Sam glanced across at Chauncey. With a look they agreed that there was no way—short of torture—to extract anything further from True if he didn't choose to explain.

"There's a PX list in mah notebook you can take along with you," True mumbled sleepily. "If there's a PX yet. Perfume, undies, lipstick. . . ."

"Are you thinking of doing female impersonations?" Sam asked tartly.

"Jest run along," True mumbled and was soon asleep, the snores beginning thirty seconds later, deep and sonorous. Had they been temple bells, thought Chauncey, they could call a whole town to worship.

Sam and Chauncey stopped for a breather at the brow of the hill dividing the Oguni valley from the rest of the world and surveyed their peaceful paradise from above.

"True's reticence is remarkable," said Chauncey.

"He may not even have seen the promised land, let alone pole-vaulted through it," said Sam. "Incidentally, how did *you* make out last night?"

Chauncey wet the tip of his finger and marked up another score in the air. "How about yourself?"

Sam's lopsided grin was smugly affirmative.

"Funny thing, though," Chauncey said, somewhat uncomfortably. "Ann Blyth—*and* the one last night, Lana Turner—they were both virgins. . . ."

"Hey, now, there's a frigging coincidence for you," said Sam. "So were both of mine!"

"Isn't that kind of odd? I mean, four girls—and all *four* of them virgins?"

"Yeah, that's stretching it a bit, all right. But what the hell, why not? Aren't they supposed to come from the cream of Fukuoka families? Nothing but the best. It's not like back in Old Chi were our neighborhood debutantes would drop their drawers for a quarter any time and then pass out free helpings on Sundays and holidays."

"Ah, Sam, you and Carl Sandberg!" Chauncey said.

The road they had previously followed into Fukuoka was blocked for repairs, so they took a detour that approached the city from the south. Fukuoka showed definite signs of coming back to life. Some streetcars were running. More pedestrians were out on the streets, and quite a few cyclists. One enterprising department store had reopened its ground floor. Teams of telephone linemen were repairing the downtown system. And the last immediate horror of the war had been removed; they saw no more bodies in the streets, dead from starvation or disease, which didn't mean, Chauncey knew, that many weren't still dying daily. It just meant that the disposal system was improving.

Fukuoka, however, still had a long way to go before it recovered its equilibrium. Rubble blocking the main streets had been cleared away, but many side streets were still impassable. The bombed-out areas were wastelands of levelled buildings, ashes, and stones.

Their hotel maid—Sumiko, Mabel's former mistress—was delighted to see them back at the Inn of Ultimate Delights, as was Aso-san, the Japanese manager, who sent a tray of delicacies to their room five minutes after their arrival.

Sam immediately switched on the radio, hoping for some news of the Occupation's progress.

"There's nothing on but music," Sumiko said. "General MacArthur hasn't yet approved news broadcasts. We all hope he will soon."

"Might be able to do something about that," Sam said craftily, but Chauncey silenced him with a hard look. They were in enough potential trouble already without compounding the conspiracy.

"How is Mabel, sir?" asked Sumiko when she had laid out their light repast.

"In heat," Sam told her simply, and Sumiko giggled.

"What's in these dishes, Sumiko?" Chauncey was lifting lids and sniffing warily. You never knew about the inn manager, whom they had dubbed "Harry" Aso.

Sumiko shrugged, knowing she had to be careful with her American friends, even though they always tried to be polite about Japanese cuisine.

"*Daketsu anko.*"

Chauncey wondered if Sam remembered that this dish of soy bean paste contained snake blood.

Sam lifted a lid. "Christ, these look like de-feathered sparrows."

"Not for you, Sam."

"The sparrows are very delicious," said Sumiko. "A

great delicacy."

"But not for delicate stomachs," Chauncey told her.

"What's in this one?" Sam asked.

"Sliced pork ovary with mushrooms, sauteed," said Sumiko, happy to be the bearer of glad tidings. "It's delicious. All through the war we had none, but now, once again. . . ."

"Sumiko, my dear," said Sam with a bow, "I insist that you sit right here and eat with us."

"Oh no, sir, I couldn't do that!" She had almost a look of horror on her genial, round face. "That isn't proper!"

"Never mind! We insist. Besides, you're hungry and we're not. And we're getting too fat, anyway. I'll take just a small dish of plain boiled rice. How about you, Chauncey?"

"Boiled rice for me, too," Chauncey answered. "Load Sumiko's plate."

"I shouldn't," said Sumiko, staring hungrily at the enormous helping Sam was preparing for her. "Aso-san might. . . ."

"You should and you will," Sam said, handing her the plate. "Now eat, my girl, and not another word out of you!"

Chauncey took out his corn cob pipe and practiced posing with it clenched in his teeth. Around HQ it was essential that he at least look like a blood relative of the great man even if he didn't feel like one. In point of fact, he felt like a bare-faced usurper. And it was only a matter of minutes before they'd have to face the crew at headquarters.

On Chauncey's desk was another one of those telltale envelopes from D. MacArthur in Tokyo, this one besmudged with curious fingerprints, obviously handled at one time or another by many members of the staff in his absence. And instead of resting on a mound of accumulated papers, it lay prominently alone in the center of his bare desk, almost as if it had been enshrined there by reverent hands.

Chauncey went through an elaborate pantomime of reading the blank sheet inside the envelope while Sam stood with eyes discreetly averted. Then Chauncey folded the letter, slipped it into his breast pocket, and the two of them headed for Colonel Dawgleish's office—and Ruby Whacker.

"Well, hi there, studs!" Ruby brayed through a cloud of

smoke. "Everything screwed on O.K.? Whatcha been doing? Out creating incidents?"

Chauncey turned on a meek though cogent charm. "Good day, Captain. We've been out in the boondocks looking for those fourteen missing girls that. . . ."

"Yeah, yeah, Chauncey, I know *all* about them," Ruby said, cutting him short. "That's all I ever hear about these days. It's enough to bring on my period early. What a lot of goddam nonsense!"

"We thought it was serious, ma'am," said Sam meekly.

Ruby thrust her overpowering bosom at him. "Stupid waste of time, if you ask me. First Corps in Kyoto's got its bowels in a rumble about it, too. Even Eighth Army's been needling General Vandel every day for some action." Ruby stamped out her cigarette and lowered her voice to the two-mile hog-calling level. "Guess I don't have to tell you sex fiends the C.O.'s counting on you to come up with the solution."

"We're getting warm,Captain," Chauncey told Ruby. "In fact we may be hot on the tail of. . . ."

"I *know* what you may be hot on the tail of, you self-styled Romeo, you."

"True sends his fond respects, Captain," Chauncey interjected diplomatically.

Ruby's face softened, lost for a moment in thoughts of the Alabaman, but then she said sternly, "I trust he's behaving himself?"

"I made him stay in the field. He's on a special research mission."

"Yeah?" said Ruby doubtfully. "Well, give him my warmest and tell him to watch it. Too much Old Parr's bad for the gonads. Don't want him knocking off too many little nips! Ha, ha!"

"Is that a laugh cue,Captain?" Sam asked innocently.

Ruby lifted her bosom with dangerous bellicosity. "If I didn't happen to be a lady, Sam Bruce, I'd split your ass for you and then hang your guts on the wash-line. Trouble with you is, you got no sense of humor. Why, True's worth ten of you. And besides, he's a real man, and a real man's just got to run his dog now and then. That's something a lady like me understands." She sighed as if she had the memories to prove it. "True sure does put me in mind of my ole

Daddy, God rest his soul. Daddy spent a year or so fiddling with the toilet tank float in the men's room of the local bus station. . . .and then went into a decline." She shook her head morosely. "Anyway, you be sure and tell True—the dear boy—that I'm waiting right here for him to come back to Fukuoka."

"She's waiting for him to come home to Fukuoka, da-de-da," Sam echoed. "Sounds like the Cat House Blues."

"You bastard!" shouted Ruby, losing her cool altogether.

Chauncey moved between them. "Shut up, Sam! Captain, True was out most of last night on the trail of a hidden arms cache—swords and things. When we left, he was just going to bed at the inn where we're temporarily quartered. And the last thing he said was. . . ." He was no good at such bold-face lying; he turned to Sam for help.

"Captain," said Sam creatively, "whatever you think of me, True *did* send you his love."

Ruby's hostility wilted. This was exactly what she wanted to hear. Suddenly all warm and animated, passion glazed her eyes. "He did?" she cried. "Why, the little devil! Hey, wait a minute! You're not just funning me, are you? Because if you are, Sam Bruce, I'll—"

"Captain Whacker, I would never fun *you*," Sam said stoutly.

Chauncey decided it was time to end the dialogue. "May we see the Colonel now?" he said politely.

"Not right now. He's in there with his ears glued to those goddam records again. I have strict orders not to let anybody in except *Douglas* MacArthur himself—" and here she rolled her eyes at Chauncey "—before precisely one-thirty."

"It's twenty-five after one now, dear lady," Sam pointed out.

"I can tell time, Bruce," said Ruby, on the verge of flaring up again.

"He was listening to a record last time we were here," said Chauncey. "What gives, Captain?"

"I guess you boys haven't been around headquarters long enough to hear all the poop, have you? The truth is, the C.O.'s hooked on Tokyo Rose's voice."

"Tokyo Rose?" Chauncey and Sam repeated almost in

perfect unison.

"The same. Been that way for months. It all started when he first heard her broadcasts down in the islands. Later he took to recording them. Somebody in the Signal Corps boondocked him the equipment. Now he spends most of his evenings just sitting around and listening to those damned recordings. His digestive system requires thirty minutes of her voice every day after lunch, he says, to settle his food."

"He's really got it bad," Sam said.

"The worst I ever saw," Ruby agreed, "why, down at the Officers' Club the other night he tried to inveigle the club manager into putting one of the Tokyo Rose records on the juke box. Can you imagine! He got real pissed off when the manager turned him down, too."

Chauncey murmured something sympathetic.

"Hey, Bruce," said Ruby, snapping her fingers, "you're the PX officer, aren't you?"

"Unfortunately."

"Well, the PX merchandise finally came in. One of the NCO's is taking care of everything right now. We set up a little shop right here in the building. Maybe you ought to drop by for a minute or two before you studs head out for the hills again. Okay?"

"Sure, Captain," said Chauncey.

"The feminine items came too, besides razor blades and shaving cream," said Ruby. "A lady really needs femmies out here. There were some magazines, too. . . . Which reminds me. I had a load of real good ones right here by my desk the day you studs took off, but some revolving son of a bitch swiped them off me."

"I had nothing to do with it, Captain," Sam said, while Chauncey hoped his blush wasn't too obvious.

"Lissen, Bruce, you may be a lot of lousy things, but I don't think you're a thief. Not yet, anyway. Some of the locals are probably guilty, but who's going to track them down? And while we're on the subject of PX supplies, I gotta complaint: There wasn't one damned squirrel-tail douche in the entire PX shipment. How's a WAC gonna take care of herself, I ask you?"

"You tell me," said Sam.

"I don't let even one day go by without a good long

application of the squirrel-tail. Like my granny used to say, it really puts snap back in the old fish. Now you take a woman whose pleasure region is all worn down to a frazzle and give her daily doses of the squirrel-tail, why, she'll have a rose in her teeth in two days and be ready to belly-dance all night in three."

She leaned across her desk, her bosom covering a full third of it. "Come closer, I got a titty-bit to tell you! General Vandel's wife was on the same base I was just before I shipped overseas. An old girl, but a nice one. And she was complaining to me about the General's lack of interest in you know what, so I asked some mighty personal questions and she admitted she'd lost her snap. I suggested the good old squirrel-tail, and once it began to work she gave the General such a raunchy time that he didn't come to headquarters once for three whole days at a stretch. . . . But I guess you youngsters aren't interested in the little niceties of female hygiene or the refinements of true romance. On and off, that's what all of you are these days. You can't keep it up to requirements. Except that True, and he's got the makings of a genuine, fourteen-carat repeater."

The alarm clock on Ruby's desk blared out one-thirty.

"You can go in, gentlemen," Ruby said in suddenly dulcet tones, as if the whole conversation had never taken place. "Colonel Dawgleish is receiving now."

The colonel had his back to them again and was wearing an Arctic-issue officer's fur cap with wires depending from the flaps. It was several seconds before Chauncey realized that the ear-flaps concealed a pair of earphones plugged into the colonel's record player. His was obviously a very serious obsession.

When Sam slid into the C.O.'s range of vision, Dawgleish ripped off the cap with the earphones and whirled around to face them, all in one lightning gesture.

"Well, well, *well*, men," he cried with false heartiness, his cheeks a rosy blush, "you finally made it back. . . . My dear young Chauncey MacArthur, friend and comrade-in-arms!" Triggered by his own words of identification, he whipped out of his chair, strode around his desk, and threw an arm across Chauncey's shoulders.

Even with this demonstration, Chauncey thought he

seemed subdued, worried. There were signs of fatigue in his eyes.

"It's about those missing girls," he told them, as if Chauncey had put the question to him. "It's been preying on my mind. I want to make the best possible showing, as we all do, and the pressure's building up daily here in Fukuoka. Actually it could reach epic proportions unless we find them soon."

"We're doing more than our share, sir," Sam said respectfully.

"Oh, I'm not faulting *you*," said Dawgleish, "I'm not bitching about your performance. It's just that the Kyushu M.G. Teams aren't the only units ordered into the search. Even the Navy's on the lookout, and you know what they'll do if they locate the girls swimming along the coast anywhere. They'll steal their clothes and then.... Look, gentlemen, we've absolutely got to find them. Now I'm not going to issue any ultimatums to you two. I know you're leaving no stone unturned. But I will offer you a heady bribe...."

"We're only human, sir," Sam said eagerly.

"If you find those girls," Dawgleish promised, "you'll get two weeks' leave."

"Two weeks' leave!" Chauncey gasped. He was sure that never in all Dawgleish's Army career had he ever been so generous.

"In Tokyo, too. And what's more, it won't be counted against your regular annual leave!"

"I think I'm going to faint," Sam muttered sotto voce.

"Now," said the C.O., "what new clues have you turned up?"

"Well, nothing really concrete, Colonel," Chauncey admitted.

Dawgleish looked dashed. "Christ, I thought you'd turn up something! You've been poking around all over the place."

"That's right, sir," Sam interjected, "and we're close. We're combing the area thoroughly. Something'll break soon, Lieutenant MacArthur and I are confident. But we'd rather not say too much until we're absolutely certain. No use turning in false alarms, sir."

"Yes, yes, very commendable. But for God's sake, be

quick about it, men. We're being pushed into a corner. General Vandel's beefed up his MP patrols. He's systematically scouring every village on the island. There isn't much chance the girls have gone to Honshu; the channel's been too carefully patrolled and all boats and trains screened since we took over."

"We'll win in the end, sir. Please relax and don't worry," Sam said.

"Goddamit!" cried the colonel. "It's my responsibility to worry! I realize you've got a tough challenge. These girls are a strange case. There were many such groups of young women who headed for the hills just before our troops landed, and perhaps understandably so. But all the others have returned to their homes by now; all are accounted for. Except this one group. And what's worse, the fathers of these girls wield powerful influence in this area. They're practically camping on General Vandel's doorstep. They've also visited the CIC and CID every day to ask for news. They're getting more vocal and hard to handle all the time. Pretty soon the scuttlebutt will have it that the Americans have either kidnapped them for some Gyrene brothel or raped and murdered them."

Chauncey looked grave. "What about the Civil Censorship Detachment, sir?"

"Thank God, so far they've not authorized the Japanese media to release any news about the affair, nothing at all," the colonel explained. "There's only one Japanese language newspaper now being published in Fukuoka, and it hasn't enough newsprint for more than a few thousand single sheets each morning due to the shortage. None go outside the city because there's no delivery. However, we're still in dire straits. . . . Which reminds me. One rumor reached me just today. Some wag, Japanese or American, says the girls were taken aboard an American submarine and shipped to Tokyo for the personal harem of General MacArthur. Now, as you know, Chauncey, I find this the most reprehensible, outrageous, and defamatory propaganda of the whole war."

"Beautiful young girls fetch a pretty price on the sex market, sir," Sam pointed out.

"Don't spread talk like that around, Bruce," the colonel cautioned him coldly. "No point in pyramiding the sordid tale. All I want you men to do is FIND THE GIRLS!!!"

He was shouting now and had begun to wave his hands in the air. There was nothing either of them could do to calm him, Chauncey realized, so he saluted the colonel, turned sharply on his heel and walked out of the office, with Sam two feet behind him.

Sam closed the door softly. "Whew! That was close."

Ruby Whacker regarded them curiously with a stony eye.

"Whatcha mean, close?" she demanded.

"Hot, stuffy, humid in there. You know, captain. The way it is out here."

"Well, yes, it is, isn't it? Boys, do me a favor, one little kindness for Ruby."

"Anything at all," said Chauncey.

Ruby reached under her desk and came up with a box of Milky Way chocolate bars. She batted her eyes at Sam and Chauncey.

"True—bless him—told me once that ever since he was a little tyke he's had this wild passion for things sweet and black, and I just know he must have been talking about chocolate candy. I want you to give these Milky Ways to him the minute you get back to the boondocks. Sweets for the sweet, tell him. And tell him there's a real honest-to-God woman waiting for him back here in Fukuoka."

"Sure, captain," said Chauncey.

"And Chauncey?"

"Yes, captain?"

"Call me Ruby, plain ole Ruby, from now on."

"All right, Plain Ole Ruby," said Chauncey.

"Just Ruby will do, dammit," she grated, glowering dangerously.

"What about me?" said Sam.

"You will continue to respect my rank, Bruce, and that's an order."

When Sam and Chauncey drew away from the PX warehouse two hours later where they had gone to collect their cases of beer and Scotch, the jeep was swaying low on its overload springs and could barely pick up speed. Their visit to the PX with Sam's NCO assistant had garnered them an immense hoard of booty: candy, flashlights and batteries, a case of chocolate toddy for Mabel, candles, an assortment of magazines, two cases of cigarettes, all kinds of canned goods including fruit, pork and beans, and the ubiquitous Spam. On the slightly gourmet side, they found canned mushrooms in a special sauce, pate de foie gras, tomato aspic, and jellied consomme. And, backed by Dawgleish's carte blanche, they were able to obtain cosmetics, nylons, panties, brassieres and other assorted female niceties from the warehouse.

Later in the jeep, Sam said, "It looks like the chase is really getting hot. We can't hold out much longer with all this pressure building up."

Chauncey agreed.

"You're always the sane, level-headed one," Sam said. "What's our best course?"

Chancey chewed on his pipe for a moment before answering. "Well, chum, as I see it, whoever brings in the girls gets all the credit, right?"

"Stands to reason."

"So if any MP's show up in Oguni, we'll try to sneak Hilda and the girls over the hill to the new temple."

"But what about bringing them back to Fukuoka? We can't load fifteen women, three of us, and one amorous ape into this jeep. It's not the Toonerville Trolley, for chrissake!"

"Don't worry," said Chauncey without much confidence. "I'll dream up something."

"Then you'd better load that pipe with hashish and make it good. I'm already quaking in my boots."

"Don't worry."

"I'm trying to follow your advice. Anyway, there's a bright side to the situation: We can dance on the rim of the volcano for a little while longer, enjoying the fabulous social life of Oguni's sophisticated foreign colony."

"Shut up and step on it," said Chauncey. "It's getting late and I have a date with Rita Hayworth tonight."

"I think I'll opt for Dorothy Lamour," said Sam. "Veronica Lake's pretty enough, but that hair hampers my style."

"Since when did you ever worry about anything above the nipple?"

CHAPTER EIGHTEEN

Yoshikita had sent Nemoto down into Oguni to reconnoiter the town while he boiled water for tea on a ridge overlooking the green, pleasant valley. Oguni was much quieter now than when he had visited it as a boy. At this hour of early evening, few of the inns showed any lights, partly because of the electricity shortage but mostly due to the lack of quests.

So much the better, Yoshikita reflected. If their quarry were here, Nemoto would have no difficulty in finding them. Even if they were trying not to be conspicuous, fourteen girls and maybe an European woman with honey-colored hair could hardly escape even a cursory search.

To occupy his time, Yoshikita once more took out the two bundles of throat-cutting knives—the Japanese word, '*nodo-giriba*', rolled nicely through his mind—and caressingly cleaned and thumb-tested the sharpness of each one. Not as sharp as true *samurai* sword, of course, which could cut in twain a silk handkerchief floating to earth, but quite sharp enough for soft young female flesh.

He wondered how he would feel when the moment came. He knew that these girls would not be able to dispatch themselves, although Japanese heroines of history had been known to do so. No, these girls were of a different age—and unworthy of the men whose spirits they were going to solace; they did not have the steel in them to make the fatal slash. The steel in them, eh? Yoshikita chuckled grimly at his own pun. Oh, it wasn't that he would take any real delight in making the throat-cut. No, indeed. He wasn't that kind of human being, he assured himself, but it was a duty. *His* duty. Stark and obvious. He would do it efficiently, coolly, and without remorse. He and Nemoto.... Or would Nemoto? Of late his companion—the same man who had cried tears of joy when they had received orders for what should have been their last mission—had begun to show signs of less-than-total devotion to this project of theirs. He would have to watch him, Yoshikita determined with a sigh. Surely Nemoto didn't doubt that their next existence would be preferable to the present one! Yoshikita's conception of Eternal Bliss was something akin to life in a *daimyo's* castle during the Sengoku era of Japanese history. The lord –the *daimyo*– stood atop the pyramid with his loyal retainers—all bescarred *samurai*—at the next level below. Then the farmers on the soil of the fiefdom and the artisans and finally the shopkeepers—the contemptible merchants—in the castle town. Every human being in his proper place; everyone knowing his station in life and accepting it. All worshipping at the three altars of loyalty, obedience, and duty. Far off in Kyoto dwelt a light too brilliant to gaze upon—the Emperor; so exalted that there was seldom reason for ordinary mortals to think on him. For he *was* Japan: the Eight Great Islands, the Land of the Morning Sun and the Ripe Rice-ears. His presence permeated the atmosphere; his concern for his faithful subjects suffused the earth on which they all walked. All that was necessary for the *samurai* to do was to focus all of his devotion on his liege lord, for it was this lord to whom His Imperial Majesty had entrusted the care of this one section of his Empire. Serving the lord faithfully was tantamount to serving the Emperor well.

Nowadays, of course, the feudal lords were no more, their place taken by organizations, governing bodies, Neighborhood Associations, patriotic groups, and military units such as the Special Attack Forces. Why the Emperor Meiji had chosen this modern scheme of things over the old feudal system was a puzzle to Yoshikita. Yes, it was a mystery, but it did not disturb him in the slightest. He had never expected to understand such matters. Just as he did not understand why His Imperial Majesty was allowing the foreign devils to desecrate the sacred soil of Japan. But Yoshikita knew that the Emperor had his reasons. He had a master plan. The Emperor—oh, the joy of hearing that blessed voice!—had ordered them to "endure the unendurable and to suffer the insufferable," and that was precisely what the entire nation was already setting out to do.

Nemoto had suggested that this might mean that he and

Yoshikita too should return to their homes, but Yoshikita had shouted him down resolutely. They—he had explained angrily to Nemoto—were still under *previous* instructions from His Imperial Majesty. Their Special Attack squadron had been ordered to hurl themselves on the American enemy and to go on from there to glory. The fact that Nemoto and Yoshikita had not done so was due to their own dereliction. And the Emperor—acting through gold-braided navy officers in Kure and Fukuoka—had blessed the unions of the fourteen death-bound pilots with the fourteen Flowers of Japanese Womanhood, which meant only that the unions would still have to be formalized and consummated, either in this world or the next. The signatures affixed recently to a scrap of paper aboard the *U.S.S. Missouri* in Tokyo Bay did not affect the Emperor's earlier intentions in the slightest.

The water was boiling so Yoshikita made himself a cup of weak green tea in the tiny metal pot they carried. He steeped the shredded tea leaves for less than a minute, then poured himself a scanty serving. He wondered if he should try to keep the water boiling for Nemoto....

Nemoto was himself toiling back up the steep road that led westward out of Oguni's secluded valley. Partially his slow pace came from hunger and fatigue but partially from his agonizing indecision over what to tell the zealous Yoshikita.

For he had found the girls at last.

At least, he was almost certain that it was they. "A dozen or more girls with an European woman'. was the description he had been given by the old man who caught fish in the river in the morning, peddled them door to door in the afternoon, and spent the rest of his time dozing or idly observing the comings and goings in what—small though it be—was after all his whole world.

At first the short, slender ensign had rejoiced at the information, seeing it only as the end of a long, long walk. Then he began to examine it from another viewpoint, for it also spelled out D*E*A*T*H K*N*E*L*L for fourteen lovely, luscious embodiments of femininity. He was between the piercing horns of a painful dilemma. If he told Yoshikita what he had found out, the girls would surely die. If he didn't, that stubborn fool Yoshikita would keep them searching and walking forever. (He had a brief, pathetic vision of himself—an ancient, stooped-over man—eternally hobbling down Kyushu's dusty roads.) .....Should he tell Yoshikita or shouldn't he?

Actually, Nemoto's principles were much closer to those of Yoshikita than an observer might have suspected. After all, he too had volunteered for the Special Attack Forces—and would have died with his fallen comrades had not his accursed Zero failed him. But Nemoto had one other problem, and this it was that caused him to veer somewhat away from Yoshikita's consistency of purpose. The long and short—mostly the former—of it was simply that Nemoto was a terribly horny young man.

He had been that way almost as long as he could remember. He had clear recollections of his mother telling the neighboring wives about finding little Futoshi making a tent of his sheet when she woke him up every morning. And while still in his early teens he had been forced to visit the neighborhood bath at those odd hours when it was almost empty because of the huge erections he sported whenever women were in the coeducational bath with him. All women from six to sixty had that effect on him.

Once he was bathing alone in the wide expanse of steamy water at ten at night when Mrs. Hashimoto, a matronly neighbor of fifty plus, came in to find Nemoto soaping himself on a stool near a wall faucet. Nemoto Junior instantly sprang to alert attention, unfazed by an admonishing dousing with cold water.

Mrs. Hashimoto sensed the cause. Tears of gratitude shining in her eyes, she walked over to him and humbly placed her hand on his fourteen-year-old head. "Buddha bless you, child" was all that she had said, in a voice husky with emotion. She had to constrain herself from patting Junior on the head, too.

To Nemoto at fourteen, Mrs. Hashimoto had seemed incredibly ancient and he would no more have considered pressing pelvises with her than he would have spat on the Emperor. Nevertheless, he could not control the tumescent reaction. It wasn't long, however, before he learned how to cure—at least, temporarily—such exuberant tumescence, and had he met Mrs. Hashimoto again under the same circumstances, he might well have given her double reason for blessing him.

In any case, horny he was and he hated to see them dispatch the girls on a journey through the spheres without first getting a little of that. Take Sujiko now; there was a girl who would make a priest burn his Book of Sutras. Even his entire library of religious tomes and scrolls. He had a raunchy vision of himself riding to glory between her thighs, each succeeding orgasm rocketing them deeper and deeper into space. Perhaps, if Yoshikita insisted on an immediate departure into the Great Unknown, he could at least persuade him to arrange for the moments of orgasm and throat-cutting to coincide.....

CHAPTER NINETEEN

True wasn't in his room when Sam and Chauncey returned from Fukuoka late in the day. After parking the jeep at the new temple, they had enlisted four novices from Correct Path's flock and had them carry their supplies over the hill to the Oguni temple.

With the aid of their new supplies, the two struck a happy dinner hour balance between Army rations and locally procured eel. To Mabel's intense vocal delight, True popped in just as they were finishing up and lost no time in scavenging.

Sam briefly reviewed their Fukuoka trip for True and then couldn't resist adding, "It looks like you got a serious thing going with Ruby Whacker. She's smitten with you."

"Then Ah've really got troubles," said True glumly, "Mah impression was that ole Ruby was just kiddin' around."

"Hell, no! She's got the hots for you," Sam said, shaking his head dolefully. "You've captured the hearts of both Raunchy Ruby and Honey-haired Hilda."

"Talent galore," said Chauncey, "and not even trying."

"Hey," said True, "you two're kiddin' me about ole Ruby, ain't you?"

Sam produced the box of Milky Ways. "Hardly," he said. "Here. These came from her. Sweets for the sweet, she said."

"Christ! Ah wouldn't let that ole fish cannery empty mah slop jar."

"You may have to one day. She's pretty insistent," Chauncey said. "And you don't need to pretend such elaborate indifference, pal. Sam and I heard you whispering her name hoarsely in your sleep a few nights ago. Before the conquest of Hilda, of course."

"That's bullshit!" True said. "Ah may snore, but Ah don't talk."

"You carry on running dramatic narratives, True. There's nothing you haven't unwittingly told us," Sam said with relish.

"What were Ruby's exact words, Sam, as she handed us the choclolate bars?"

"'Tell him there's a real honest-to-God woman waiting for him back in Fukuoka.'"

True stopped eating and abruptly smacked a fist into the palm of his hand. "Nossuh! Ah'm damned if Ah'll piddle around with an ole cesspool like that Ruby Whacker when Ah got me a gal right heah in Oh-Gooney that won't lay down. She's the most....."

"I thought the essence of Hilda's charm was that she *would* lie down," Chauncey said.

"Huh?"

"Quit stalling, True. Give us the straight scoop on Hilda. When're you going to introduce us to her?"

"Maybe not evah for you, Sam." said True defiantly. "Ah don't trust that mouth of yours."

"There's more to it than that. Level with us."

"Well, Hilda's bashful, for one thing. She knows you all watched her bathin' nekkid as a Brass Monkey and....."

"But you watched her, too," Chauncey pointed out.

"That's different. Ah got mah rights."

"You didn't have then," Sam reminded him.

"Does she speak English?" asked Chauncey.

"She'd have to. He's only half-lingual."

"Sure does," said True proudly. "Better'n me, in fact."

"That would hardly qualify her as an expert," said Sam.

"Have you discovered what she thinks we're doing here in Oguni?" asked Chauncey.

"Well, her and me, we've been right busy with other things and haven't talked much about the Army and truck like that. But Ah kinda hinted around that we was heah on a special secret mission for General MacArthur, and that Chauncey is blood-related."

Chauncey groaned. "My whole life's becoming a tissue of lies."

"Does Hilda know what's been going on between us and the girls?" Sam asked.

"Ah'm not too sure 'bout that, but Ah know theah's something worryin' her. Yessiree. Ah see it in her eyes now and then. Fear. Pure and simple. And Ah can't get her to tell me what she's so scared of."

"Now that you mention it," Chauncey mused, "I've seen the same thing in some of the girls. Only a few times, like when they thought no one was watching......"

"For God's sake, Chauncey, give your imagination a rest. And let me get some, too. We've got another performance at nine and mustn't disappoint our fan-club."

It was not the fan-club, however, that was disappointed. Instead, it was Chauncey, Sam, and True.

For the girls and their teacher did not come to the bath on schedule. True reconnoitered Hilda's room and found it in disarray, as if she had packed only the more necessary items of her scanty travelling outfit in exceeding haste and fled. Ignoring the past need for concealment, True plunged down the corridor, shoving open sliding doors right and left, hastily peering within, rushing on.

At last there could be no doubt, no misinterpretation. The Swiss woman and her fourteen charges had disappeared. They had even left some of their precious movie magazines behind: one copy of *Hollywood in Bed* and three of *Cute Cinema Cut-Ups*.

Shocked and disconsolate, True gathered the magazines up and hurried off to tell Sam and Chauncey.

The jeep raced through the darkness westward away from the valley of Oguni with Chauncey and True urging Sam at the wheel to greater speeds.

"Hang the danger!" Chauncey was saying, "we've got to catch them."

On a downward slope Sam pressed the gas pedal to the floor and the jeep fairly flew along the dirt road, its headlights two fast-moving cones in the gloom of the Kyushu countryside.

"We've only got a fifty-fifty chance that they came this way," Sam grated.

"With only two roads out of the valley," Chauncey said, "one guess was as good as the other."

"I'm afraid we've already lost too much time," Sam said as the jeep raced past an occasional thatch-roofed farm house. "They'd been gone a couple of hours already when we missed them, and then it took another hour to climb over the hill and get Correct Path to send that apprentice-priest back into Oguni to ask around for us."

"But they can't get far a-riding in rickshaws," True protested.

"I don't know about that," Chauncey demurred. "Those old rickshaw men have been running every time I've ever seen a rickshaw—and they've got themselves a three-hour head start."

"Ah wonder what we did to spook 'em like that?" True asked, the wind of their velocity forcing him to lean well forward toward the others in front to make himself heard.

"I suppose Hilda must have found out about our little Affairs of the Heart," Chauncey replied.

"Huh!" Sam snorted. "You mean Affairs of the Parts Private, don't you?"

"The very vulgarity of your mind has always been its dynamic," Chauncey noted with restraint.

"Anyway," Sam went on, unperturbed, "it was a lucky thing that Correct Path's boy thought to look in the rickshaw stand. Eight rickshaws gone and only a sleepy little girl to say that they had all left for the Inn of the Playful Hermit a little after eight. From there she had no idea where they had gone—or when they might be back."

"But why," asked Chauncey, suddenly striking his left palm with his right fist, "did they run out on us like that? *Why?*"

CHAPTER TWENTY

As luck would have it, the three Americans had taken the wrong road and had driven as far as Hida before coming to that conclusion. They then retraced their steps back to Oguni, parked their jeep at the new temple at two in the morning and climbed wearily back over the hill to their hideaway.

Early the next morning they poured their only five-gallon can of gasoline into the nearly-empty tank and took the other road southeast-ward out of the valley toward Bungo-Mori. They were bleary-eyed and irritable from lack of sleep but determined to press on with their search. The fifteen fugitive females had come to mean too much to them: ease and relaxation, sexual adventurism, and—to at least one of their number—true romance.

Cursory inquiries of two men and one woman in Bungo-Mori uncovered no trace of the missing women so they pushed on and took one of the three remaining roads out of town, this one to Yufuin. Before reaching it, however, Chauncey had figured out that the rickshaws could not possibly have got that far even if the rickshaw coolies had sprinted every single minute since eight o'clock the previous evening.

Back-tracking to Bungo-Mori, they reached that town of twelve thousand—situated at the base of the Kuji Plateau—in the nick of time, for there their five gallons of gasoline gave out. The first three filling stations where they tried to buy more had been closed so long that the locks and chains on the pumps were nearly unrecognizable with rust. At the fourth, Sam used his forty-five to shoot the lock off the door, and he and Chauncey ransacked the interior while True used a crow-bar to pry open several fifty-gallon drum cans lined up in back of the station. The Alabaman's efforts were unproductive, but Chauncey found a can atop a high shelf that sloshed when he lifted it. On the can was written *kanji* meaning, "For Emergency Use Only." It held between two and three gallons of the precious fuel they sought.

"Well, let's get on with it," Sam said after emptying the can into their tank.

"Hold on," Chauncey said. "If we go on with only that little gas, we'll only run out again before long."

"So what are we going to do? Just sit?"

Chauncey thought for a moment, then said, "That much gas will get the jeep back to Oguni. Let's put Mabel aboard and hire someone to drive it back to Correct Path's temple with a message to keep them for us until we get back."

"And then?" Sam asked impatiently.

"We keep on looking for the girls. Maybe they're here after all. Or maybe we passed them somewhere back there. They could've pulled off the side of the road when they heard the jeep coming or for some other reason."

"Well, it's your show," Sam said with a clear lack of enthusiasm.

As it turned out, Chauncey was right. They had passed the rickshaw caravan north of Bungo-Mori where it had left the road to find shade in a stand of trees and give the coolies a chance to catch up on their lost sleep.

Sam and True had settled themselves comfortably in the shelter of a wayside shrine to the Goddess Kannon to watch the road from Oguni, while Chauncey continued the search through the inns of the quiet town, which had been frightened into an unnatural stillness by their presence.

First to come in the early afternoon were only two rickshaws, their cloth flaps carefully concealing the identity of the passengers in the cabs of the two-wheeled vehicles and the coolies loping along on old but seemingly tireless legs that looked as if they were made entirely of metallic tendons and and hard-knotted ligaments.

Suspicious but uncertain, True and Sam let these pass. Five minutes later the main body of six rickshaws passed at the same pace. The Americans gave them a slight head start, then followed them into Bungo-Mori.

Chauncey too sighted the procession when he was returning to join True and Sam at the wayside shrine, and the three fell in together as the rickshaws winded their way through narrow, crooked streets away from the center of town. At an isolated inn, the lead rickshaw finally came to a halt and the three Americans watched covertly from a distance as Hilda Ritter stepped quickly inside, evidently to inquire if lodging was available. In a minute, she emerged and walked along the rickshaw line, speaking to the passengers and pointing out to the coolies where to park their vehicles behind the inn. Then, in a rush, all the girls hurried into the inn and out of sight.

"Well, you can leash the dogs, men," Sam said with a satisfied grin. "We've treed the quarry again."

"Let's give them a chance to get settled, then go in and register ourselves," Chauncey said. "Maybe we can even join them in a pre-dinner bath. They'll probably be wanting one pretty soon after that dusty ride."

"I never scored under water," Sam ventured.

"Yo'all are givin' me a hard-on, a-talkin' like that," complained True, pulling at his crotch.

The reunion was cunningly planned and masterfully executed. After registering under the half-frightened half-suspicious gaze of a youthful clerk at the front desk of the inn, the trio padded silently along the highly-polished corridors to their rooms toward the rear of the first floor. Tossing their musette bags in a handy corner, they quietly reconnoitered the two floors of the small, residential inn, determining that Hilda and her fourteen charges occupied eight rooms of the otherwise empty second floor while two of the first-floor rooms were in use by a couple and by a mother and her child. Their own rooms were two doors down from the communal bath, which was in size not unlike the one in the Inn of the Playful Hermit in Oguni. When they at last heard the slithering of many slippered feet past their rooms toward the bath, the three Americans waited until they calculated that the female contingent would be undressed, soaped and rinsed down, and deeply ensconced in hot water, then stealthily made their own way through the men's dressing room, where they shed their uniforms, and into the bathroom itself.

A gasp—almost palpable in its unified intensity—rose through the steamy air. Then bedlam ensued.

Hilda, who was sitting in a supervisory stance on the rim of the pool, screamed in outrage and plunged into the water. Two of the girls seated near her followed suit. On the other hand, Ann Blyth, Lana Turner, and Katherine Hepburn, all of whom had been contemplatively soaking in the pool. climbed out quickly and came rushing up to Sam and Chauncey, unmindful of the fact that they were naked as peeled grapes. They added to the confusion with cooing expressions of pleased surprise and endearment. Some laughed, others cheered, and one wailed, although no one knew whether from embarrassment or from distress at being on the far side of the pool from the Americans.

Grinning sheepishly at the commotion they were causing, Sam, Chauncey, and True stood their ground, wash cloths held in strategically modest positions in front of them.

"Hi! "Sam essayed a trifle weakly, not realizing that he spoke in English.

"*Hai!*" most of the girls chorused in return, using a Japanese word of the same pronunciation but having an affirmative connotation.

Chin deep in the water and with her angry eyes averted, Hilda Ritter commanded, "Get out! Go! You . . . . savages!"

"Why, Hilda honey, we just got heah," True objected,

"I believe this is a communal bath, isn't it, Miss Ritter?" Sam inquired, then added, "I'm Lieutenant Sam Bruce and this is Lieutenant Chauncey *MacArthur.*" He paused to let that sink in. "And, of course, you are intimately acquainted with our comrade from Mushville, Lieutenant Truman Foote, sometimes called Trench by his admirers."

"Intimately?" Hilda flared shrilly. "Are you suggesting that . . . . ." She sputtered in her anger. "Anyway, don't just stand there. If you insist on staying in this room, at least have the decency to get down here into the water."

Within two minutes the three men and fifteen women had arranged themselves in positions of their varied preference in the spacious pool. With the exception of Hilda Ritter, everyone seemed quite pleased with this turn of events, and smiles and significant glances were flitting back and forth over the surface of the water with growing abandon.

The still-glowering Hilda did not miss this nor the gradually lessening distance between two of the Americans and several of her charges. The situation was explosive, so she tried to defuse it.

"Well, as long as you're here, you might as well speak your piece," she said sharply.

"First of all," Sam said, rising up to nipple depth in the water and deepening his voice, "we want to know why you ran out on us back there in Oguni."

"Ran out on you! Well, I like that!" Hilda cried. "Who are you to say where we can go or when?" The strands of her water-darkened blond hair swayed with the angry movements of her head. "We decided to leave Oguni, and that's all there is to it. Besides, why should you care?"

"Why, Hilda, Ah thought you and me, we was kinda . . . ."

"Don't be preposterous, you wretched . . . . .brown-necked yokel!"

"That's 'red—necked', m'am," True corrected.

"Thank you," Hilda said stiffly.

"Ah can tell," True averred warmly, "that you ain't plumb indifferent to me."

Sam cleared his throat to regain their attention. "Besides, Miss Ritter, Lieutenant *MacArthur* and I . . . . well, we wanted to see some of these girls again and . . . ."

Hilda's eyes flashed suspiciously as she quickly surveyed the faces of the fourteen girls. "Have any of you been . . . ." she started to ask, then abruptly realized from the blank looks of polite attention on all faces that they had been speaking in English, that none of the girls had understood a word that had been said.

"Well, maybe it's just as well," she said, then lapsed into silence.

"*Sensei*, why don't we tell them?" softly suggested Irene Dunne, who was known back home as Saseko Komara.

"Be quiet!" instructed Hilda.

"Tell us what?" demanded Sam, ears a-twitch.

"Nothing important," answered Hilda shortly. "Just a small matter . . . . of a feminine nature." In her distraction, she had risen slowly out of the water to an extent that fully exposed her magnificent breasts.

True gawked, Sam leered, and Chauncey trembled . . . . until Hilda traced their intent looks to their goals. Flushed and confused, she sank back too quickly and too deeply into the steamy water, then re-surfaced sputtering.

"You needn't be shy, Miss Ritter," Sam advised. "Not with equipment like that."

"You, Lieutenant, are a lecher," Hilda stated coldly. "If you have nothing else to say, I think I'll just go back to my room."

The Americans clamped their lips shut tightly, then waited in bright-eyed anticipation.

"All right, *all right!*" Hilda cried in exasperation. "Then I *won't* go back to my room."

The three lieutenants sighed in temporary defeat.

Turning to the girls, Sam asked brightly in Japanese, "Have any of you girls ever heard of a game called Post Office? It's very popular among upper-class young ladies and gentlemen back home."

"Oh, for God's sake, stop it!" cried Hilda.

"No harm intended, Miss Ritter," Chauncey said. "We just wanted to . . . ."

"I *know* what you just wanted to do, Lieutenant. I know quite well. That's why we're leaving here tomorrow morning."

"Wha . . . . at?"

"I'll give you exactly three minutes to say goodbye to the girls. Then, if you really are officers and *gentlemen,* you'll turn your backs while we leave the bath."

"Hilda honey, Ah wish you'd . . . ."

"Goodbye, Lieutenant Foote," Hilda said adamantly.

Sam and Chauncey bade the equally disappointed girls farewell, then glumly moved to the far side of the pool and reluctantly turned their backs.

It was at four the next morning, however, when they said goodbye a second time to Ida Lupino and Deborah Kerr, while True snored obstreperously in his bachelor *futon* down the hall.

CHAPTER TWENTY-ONE

At noon the safari of eight rickshaws pulled off the road between Bungo-Mori and Bochu into a bamboo grove. Hilda Ritter dismounted from the lead vehicle and instructed the leathery, wrinkled old fellow between the poles of her rickshaw to distribute the *bento* prepared for them at the inn to the other coolies. After satisfying herself that they were sufficiently concealed from the road, she led the fourteen girls still deeper into the cool, green interior of the grove for their noon meal.

"Takako-san," she called to the girl known as Claudette Colbert to the Americans. "Pass out the lunch boxes, please. And Marako-san, are you feeling any better now?"

"Yes, thank you, *Sensei*," answered the girl who had barely been able to climb into the rickshaw that morning. Marako was the one who had decided that she liked the name and appearance of Ida Lupino.

"What was it, dear? I noticed you holding your . . . . . stomach."

"Just. . . .uh, cramps, Miss Ritter."

"You mustn't overdo things, dear."

"That's good advice, Miss Ritter," Ida murmured, averting her face. "But sometimes it's so hard. . . .to restrain oneself."

The Swiss woman looked at her in sharp curiosity, then shrugged off the thought.

"How far do we still have to go?" Ida/Marako asked, uncomfortable under the teacher's scrutiny.

"Quite a way, I'm afraid. I just hope we reach Bochu by evening. I don't know why. . . .but three of the coolies were so slow this morning. It seemed as if we had to stop every fifteen minutes to let them catch up. It's rather odd, come to think of it, especially since they look like the largest and strongest of the lot. And I thought I heard a kind of. . . . .wailing from them now and then, too, but perhaps it was merely one of those coolie chants."

"What about those two dreadful ensigns, Miss Ritter?" Ida/Marako asked in haste to change the subject. "Do you think they will find us?"

"I don't know, dear, but I'm terribly worried. After all, those barbaric Americans found us."

"But they had a jeep. . . . . "

Hilda's eyes glinted as she asked, "How do you know that, Marako? I don't recall them saying anything like that in the bath last night."

"Oh, we heard it from one of the maids in the inn, Miss Ritter. She saw them leave for Oguni in it early this morning."

"I see," Hilda said, still watching Marako's face.

"I wish they were with us," Ida/Marako said in a burst of wistfulness.

"Marako-san!"

"I mean, they'd be such protection, wouldn't they? What with those two idiots Yoshikita and Nemoto loose. . . . . "

Hilda could not—in good conscience—deny that, so she took a bite of *sushi* from her lunch box.

In another part of the bamboo grove, the eight coolies had doffed their wide-brimmed, low-cone-shaped hats and stood clustered together for a moment while the rice-filled *bento* were passed out. After a few words with the others, three of them staggered off to one side and collapsed on the ground.

"Ah think mah feet are a-fire," said one in a fair approximation of English.

"Maybe we could get three of the girls to trade places with us this afternoon," groaned the second coolie.

The third said nothing, preferring to devote his undivided attention to massaging his leg muscles, which were threatening to go into spasms momentarily.

"You and yoah fat-headed ideas!" True snarled at Sam.

"You should complain, mushmouth. At least you got some sleep."

"And that's bout all Ah got."

They had no sooner finished their *bento* than the head coolie came over to them and said in Japanese. "The Swiss woman is calling us."

Chauncey nodded and rose painfully to his feet.

"I still get the feeling that Hilda is running from something."

"From us, maybe," Sam conjectured.

"I don't know," Chauncey mused. "I saw that scared look in her eyes again last night."

"And Ah gave that ole coolie a whole carton of smokes to let me take his place," True said in disgust at his own stupidity.

"If we get as far as Bochu," Sam said, putting on the wide coolie hat with which each had effectively concealed his non-Japanese face and hair, "I vote we call it off. Let 'em go on without us. What the hell, there's no piece of tail on earth worth pulling a bloody rickshaw eight hours for."

"Not even Rita Hayworth or Dorothy Lamour?" Chauncey asked.

Sam gave the choice his serious consideration for a long moment before shrugging and turning to follow the other coolies to the waiting rickshaws.

At the inn in Bochu, the three lieutenants bunked with the five other coolies in a spacious, eighteen-mat room, which was situated behind the kitchen and was used in better times by touring groups from farmers' cooperatives. Nowadays, however, the inns were nearly empty of guests and the traveller could have his pick of rooms and arrangements and practically set his own room rate.

As soon as they entered the room, they dragged out the *futon* from a closet and collapsed on them groaning and cursing. The five genuine coolies, who were two or three times their ages, sniggered and whispered among themselves about the physical weakness of the conquerors, but they were too uncertain of the temper and intentions of the Americans to cross a certain line of circumspection. The whole affair was something of a puzzle to them and they were mightily envious of their three co-workers who had already received a carton of cigarettes (worth the equivalent of two months' wages on the blackmarket) each for returning to Oguni and keeping their mouths shut. Obviously these wealthy American officers, who had still more cigarettes in the musette bags stowed away in the last rickshaw, could have afforded to ride themselves, and obviously they were fooling no one except the foreign woman, for the Japanese girls were very much aware of their presence and very much concerned about their well-being.

Well, it was beyond the comprehension of the coolies. The prefectural authorities had warned the people by radio late last month that they could expect the incoming Americans to act in a weird and outlandish manner, and despite their growing lack of faith in the utterances of Japanese officialdom, this at least was one prediction that they were beginning to appreciate fervently. Surely none but the certifiable would pull a rickshaw if it had not been the occupation of his forefathers and fate had not ordained that it be his *hombun* in life.

With one last look—and chuckle—at the already snoring Americans, the five coolies left for the communal bath on the far side of the kitchen. After a leisurely scrubbing and soaking, they returned to the room, ate their dinner, and went out to stroll around Bochu in the mild September dusk. While they were gone, Carole Landis, Rita Hayworth, and Dorothy Lamour tiptoed in to hang up the coolie outfits the Americans had borrowed and improvised. (Fortunately, most coolie clothing was large and concealing—like the hat, loose—like the *happi* coat, or accommodating and would fit all sizes—like the loin cloth. The lieutenants were wearing their own T-shirts so the only items of apparel they had needed to buy were *chika-tabi,* the rubber and canvas footwear with the split next to the big toe. This tidying up accomplished with only a few irrepressible titters, the *yukata*-clad girls knelt by the *futon* and began to massage a soothing ointment into the calf and thigh muscles of the Americans, who were so exhausted that they did not become aware of these ministrations for several minutes.

"You have had a long and tiring day," said Rita as Chauncey slowly pried one eye open. He tried to speak but succeeded only in uttering a single croak.

"After this, we will take you to the bath and let the hot water work more of the soreness out of your muscles," Carole said to True who was softly moaning with his eyes closed.

"Also," began Dorothy, with a note of ill-repressed excitement in her voice, "we have arranged three single rooms for you elsewhere on the first floor, where we will take you for dinner when you have finished your bath."

"We thought you would prefer to be alone," chirped Rita in reply to Chauncey's raised eyebrows.

"Alone with us, that is," added Carole.

Propping himself up on an elbow, True said in English to Sam and Chauncey, "Ah was kinda planning on keeping mahself pure for Hildy. . . . ."

"After she called you a 'preposterous, brown-necked yokel'?" asked Sam.

"Aw, she didn't mean nothin' by it," grinned True, watching Carole Landis massage his upper thigh muscles, "but then again, Ah don't want to hurt this lil gal's feelings none, seein' how she's tryin' to be friendly an' all."

"Do you think you can make it to the bath now, with our help?" the vivacious Dorothy Lamour asked.

"We'll try," said Chauncey gamely.

Seeing that the bath was as silent and dark as a tomb, the girls boldly accompanied the Americans into the male dressing room to help them remove the inn *yukata* they had donned for the brief but pain-ridden trip down the corridor past the inn kitchen. Then, while Dorothy, Carole, and Rita undressed in the other locker room, the men slowly made their way into the bath, turned on the lights, and inched down into the welcome heat.

"Well, do we quit here—or do we go on?" Chauncey asked the others hoarsely.

"I don't have any choice," Sam stated with calm resignation. "I know I won't be able to get out of bed for at least three days."

At that moment their three companions entered the large steamy room from the door marked *Joshi*. They were, of course, mother-naked and apparently quite unconcerned about the fact. They chattered glibly and gaily among themselves as they arranged stools, pails, soap, and wash towels to their satisfaction. The wall faucets, from which they drew water for rinsing, were so located that Dorothy went to the east side of the sixteen-by-twenty-foot pool, Carole went to the west, and Rita to the south.

"I don't think I'll ever get accustomed to it," Sam said in English to Chauncey, whom he could now see only dimly on the far side of the pool through the rising steam.

"To what?"

"To these girls. . . . . .and their wonderful attitudes," explained Sam with a sigh. "They're like pagans from some far-off paradise. No shame, no false modesty. So natural and pure in their own way."

"Pure?" Chauncey snorted. "Why, we've got teeth-marks on our necks and scratches all over our backs."

"But that's just what I mean!" Sam cried. "Our so-called civilized values! If a girl is naturally passionate and openly likes sex, we think that there's something lewd and depraved about her. God, what hypocrites we Westerners are!"

"Hey, yo' all still over theah? " called True.

"Yeah, we'uns is still over heah," replied Sam in deliberate mimicry.

While the men talked through the clouds of steam, the three girls sat on miniature stools and bathed themselves with the thoroughness of a surgeon approaching the operating room. First they used the wooden pails to ladle hot water from the pool over themselves and then applied soap with a lavish hand. Hot water and soap, hot water and soap in a seemingly endless cycle. Finally, after three more hot water rinsings, they evidently decided that they were clean enough to enter the pool itself,

"Dorothy-san," Sam said in Japanese to that girl as she snuggled down into the water beside him, "I don't think I can make it tomorrow."

"Poor Sam-san," she commiserated, kneading his shoulder muscles.

"Why can't we just stay here in Bochu for a while?" Chauncey asked Rita over on their side of the pool. They could all hear each other better than they could see, as the cooling air of night met the hot water of the bath.

"Oh, no!" cried Carole. "We *must* go on."

"But why?" asked Chauncey. "All of you act as if you were running away from something. The war's over; there's no danger."

None of the girls said anything.

"If you're in any kind of trouble," said Sam, "we would

do anything we could to help you."

"Oh, I wish you. . . ." began Carole.

"Be quiet," hissed Dorothy.

"But. . . ."

"Remember what Miss Ritter told us." Dorothy warned Carole.

"Anyway," said Sam after a long moment of unproductive silence, "with my legs in the condition they're in, I doubt that I'll be able to. . . ."

"We'll get your legs in shape," volunteered Rita brightly, her voice a sound without body in the fog. "Chauncey. . . and True and Sam, too. . . .all of you get out of the bath and sit down on the edge. Here, I'll help you up, Chauncey. Easy. There. Now sit down. That's it. Let your legs dangle down in the water. That's right. Now we'll stay down here in the water and massage your legs."

Dorothy and Carole arranged their companions in similar positions and all three fell to leg massage with considerable dedication, the depth of the shallow pool being such that their unadorned breasts came just up to the level of the men's knees as the girls stood in the water. And during the course of their vigorous massaging movements, the nipples of their breasts time and again brushed against those knees.

Eventually—and despite general debility and fatigue, this feathery contact against a background of lovely, eager, and devoted femininity produced another entirely predictable reaction in—or on—the men.

Rita Hayworth made no bones about it. With a gay laugh, she said, "I see that your leg muscles are not the only ones that are stiff."

"Over here, too," called Carole with evident delight.

"Mine, too," chortled Dorothy.

"Dr. Landis," asked Rita, "don't you think another kind of treatment is indicated in this case?"

"I do, indeed,"

"What do you recommend?" pursued Rita.

"Perhaps *kozetsu amma*,.. suggested Carole, pushing herself in between True's legs. "What do you think, Dr. Lamour?"

"Your diagnosis and prescription are excellent, Doctor. *Kozetsu amma* should take care of the other stiff muscles in a jiffy."

— 143 —

"I'm not sure that I know how," complained Rita.

"Oh, Rita!" exclaimed Dorothy in evident exasperation. "The entire second chapter of that illustrated book I lent you this summer was all about nothing else. And that chapter was so worn when you returned the book that the pages were falling out."

"I remember it now," admitted Rita heatedly, "but it was my little sister who had the book most of the time."

"What the devil does *kozetsu amma* mean?" called Sam to Chauncey through the fog but got only silence for an answer.

Because by then none of the Americans needed to be told that it meant 'tongue-and-lip massage.'

At the same time the three couples were undressing and entering the bath, Hilda Ritter was discovering the absence of three of her charges on the floor above. She had gone into Ida Marako Lupino's room to see if that young girl needed any medicine for her. . . .uh, stomach cramps and had noticed the absence of Ida's room-mate for the night, Dorothy Lamour. Ida had tried to cover for Dorothy by saying that she had just gone down the hall to one of the other rooms, but the Swiss teacher was having none of that. She resolutely went into all the rooms and thereby uncovered the absence of Rita and Carole as well.

"If we were anywhere near those three Americans. . . . ." she thought, then abandoned the suspicion. The Americans were back in Oguni or perhaps even Fukuoka by now. But as she went down the stairs of the inn to the entrance, she had to admit to herself that she almost wished the three American officers were near at hand. She had had too much experience with Japanese fanaticism during the long war years to think that those two dreadful ensigns of the Special Attack Forces would abandon the search for their prey so easily. And that Yoshikita-san, well, he was just a fanatic's fanatic.

A sleepy desk-clerk bowed and said that he had not seen any of her charges leave the inn, then closed his eyes and leaned back in his chair again.

What would he know, thought Hilda. They might have gone out for a walk. Changing from indoor slippers to outdoor *geta,* she grimaced as the wooden footgear pinched her larger foreign feet. Then she crossed the cobblestones of the small inn courtyard and opened the gate a few inches to look out.

What she saw prompted her to close the gate again in a rush, then hurry back into the inn, panic welling up within her. Oh dear God, she thought, those terrible men are out there again, just as they had been in Oguni. None other than Yoshikita and Nemoto were standing near a lighted shop front on the other side of the street. Luckily they had been talking to each other and had not seen her open the gate. Frantically Hilda jammed her feet back into the slippers and ran past the gaping clerk.

Her heart thudding behind her ample, well-formed bosom, she tried to get a grip on herself and think clearly. First, she *had* to find the three missing girls. They weren't upstairs, and she couldn't go outside to look for them. Where else could. . . . The bath! Quick, try the bath. That's where she'd found three other 'missing' girls back in Oguni. Where was it now? Oh yes, down this hall and to the right. Ah, there's a light on inside! They must be. . . . But quietly now! It could be someone else in there.

On tiptoe, Hilda went as quickly as she could through the women's dressing room and silently inched open the door to the interior of the bath. Dear God, dear, dear, dear God, she was chanting to herself, let the girls be inside. Then show me how to save all of them from those two monsters in the street! The coolies? No, those old men would never face navy officers. Not in Japan! If only those Americans were here! Why did I ever. . . .

For a moment the interior of the bath was too steamy for her to see clearly. Then a draft wafted in through the half-open door and swept through the wisps of fog so that she could distinguish the outlines of forms.

Yes, forms. Three? Yes. Three men, each on a different side of the pool. Sitting on the tiled rim. No, reclining back, propped up on their elbows. What on earth were they. . . . Damn that steam! There, she had a good look at the face of one of them. It was. . . .could it really be?. . . .one of the Americans! In pain? That agonized expression! The closed eyes! What was happening to him? And the other two? There! Creatures black and hairy were voraciously attacking their. . . . . .clinging to their lower parts, bobbing up and down. . . .what on earth! Oh, my dear God, no, no! It couldn't be! Don't let it be! Not her three missing girls, not doing. . . .*that* to the Americans!

Stifling a scream, Hilda closed the door all but an inch and stood there with one hand over her pounding heart. Unconscious of her voyeuristic role, she watched the scene of growing abandonment while trying desperately to decide how to meet the threat outside in the street. Somehow she would have to utilize the presence of the Americans to combat the murderous Japanese pilots. Hmmm, the Americans looked strong enough. . . .and three to two were good odds. Besides, they probably carried weapons, didn't they? Yes, she thought with narrowing eyes, they would have to do in this emergency. Brown-necked or red-necked yokel and what else have you, they would have to do!

That was the Alabaman over there, she thought, as the draft continued to increase visibility. And that little minx Fukako! Where did she ever learn such. . . . Hmmm, the Alabaman certainly seemed to be enjoying her attentions. Enjoying hell, she smiled to herself, he was *loving* it! She felt an emotion that she refused to identify as incipient jealousy. Look at that! The size of it! Flushing, she tried to look away but found that she could not. Her eyes were glued to the action and she could not bring herself to even blink them.

She recalled, now with distinct regret, that night back in Oguni, when the lieutenant from Alabama had chased her from the bath to her room. She had finally let him come in because she took pity on him and they had talked in whispers and sipped tea for nearly an hour before she told him he had to leave. And then he had begged so ardently to be permitted to stay that she had at last told him he could sleep outside on her balcony. Perhaps she shouldn't have been quite so. . . . . . .unrelenting in her stand.

She tried to make herself feel shame, but all that she felt was. . . .warmth. An undeniable warmth that centered in her. . . .lower region. A damp glowing warmth—and it rose from her loins as an idea began to take shape in her mind. Perhaps there was a way to serve both of her purposes at the same time. . . .

Silently Hilda closed the door and took a deep breath. She could wait a minute or two. It would be needlessly cruel to interrupt now. Yes, she thought she now had the solution. . . . .

CHAPTER TWENTY-TWO

Back on the second floor of the inn, Hilda Ritter went about putting her plan into action with Swiss efficiency and dispatch. First, she went through the empty rooms until she found three that suited her purpose, then she marshalled her students and had them move all belongings into those rooms. Next, she summoned Hiroko Maguchi (Barbara Stanwyck) to her side and told her:

"The missing girls are in the bath. Run down and fetch them quickly."

Hiroko bowed and started to leave.

"And tell them, Hiroko-san, to bring the three Americans with them."

Hiroko clapped a surprised hand over a startled mouth. "How did. . . .."

"Never mind. I know the Americans are there. Tell them all to come quickly."

Hiroko turned away to hide her grin and hurried off.

In less than three minutes Hiroko was back with the missing three, their long black hair still dampish from the steam and their eyes shining in secret satisfaction. Several of the other girls clustered around them, and there was a fast exchange of whispered confidences interspersed by low-pitched peals of delighted laughter.

After counting heads to see that all were present, Hilda asked if the Americans were coming.

"They went to get their things from the coolies' room," Hiroko explained. "They'll be here in a few minutes."

"All right, girls," Hilda said. "Listen to me carefully now. This is very serious."

The fourteen girls bowed their heads and clasped their hands below the waist in the proper pupil-listening-to-teacher attitude.

"Ensigns Yoshikita and Nemoto are outside in the street."

A gasp of genuine dismay ran through the room.

"But I have a plan," Hilda went on, speaking quickly. "I've moved all of us into these three rooms. I will sleep in the smallest one, and the seven of you will sleep in each of the two larger ones." Inwardly, Hilda sighed with relief. No one was questioning why she should sleep alone. "In a minute the three American officers, who have been so persistently intent on. . . .getting to know us better, will be here. . . .and we're going to give them a chance to do just that."

"What is that, *Sensei?*"

"Get to know us better. You see, we will persuade them to stay with us, one in each of our three rooms, as guards." Hilda rushed on to distract the thoughts of the group from the obvious fact that their teacher would be alone in her room with one of the Americans. "These men are combat veterans, and I hope they carry weapons. And they appear to be capable and strong." She flushed at a certain unbidden remembrance. "Obviously, this will mean some sacrifice on our part in feminine. . . .uh, decorum, but I feel that this sacrifice must be made. To save your lives."

The girls nodded in grave agreement.

"You must all promise me that you will never say anything about these. . . .uh, arrangements when you return to your homes in Fukuoka. Your families might not understand. Your fathers in particular might believe that I have consigned you to a. . . .hmm, a fate worse than death."

"We'll never breathe a word of it, *Sensei*," Keiko Koshi (Shirley Temple) said breathlessly. The others nodded solemnly, their eyes bright in anticipation.

"But what are we going to tell the Americans, Miss Ritter?" asked Michiko Chino (Veronica Lake). "I mean, about Nemoto-san and Yoshikita-san."

"For the moment, nothing. The Americans obviously want to be with us, so we're giving them that chance. Of course, I think that we should treat them very well. . . .very well, indeed. . . . .to encourage them to travel with us, don't you agree?"

They all did. Very readily.

"Now, about tomorrow," began the Swiss woman, confidence in her machinations growing as she gave them oral expression and obtained the acquiescence of her charges. (Not that she thought for a moment that they would demur. Oh, no! Not after seeing that idyllic scene of pure affection in the bath below! The little imps. She was sure that some of the others as well were parties to similar hanky-panky. Talk about butter not melting in mouths!) "We're going to leave Bochu and take the road that goes along the slope part of the way up Mt. Aso, circle the mountain, and descend the other side. I was talking to one of the coolies—the *real* coolies—yesterday and he told me about this road. Or really only a path. It's very seldom used, and not many people know of it."

"But won't those two idiots follow us?" asked Sachie Iki (Betty Grable).

"I'm coming to that. Oh, Sachie-san, will you please stand over by the door and let me know when you hear the Americans coming? Thank you, dear. Now tonight I'm going to have our coolies take the rickshaws down some back alleys until they get out of town, then park them a mile or so away on the road to the mountain. Three of them will have to come back for the other rickshaws, of course. And I'm going to give the head coolie some money and have him make arrangements with the local *kumiai* to sneak eight more rickshaws—all covered, like ours—into the rear courtyard of the inn as soon as ours have left. Tomorrow morning these eight will leave here early with all the maids in the inn aboard and go quickly to the railroad station. The maids will be carrying *furoshiki* and small bags and they will casually mention to the other coolies that they are travelling to Kagoshima. At the station they will buy tickets to that city, board that train—which leaves at seven forty-five, and ride as far as they like. Then they will get off, do some sight-seeing—I will give them enough money—and catch a train home."

Sachie/Betty signalled that there was still no one in the hallway; the others were listening intently to the attractive Swiss woman.

"Then we will walk to where *our* rickshaws are waiting and start out to cross Mt. Aso. Hopefully, Nemoto-san and Yoshikita-san will see the other rickshaws leave here but will not be able to catch up with them before the Kagoshima train leaves. . . .I will arrange the timing so that the maids have only a munute or so to wait in the station. Then when those crazy pilots get there, they will—I hope—ask around and learn that a group of girls like you caught the Kagoshima train."

"But they won't have a European woman with them, will they?" asked the mentally alert Michiko/Veronica.

"That is the one flaw in my plan," admitted their teacher. "However, I will have the tallest maid carry both an umbrella and a parasol in the rickshaw with her to the station. If it's raining, she'll use the umbrella and if the sun is shining, she'll use the parasol. Very low over her head, of course, to conceal her hair and features as mucn as possible."

"I have a scarf she can wear around her hair, *Sensei*," volunteered Mameko/Dorothy.

"Fine. Let me have it now, please. Thank you, Mameko-san."

"*Sensei*, are we going to have the Americans take us back to our homes?"

A frown creased Hilda's forehead. "Frankly, I still haven't decided what's best to do. If we go back to Fukuoka now. . . .without somehow solving the problem of Nemoto and Yoshikita, there would be little to prevent them from. . . .carrying out their plan there. Eventually, I mean. Your fathers couldn't put guards around you for the rest of your lives. Also, we don't know what kind of reception your families will give you."

"But can't the Americans do *something*?" asked Kusako/Rita in a half-wail, her pretty face revealing her fright. "After all, one of them *is* General MacArthur's nephew!"

"I know, I know," said Hilda. "And maybe they can help. Anyway, that's why I'm getting them to join us. But if I tell them the problem now, they might insist on taking us back to Fukuoka right away. I mean, they might not understand how stubborn and *fanatical* those two pilots are liable to be about this."

"Couldn't they just capture them now, right here in Bochu?" asked Kusako/Rita.

"They could *try*," replied Hilda. "But if they tried and failed, then Nemoto and Yoshikita would be warned. . . . and more cunning and vengeful than ever. We can't afford to ignore the chance that the pilots might kill the Americans. After all, they are in their own country, and there are no other American forces near here."

This grim possibility sobered the girls considerably.

"Anyway," Hilda said, forcing a smile on her attractive face, "we'll have the Americans with us tonight, and I'm sure we'll be safe here inside the inn."

"Oh, *Sensei!* I hear someone coming," warned Sachie/ Betty.

"All right now, girls," said Hilda lowering her voice. "Get ready. Let's go all out to make them comfortable and content. If we entertain them royally, they may be our salvation. Tsutako-san, you order the very best food and *sake* from the kitchen. Sujiko-san, get the softest *zabuton* out of the closet. And all of you: remember to massage them well! They can't go with us if they can't walk."

As the door slid open, Hilda had one last worrisome thought about her own qualifications to adequately "entertain" Lieutenant Truman Foote. She wished she had studied that book that Mameko (Dorothy) lent Kusako (Rita) last summer. Still, she had just witnessed a performance of the real thing, so perhaps she could pass muster.

"Chauncey-san," asked Ann Blyth from a position behind and slightly above him, "should I get out and walk?"

"That's. . . .a good. . . .idea," panted Chauncey hoarsely, his voice that of the doomed. "I've got to. . . .take a break, any. . . .way."

The rickshaw safari was making its way diagonally up the long, low slope of Mt. Aso in central Kyushu. The hour was nearing noon. Five rickshaws made up the first segment of the safari and were at least two hundred yards ahead of the other three. This rear echelon was led by Chauncey MacArthur with only one—he had won the toss—passenger: Ann Blyth. True came next with Lana and Deborah and then Sam with Claudette and Shirley. If anything, the faces of Sam and True were even paler and more drawn than Chauncey's, their panting deeper, their groans hoarser.

"I hardly got to see anything of you at all last night, Chauncey-san," said Ann, pretending to pout and lowering her head so that she could look up at him more devastatingly through her long, long lashes. With the lieutenant's trembling aid, she had descended from the two-wheeled vehicle, and they were waiting for the tail of the safari to catch up with them.

Chauncey spread his hands in a helpless gesture.

"There were several things that I wanted to. . . .hmm, discuss with you," Ann went on, "but the other girls sort of of. . . . . . monopolized you."

"Rub my legs, will you?" asked Chauncey, his eyes glazed and inattentive.

"Several things that I read in a book last summer."

"God, what a studious little witch you are!"

"Oh, it wasn't that kind of book," Ann exclaimed, missing the irony. "It was all about. . . . ."

"You don't need to tell me," said the 'nephew' of the illustrious general, who remembered all too well the events of the sleepless night just past. He had bedded down with Ann and the other six hoping that he might be able to sneak in a little sex, missionary-style, later with this lovely creature now kneeling in the lava dust at his feet but instead was treated to the entire panorama of sex in the Orient, all energetically and ably portrayed to the mystifying background of a running commentary of whispered page, chapter, and position numbers.

Sam Bruce pulled his rickshaw up beside Chauncey's, dropped the two shafts to the ground, and staggered off to the side of the path.

"You. . . .may not believe this," he said in English with a shuddering expiration of breath, "but I really wish I was back on Okinawa."

"Did you get a good night's sleep?" Chauncey asked innocently.

"Sleep, hell!" the Chicagoan snorted. "Say, have you ever heard of the Forty-Eight Postions?"

"Yeah, someone told me that the Japanese consider that par for the course."

"Well," said Sam, motioning for Claudette and Shirley to get down and begin work on his legs, "now there're forty-*nine*!"

"Hmmm," began Chauncey reflectively, "I'd have guessed nearer a *hundred* and forty-nine."

"When I finally got to sleep at dawn, my seven busy little darlings were talking—dead seriously, mind you—about adding a new chapter to some damned book they'd been studying."

"It was some night."

"Criminal understatement," said Sam.

"You know," Chauncey began, looking around as if to reassure himself that there was no one who could understand English nearby, "there's something funny going on. . . ."

"Funny, he says!"

"I mean it, Sam. It's downright mystifying, in fact. Back in Oguni Hilda couldn't wait to get away from us and now. . . . ."

". . . . .she won't let us out of her sight," finished Sam. "Making the girls bow and scrape and wait on us hands, feet, and. . . .everywhere else. Father Divine would eat his heart out if he could have seen us last night."

"And then why did we have to walk from the inn this morning all that way to the rickshaws?"

"Ask someone who knows, buddy, not me. What *I* want to know is how long we're going on with this farce. We can't continue like this, Chauncey. The human body can only take so much. Besides, we're overdue back at headquarters. Old Dawgleish will be unleashing his hounds." Sam's lopsided grin appeared briefly in appreciation of this weak sally.

"I'm about ready to call it quits, too, Sam, but what the hell, we can't just leave these five girls out here in this wilderness! And besides, what would we do here ourselves?"

"Rest, man!" said Sam crossly. "What I've been wanting to do all along, ever since we embarked on this excursion into sheer idiocy."

"Well, let's stick it out at least until we all get back to something closer to civilization. Maybe by then Hilda will have let us in on the true story."

"Speaking of True, here he comes."

"Dawg bite it!" the Bulwark of Alabama exclaimed as he staggered up between the shafts of his rickshaw.

"And not only dogs," commented Sam.

"Huh?"

"Never mind."

"Ah'm in love," True announced simply.

"After last night?" asked Sam.

True nodded happily.

"But I thought we sent Mabel back to Oguni."

"Up yours!" snarled True. "Ah got me a woman that just won't quit."

"I wish I had one that *would* quit," said Chauncey fervently.

"Now that you mention it," Sam commented, "Honey-haired Hilda *did* look somehow more satisfied, more........hmm, *mature* this morning, didn't she, Chauncey?"

"More mature, maybe, but she's still frightened about something."

"Maybe she's scared of a stiff."

"Hah. . .hah."

After a few more minutes of rest and respite, the three lieutenants painfully got back into harness and moved on up the gradually ascending path in an effort to catch up with the others before the noon break.

At the highest point the path would reach, the rickshaw procession stopped and Hilda had the head coolie distribute the rice-packed *bento* from the inn in Bochu. Except for True's, which she delivered herself, then spoke to him in anxious concern for several minutes.

Although the summit of the low-cone-shaped volcano was still above them, the view from where they stood was magnificent. The lower hills of central Kyushu spread out on all sides like waves in a green sea. Below them the slopes of Mt. Aso were forested while above they were tree-less, and the rickshaws would make their way in and out of stands of pine trees for the next hour as they started down the long slope that wound north and away from the volcano, which, the Japan Tourist Bureau boasted, held the largest crater on earth.

After an all-too-short rest, the coolies—both Japanese and American—were hitched up to their carts for the afternoon run.

"At least it's downhill all the way," noted Chauncey, trying to extract a small measure of optimism from an otherwise grim prospect.

One serious omission, however, had been made. In the trip so far, the three lieutenants had pulled the rickshaws only over the comparatively level road to Bochu and then, this morning, *up* the side of Mt. Aso. ("Ah wonder if ole Harry Aso comes from anywheah 'round heah?" True had asked when he first heard the name of the volcano.) This afternoon would be their first experience with a long downhill slope.

The omission? Each rickshaw was equipped with an emergency brake (a small metal ring attached to a wire running along the bottom of the right-hand shaft), but no one had thought to tell the Americans where they were or how to use them.

CHAPTER TWENTY-THREE

As usual, the five native-drawn vehicles went into the lead and were soon about fifty yards ahead of the other three. Even so, Chauncey and his team were making increasingly good time on the downward slope and were beginning to think that everything might turn out to be all right yet, when the Fresno Flash noticed that Sam was trying to pass him.

Pulling over to one side as far as he could, he called to Sam as the Chicagoan sped past, "Feeling pretty good, huh? Better take it easy, though. We've got a long way to...." By then Sam was well ahead of Chauncey on the narrow path that the head coolie had told him was about nine miles in length, fairly straight and downhill all the way.

"Get outa mah way!"

Here comes True, thought Chauncey. Why was he too in such an all-fired hurry? Then it dawned on him that True and Sam each had two passengers to his one and that the additional weight added that much impetus. Still, he'd better not get too far behind, Chauncey decided, lengthening his own stride and trying to ignore the burning pain in his legs.

True's shout had caused the native coolies to look back and when they saw the last three rickshaws bearing down on them at quite respectable speeds, they pulled over to the side and cheered as the American-drawn vehicles flew past.

When Hilda Ritter looked out, however, she saw the suddenly miraculously faster Americans, whose faces were now beginning to register incipient panic, and she came to a mistaken and dire conclusion.

"Oh, dear God!" she wailed, her heart in her throat. She turned to the girls behind her. "They've sighted Nemoto and Yoshikita! They're right behind us! Follow me, girls!" Nudging her own coolie in the ribs, she urged, "Go on, go on! I'll double your wages if you'll keep up with those other rickshaws!"

Sensing an advantageous situation, the head coolie started off with deliberate lassitude and nonchalance.

"I'll *triple* them!" Hilda cried. "Do you hear? I'll triple all your wages! Just don't let those other rickshaws out of your sight!"

Grinning, the head coolie yelled something to his four co-workers behind him in the Oguni dialect, and the race was on.

Aside from short dashes, the fastest official pace ever recorded over level ground for a rickshaw with one passenger aboard was eight miles per hour, but the head coolie—a man who had devoted his life to the cause of rickshaws—later estimated the speed of the three American entries at the end of the first downhill mile as something closer to twenty. And this speed increased with each remaining mile of the nine-mile downward course.

Knowing nothing of the illusionary pursuit by Nemoto and Yoshikita, the five girls in the first three vehicles were taking the whole thing as a lark. Convinced that it was a spontaneous race prompted solely by high animal spirits, they cheered their own mounts on and gaily called bets back and forth to each other.

The Americans had neither the time nor inclination to disabuse them of this notion.

By the end of the second mile, however, even these carefree spirits in colorful *kimono* had begun to sense that something was amiss, that creatures constructed by Buddha were not intended to maintain—to say nothing of increasing—this mad pace for sustained periods over a path that would make a mountain goat stop and ruminate. Their cheery cries began to diminish, then died away. . . .to be replaced by worried questions directed at the unheeding backs of their flying steeds.

Hilda and the other nine girls had been terrified from the beginning—on two counts: the presumed approach of their nemesis (in the form of two pilots of the Special Attack Forces) and the breakneck speed at which they were descending the long path that stretched out mile after mile down off the volcano.

Even the native coolies were beginning to wonder. What had started out as a light-hearted race with the high-spirited

Americans was degenerating into a senseless plunge down toward potential tragedy. But they gritted their stubby, brown teeth and put forth the finest effort of their rickshaw careers. After all, triple wages in these hard times were like rice-dumplings from the Goddess Kannon. They thought of the many hungry mouths awaiting them in their homes in Oguni, then sprinted on.

At the end of the third mile, Sam's feet were barely touching the ground. The momentum of the rickshaw pushing down on him was so great that he was flying along in great, ostrich-like strides, each one fifteen feet or more in length. By using the fleeting and all-too-infrequent contacts of his toes with the lava dust of the path, he was able—but just barely—to keep the rickshaw from spurning the path in favor of open slope.

By the end of the fourth mile, True was filled with terror in its purest form. He was afraid to shut his eyes and afraid to leave them open. Both sides of the path were nothing but a blur to him as he sped along, heedless of the cries and pleas from the two girls riding behind him. Ahead of him, the path appeared to stretch on and on endlessly down the awesome slope. Occasionally, when fear momentarily loosened its grip on his throat, he rent the air with a pitiable cry for divine intervention.

By the end of the sixth mile, clouds of blackish lava dust were boiling up behind each vehicle, reducing visibility and making flying conditions over Mt. Aso even more hazardous. With only Ann Blyth to add ballast to his two-wheeler, Chauncey was running a poor third but still well in advance of the hotly-pursuing, triple-wage-inspired coolies from Oguni. For a brief instant, Chauncey considered flinging himself off to one side of the path, but a glance over his shoulder at the horror-struck face of the Number One Houri in his newly-acquired harem brought out the true grit in him, and he vowed to see the ever-accelerating race through to its doubtless bitter termination.

The last three miles sped past in six minutes, but the awful momentum of the plunge carried all the rickshaws on for a quarter of a mile over perfectly flat ground before Sam and True could bring their vehicles to a shuddering halt.

Chauncey, however, pulled off the path before his speed was sufficiently reduced, thereby causing his right-hand wheel to slam into a large rock. The rickshaw veered sharply to the right and spilled both Chauncey and Ann into the dust. Neither was hurt, but the wheel was bent beyond the capabilities of on-the-spot repair.

The caravan was now a study in immobility. It was strung out to the right and left of the path for several hundred yards, the rickshaws standing unattended where they had finally come to a well-earned rest. Most of the coolies—Japanese and American—were sprawled out in the dust taking great gulps of air into tortured lungs. One was kneeling in prayer, chanting the Lotus Sutra in a shaken voice.

Hilda and the fourteen girls were standing around in dazed attitudes. Those who could speak at all were wondering in whispers at their incredible good fortune in emerging unscathed. Others were gazing awe-struck back up at the slope they had just descended with such alacrity. Hilda too was looking back—but for a different reason. She still expected to see Nemoto and Yoshikita come running after them at any minute. Squaring her shoulders, she steeled herself and marched forward to where the three Americans lay comatose in the dust.

"How far back were they when you saw them?" she demanded of Tsutako/Ann.

"Who, *Sensei?*" asked Ann, her voice still unsteady.

"Why, Nemoto-san and Yoshikita-san, of course."

"We didn't see them at all."

"Then why on earth did you go speeding past us like that?" asked Hilda in exasperation.

"I don't know," answered Ann. "The Americans just started running, that's all."

"Just who are Nemoto and Yoshikita?" muttered Chauncey, his mouth half-stopped with the dust on which he was lying face down.

Hilda reflected for a moment, then said, "I suppose I'll have to tell you the whole story. But not right now, for God's sake! Tonight, when we get to an inn."

"I can hardly wait," said Sam drearily.

"But *why* did you start racing down the hill?" Hilda wanted to know.

"Dammit, woman," Sam exclaimed, sitting up, "those rickshaws don't have brakes. Or if they do, we don't know where they are. They just started going faster and faster and we couldn't stop them."

The Swiss teacher considered this intelligence for a few seconds. "Of course, you could have jumped aside and let the rickshaws go on."

Sam drew a circle in the dust with the toe of his *chikatabi* but said nothing.

"I see," Hilda said softly, her face lighting up in full cognizance of what had happened. "You risked your lives to save these five girls."

"Say," Chauncey said to change the subject, "I've got to do something about that bent wheel." He turned and walked back up the road to the head coolie, talked to him for a minute, and then limped back to the others.

"He says there's a little town two miles up ahead where we can get the wheel fixed."

"Tell you what," Sam proposed. "We'll tie your wheel onto the back of one of our rickshaws and drop it off at the first repair shop we come to. Then we'll put up at an inn and tell the repair shop man where we're staying. He can tell you where we are when he brings the wheel back here to you. All right?"

"How about Ann?" asked Chauncey dubiously.

"She can keep you company," Sam said with a wink.

With this agreed on, all the others mustered themselves into an exhausted line and prepared to leave. Hilda took Tsutako/Ann aside and whispered, "Keep off the path, dear, and watch for Nemoto-san and Yoshikita-san. They might be behind us, after all."

Ann nodded her understanding.

"And another thing: you might as well tell Lieutenant MacArthur the whole story about those two. I'll tell the others over dinner at the inn. We'll see you soon," she said and waved goodbye.

It was to be more than just a few hours, however, before Chauncey and Ann were able to rejoin the rest of the party. The only rickshaw repairman in the hamlet of Yoshida up ahead was watching a midwife preside over the delivery of his first son when the bent wheel reached his shop, and it was not until nine-thirty that night that he would deign to start work on it.

By working occasionally between generous self-congratulatory draughts of *sake,* he was able to straighten the wheel in just over two hours, and his apprentice delivered it—with the name of the inn—to an anxious Chauncey and Ann crouched behind a rock a little way off the path at one o'clock in the morning. He had gone past their place of concealment three times in the darkness before he decided to try calling for them.

It took another thirty minutes for him to remount the wheel, after which he led the way to Yoshida, with Chauncey following between the shafts of the rickshaw, his bleary eyes glued on the wavering, weak beam of the apprentice's flashlight ahead of him.

It was well after two a.m. when Ann and Chauncey finally reached the inn. . . .to find Hilda and True exploring each other in an eight-mat room and Sam and the other thirteen girls engaged in diverse feats of acrobatic skill in a spacious, twenty-four mat room usually reserved for dinner parties.

CHAPTER TWENTY-FOUR

The *Eifuku-kan* (Inn of Eternal Happiness) offered for breakfast the following morning rice, bean-curd soup, pickled giant radish, salted trout guts, and cold fried egg. Lieutenant Truman Foote wondered aloud at the absence of eel, although not necessarily as an expression of disappointment.

"This is not a Class-A inn, dear," explained Hilda Ritter who was nestled intimately at his left side.

Ann and Chauncey sat across the low, red-lacquered table from them in True's eight-mat room. Sam and the other thirteen girls were still deep in exhausted slumber in the larger room across the hall. Attempts to arouse them had been futile, so Hilda had suggested that they be allowed to sleep until mid-morning.

Ann and Hilda were eating with good appetites, Chauncey was starting his motor with cups of pale green tea, and True was staring morosely off into space.

"Actually," Chauncey was saying, "I'm feeling pretty good except for my sore leg muscles. I got a few hours of sleep and. . . . ."

"The head coolie says that your muscles will toughen up in a few months," Hilda offered brightly, not noticing the involuntary shudder that ran through both Americans. Glancing with unexpected shyness up at True, she went on, "I'm feeling better, too. Especially since Ann here. . . ." they had told her last night about the adoption of movie stars' names, and she was trying to learn them " . . .said you didn't see Nemoto or Yoshikita yesterday."

Ann looked up from her bean-curd soup at the mention of her name but not understanding the English conversation, said nothing. Her fresh beauty was doing much more than the tea to persuade Chauncey to face the day.

"I wonder if they really caught the train to Kagoshima?" mused Chauncey in reference to the two pilots of the

Special Attack Forces.

"Oh, I hope so!" exclaimed Hilda fervently, "Those terrible, terrible men! Just imagine: wanting to force fourteen lovely young girls—right on the doorstep of all life has to offer—into a mass suicide for the sake of a ridiculous set of outdated, dangerous traditions!"

"I agree, Hilda," said Chauncey, "but the question is what to do about it. Even if they did go on to Kagoshima, that will delay them only a few days. They'll either come back to Bochu and try to pick up the trail there, or they'll go to Fukuoka and set up watch on the girls' homes."

"Can't *you* do something about it?" Hilda asked in pointed reference, Chauncey believed, to his distinguished relation in Tokyo.

Chauncey was weary of the pretense but in no mood to start breaking down the elaborate structure of prevarication Sam had so cunningly contrived, so he temporized: "I could get you official help and protection, all right, but that would only be postponing the ultimate solution of your problem, wouldn't it? I mean, if those two—Yoshikita and Nemoto, did you say?—are actually *that* fanatical, sooner or later they would. . . ."

"I know, I know," said Hilda in despair. "But I had so hoped that you three. . . ."

"Say, I've got an idea," said Chauncey, mindful of the original purpose behind their search for the missing girls, "Let's circle back to Oguni!"

"But that's where they found us! "

"Exactly. And that's why we should go back there, don't you see?"

"Hmmm," mused Hilda.

"Yeah, and we could stay in that ole haunted temple again huh?" chimed in True, the prospect of a period of recuperation dawning on him and partially dispelling his morose view of things.

"That's a wonderful idea, dear," agreed Hilda, who, Chauncey suspected, would have wholeheartedly agreed with True on that particular morning even if the Alabaman had proposed that they all paint their bodies blue.

It took the party four days all told to return to Oguni. During the first two days the caravan meandered leisurely and with intentional zig-zagging northward to the rail center of Kurume on the Chikugo River. There they had to part company with the Oguni rickshaw coolies in order to keep their destination secret. Hilda paid them their promised wages from the more than ample funds which the Fukuoka girls had taken from their bank savings, while the Americans sold cigarettes on Kurume's burgeoning black market and gave the Oguni men money for the transportation of the three coolie-less rickshaws back to their owners.

"Ah kinda wish Ah could keep the ole gal," True said wistfully as he rubbed the worn shafts of his two-wheeler for the last time.

"Yeah, I know," agreed Sam. "And to think that only a few days ago I would have gladly drenched her in gasoline and put a match to her."

"Speaking of gasoline," said Chauncey who was dry-eyed but touched, "we'd better get some from that marine battalion that's just set up shop here. We don't have any back in Oguni, remember?"

After waving goodbye to the Oguni men, the three lieutenants went back to their rooms in the inn and took off their coolie outfits, which they vowed to preserve and treasure as mementoes of their Kyushu Campaign, and changed into their uniforms, which had been laundered and ironed for them by willing members of their harem of houris.

After several cautious inquiries, the Americans learned that bus and rail service between Kurume and Hida still had not been resumed. This left them with three transportation choices: other rickshaws (which they decided would attract too much unwelcome attention in these more populous regions), *hizakurige* (as the Japanese called Shank's Mare), and *yakata-bune.*

Yakata-bune were shallow-draft river excursion boats of various sizes, the larger propelled by one-lung diesel engines and the smaller by stern oars. All were equipped with low roofs for weather protection but were open on the sides. They plied Japan's rivers and lakes and provided mobile settings for parties as well as opportunities for sight-seeing and fishing. In these times, however, persons with the means and time for such pleasures were so few that a dozen boatmen rushed to offer their services when Chauncey entered the riverside shack that served as headquarters for the Kurume *yakata-bune* association and asked if he could hire two boats to carry a party of eighteen persons up river as far as Oguni.

Chauncey inspected the *yakata-bune* tied up along the river-bank and selected two that appeared to best fit the size and requirements of his party. After asking how long the trip would take, he arranged a departure hour that would put them alongside Correct Path's new temple just this side of Oguni in the early dusk of the following day. From there, the Americans and Hilda had decided, they would cross the hill and move into the abandoned temple in the dark, hopefully unseen by anyone in Oguni.

The voyage up river was a restful interlude between what had happened and the even more outrageous events still to come. On later reflection, it seemed to the three Americans that time—for them—had been suspended during the trip as they lounged about the boats, drinking the beer they had bought in Kurume and getting to know Hilda and her fourteen pupils better.

With no facilities aboard either craft to provide the privacy for sexual embrace, the passengers contented themselves with platonic excursions into each other's minds, and Chauncey and Sam—Hilda kept True off to herself—were both surprised and pleased to observe what distinct personalities each of their fourteen girls possessed. What had until now been a *group* of lovely, lively, petite, colorfully-garbed, sexually curious and zestful brunettes began to come through to them as one girl named Ann Blyth (Tsutako Sugimura) who was loyal, amorous, and had a mole on her left ear lobe, a second girl named Sachie Iki (Betty Grable) who had pert features, a rebellious spirit, and doted on tangerines, a third named Mieko Shimizu (Lana Turner) who spoke softly but seldom and who was always listened to, a fourth named Fukako Okuyuki (Carole Landis) who was the group's Doubting Thomas and who could vie with professional singers in her rendition of *Kojo no Tsuki* or *Moon over the Old Castle,* a fifth named Hiroko Maguchi (Barbara Stanwyck) who dreamed of the movie actor Kazuo Hasegawa and who kept them in stitches with her excellent imitations of the dialectal speech of the

Oguni coolies, a sixth named Keiko Koshi (Shirley Temple) whose sad, wistful countenance belied the passions within, a seventh—the unwilling fiancee of Ensign Futoshi Nemoto— named Sujiko Honekawa (Katherine Hepburn) whose curiosity was almost patholigical and who cursed with commendable inventiveness when out of Hilda Ritter's hearing, and so on down the row of fourteen.

Other lines of identification were also being drawn. Hilda having staked out True as her own, the girls divided themselves into two equal groups, one becoming Sam's stable and the other Chauncey's. To Sam clove Dorothy Lamour, Betty Grable, Irene Dunne, Claudette Colbert, Carole Landis, Ida Lupino, and Deborah Kerr, while to Chauncey the ones to pledge their sexual allegiance were Shirley Temple, Barbara Stanwyck, Rita Hayworth, Katherine Hepburn, Lana Turner, Veronica Lake, and, of course, Ann Blyth. Nor were these lines drawn—odd though it seemed—on the basis of previous physical coupling. Sam had laid down with some of Chauncey's stable and vice versa. Nor was it a matter of stand up, raise your hands, and be counted. For reasons of their own, the girls had drifted easily into one camp or the other by the end of the first day on the river. After that, one boat became Chauncey's and the other Sam's, while Hilda and True went from one to the other as the Swiss teacher's responsibilities moved her. (In the calm lower reaches of the Chikugo River, they could step from one slow-moving *yakata-bune* across to the other when the boats were side by side.)

The first day on the Chikugo had been a study in geographical progression for the Americans. The river that watered the north-central rice plain of Kyushu afforded them an ever-changing view of just defeated Japan, from badly-bombed Kurume eastward through or past smaller communities that, while not directly damaged, were nonetheless victims of war: apathetic accumulations of homes and buildings that seemed to be clinging to the edge of bare survival and looking out at the unaffected river with listless, uncaring eyes. But the rice crop had to be brought in, and here in Kyushu—where harvest came earlier than in Honshu and Shikoku—farmers were beginning to bestir themselves to make preparations. For without rice the half-dead nation would surely expire completely.

On the roads that paralleled the river could be seen an occasional American military vehicle and, more often, Japanese trucks that burned charcoal. Also carts pulled by bullocks, two-wheeled hand-carts pulled by humans, bicycles, rickshaws, and pedestrians—many of whom were Japanese soldiers and sailors walking wearily home. For the most part the military men travelled singly or in pairs and appeared subdued, introspective, and hesitant to take the plunge that they would soon have to take back into the civilian community. The Japanese don't like losers.

Toward evening of that first day, the two *yakata-bune* tied up at a stand of trees edging the river and the boatmen cast throw-nets into the water until they had landed enough fish to feed the company. (Several eels wriggled sinuously among the otherwise finny catch, but Sam, who was building up a lifelong enmity for the slimy creatures, sternly ordered that they be excluded from that night's bill of fare.) Hilda, Ann, and Dorothy sat gracefully on the *tatami* flooring beside their masters and kept their glasses filled with beer. The rest of the girls chose up chores and cleaned and grilled the fish, steamed the rice, sliced the pickled vegetables, set the table, laid out soy sauce and Ajinomoto, and distributed wooden, throw-away chopsticks.

As dark came on, the boatmen lit the prow and stern lanterns, and the party ate under their semi-illumination in the gently rocking boats. After dinner, the Americans drank more beer, watched the moon rise and put the lanterns to shame, and discussed in sultanic overtones the more or less desirable qualifications of their female attendants, who cheerfully flitted about tidying up after dinner and laying out *futon* for the night.

"This is what the whole thing's about, men," Chauncey observed, his head nestled against Ann's pubic bone.

"Why can't we just go on and on up the Chikugo like this," asked Sam, raising questioning eyes to the dark skies over Kyushu, "till the end of time?"

The splendor of the hour was such that nothing else would do but for True to bring forth his harmonica and entertain the ladies with a selection of such Japanese favorites as *Soochow Nocturne, China Nights, Tale of Nagasaki, Harbor Blues, Demon of Greed,* and *Song of The Apple.*

CHAPTER TWENTY-FIVE

After Mabel's somewhat hysterical reunion with True at the new temple, the Americans enlisted the aid of some of Correct Path's acolytes and then led their companions over the hill and down into Oguni in the gathering dusk. They still wanted to keep their presence in the resort town unknown, although for a different reason this time.

After rewarding the acolytes, Sam and Chauncey—True had his hands full with two competitive females of different species—lit candles, opened and aired out long-unused rooms, and distributed luggage and rations.

Sam drew Chauncey aside. "We'll have to go back to Fukuoka for more supplies. With this crowd, these won't last more than a day."

"We're overdue, anyway. Let's take off early in the morning, so we can get back by tomorrow evening. We can leave True here to watch over the girls."

"Which reminds me," Sam began, lowering his voice. "These rooms aren't big enough for us to sleep with more than a couple of girls apiece, and I was wondering who we should put where for the night."

"As tired as I am, I could care less."

"Yeah, yeah, I know, but we want to be fair about this thing, and I just found out today that two of the girls are still virgins."

"Surely not!" Chauncey exclaimed, shocked. "Which ones?"

"Irene Dunne and Betty Grable."

"Oh, come off it, Sam. Why, that night in Bochu, Betty and I. . . ."

"Yes? Go on, professor."

"Hmmm. Well, come to think about it, I guess I didn't. . . .*we* didn't exactly. . . ."

"That's what I mean," said Sam, grinning lopsidedly. "It's a matter of definition. Like virgin above the waist or below."

"I see your point."

"Well, Irene and Betty are kinda upset about it. You know, not getting their fair share and all that. Of course, they're both in my stable, so I feel responsible for keeping them happy."

"So what's the problem? Take 'em both to bed with you tonight, and tomorrow morning it'll be 'Look, daddy, I've got a cavity!'"

"Don't be so damned callous, Chauncey! Two in one night? That's above and beyond the. . . ."

"So you want me to do part of your job for you, is that it?" asked Chauncey wearily. The cumulative effects of the circular chase through central Kyushu were catching up with him.

"For harmony within the group, Chauncey! Don't be so. . . ."

"Really, Sam, I think we'd better leave them just as they are. For a little longer, at least. I've got a funny feeling about this whole damned thing. Do you know what the odds would be back home against picking a group of fourteen girls their ages at random and finding that they're all virgins?"

"I know, I know, but the situation's different here, don't you see? First off, our little dears all go to a girls' school, so little contact with boys, right? Second, they're all from the top crust, which means the parents should be able to erect more barriers between their darlings and hanky-panky in various guises. And. . . ."

"I don't care what you say, Sam, it still doesn't make sense. Fourteen good-looking girls in their late teens and all virgins? It's against all the laws of nature and reason. It makes me feel as if I'm opening Pandora's Box whenever. . . ."

"She must be one of yours. I don't have any Pandora in my harem."

"You're a laugh a minute, Bruce, old boy, but the answer is still no, *no*, NO!"

The sun was precisely halfway over the eastern horizon when Sam and Chauncey reached the top of the hill behind the abandoned temple the next morning. The valley of Oguni behind and below them still lay swathed in semi-darkness and sleep. At the new temple they poured the gasoline they had procured in Kurume into the almost-empty tank of their jeep and struck out for Fukuoka.

Although it seemed that they had been away for ages, there were relatively few changes in Fukuoka itself—except for the blossoming of a crop of English signs over shops whose owners had decided that the flushed-with-victory American troops had imported E*C*O*N*O*M*I*C O*P*P*O*R*T*U*N*I*T*Y with them. Among the signs that caught and held their bemused attention were, over an outlet for sexually stimulating devices, "Madame Butterfly Erotic Museum" and, over a fur store, "We Make Fur Out of Your Skin." Two tailor shops proclaimed "Dresses for Ladies and Gentlemen" and "Ladies Have Fits Upstairs." The real puzzler, however, was a store front with the intriguing legend, "Come In and Have Your Thing Engraved!"

In better spirits now, they slipped into the Inn of Ultimate Delights as unobtrusively as possible, bent only on picking up clean uniforms from their quarters. They were hoping to avoid any evil concoction that "Harry" Aso might be broiling on his kitchen *hibachi,* afraid that he would thoughtfully send some of it up to them, if he knew they were around, before they could make good their escape.

At Team Headquarters, no Tokyo-postmarked letter sat on Chauncey's desk, for which he was almost grateful. Sam had a letter from his mother and True one from his aunt back home, giving—they later learned—a long sorrowful account of his prize stump-broke mare's recent demise and funeral.

By the time the mail was read, Chauncey decided they ought to pay a visit to the C.O.

"Funny that Ruby's not on duty," noticed Chauncey as they started for the colonel's sanctuary.

"If she's not in the crapper, she's probably out for a shave," Sam conjectured.

The colonel was still at it: Arctic-issue fur cap concealed the earphones, and Tokyo Rose's voice was insinuating itself deep into his soul. Dawgleish sat crouched over in his chair, eyes shut, a dreamy smile on his lips.

Chauncey coughed loudly; the colonel jumped.

"God, Chauncey boy, am I glad to see you!" Dawgleish doffed his headgear and sprang around the desk to pump Chauncey's hand. "I hope you found them?"

"Not yet, sir," Chauncey replied morosely. "We hope it'll be very soon, though."

The colonel wilted visibly and sat down heavily, looking darkly dejected.

"Well, well," he mumbled. "What this outfit needs is a roaring success, not a failure. . . .Oh, I know it's not your fault, Chauncey. I realize that you and your men are trying, really trying. Like a needle in a haystack, I know that. But those damned girls just *must* be found; they're all we ever hear about. Everybody from General MacArthur on down the line to the lowest buck private is yammering at the top of their lungs about them."

Turning to show his profile, Chauncey chewed on his pipe and nodded reflectively as the colonel continued mournfully: "You wouldn't believe what's been going on in your absence. The girls' fathers are now thoroughly brainwashed—for the worst. They're beginning to believe that their daughters are now flat on their backs in some Marine brothel and that we're all lying in our teeth when we say we don't know where they are."

"Oh, they should know, Colonel," Sam vowed angelically, "that none of us would ever think of lying."

"General Vandel was all in favor of clapping the fathers into the brig for such an insinuation, but he's received strict orders from Tokyo to handle them with kid gloves."

"A wise move," said Chauncey.

"I thought so, too," the colonel agreed. "It seems General MacArthur's afraid that this one incident might determine the future tone of the whole Occupation. He's advised Vandel that he wants the willing and voluntary cooperation of the Japanese. He hopes he won't have to grind them into the dirt. Now the rumor has it that he's talking about coming down here himself to take charge of a large-scale, door-to-door search."

"Oh, no!" exclaimed Sam, genuinely alarmed now.

"I wonder, Chauncey," the colonel speculated, "if I shouldn't tell Tokyo Headquarters who's working on the case—personally?"

Chauncey had to block that maneuver right away. "Tokyo already knows, sir," he said brightly. "I write to Tokyo often."

"Well, that's a comforting bit of knowledge," Dawgleish said with obvious relief. "Now if *he* should come down here, perhaps he won't land on our Team too hard. After all, we're trying. . . . ."

"We really are, sir, and we can't do any more than that, no matter how it looks to Tokyo. I've conveyed that impression, so I wouldn't be too alarmed if I were you. . . ."

"We're concentrating on the center of the island now, Colonel, from Hida south and east," Sam said.

"Ah, that's just where General Vandel intends to shift the bulk of his search operations starting tomorrow."

"Tomorrow?" Sam's voice rose sharply.

"What's wrong with that?" demanded the colonel, "aside from the fact that the Marine swine are our natural enemies, they're being very thorough. That's the only major section of the island they haven't combed with a magnifying glass. Do you object, Bruce?"

"But they might find the girls first, Colonel. We wanted their discovery to be a feather in *your* cap."

Only slightly mollified Dawgleish grumbled, "All this commotion and trouble over fourteen missing girls. So what the hell if they *are* virgins? Virgins-smirgins, I say. That's not sufficient reason to call out the Marines."

"Excuse me, Colonel, what was that you just said?" Chauncey asked anxiously, heart almost protruding from his mouth.

"About all of them being virgins? Oh, of course, you don't know about that, do you?"

"I certainly don't, sir," Chauncey said weakly, trying to get a purchase on himself.

"Well, that business of all of them being virgins didn't come out until their fathers really began to suspect that the Marines might have them in one of their regimental Houses of Joy or whatever it is they call those damned places they try to keep us army men out of. They told General Vandel that their daughters had been virgins when they disappeared and that, by Buddha, they expected them to be virgins when they came back."

"Well, Colonel," said Chauncey, clutching at a very weak straw, "you know how parents are. They all like to *think* that their sweet little angels are wholly holy. . . .or should I say wholly un-holey? Hah, hah. . . ."

"There's that good old MacArthur brand of humor again," cried Dawgleish, blowing his nose to hide his true reaction, "but this time you're way off base, Chauncey, my boy. I hate to say it, but I'm afraid you are. You see, the truth of the matter is that those fourteen girls were all given physical examinations recently. Not once, but twice."

"But *why,* for God's sake?"

"A navy doctor had to check them all when they were first being considered as candidates for marriage to those pilots. Hell, I understand there were several hundred applicants at first and that they washed most of those out with the virginity test."

"And the second time?" Chauncey asked weakly.

"Two days before the weddings were to take place, the day before they all bugged out."

"And all fourteen passed?" asked Chauncey, his voice fainter still.

"With flying colors and whole hymens."

"Awfully stuffy in here," said Sam quietly; his color had turned greenish.

"I wonder if their chaperone knows about that?" asked Chauncey.

"I fail to see what difference it would make," answered the Colonel, "but she might not. Evidently she had nothing to do with the whole ridiculous affair until very shortly before the girls disappeared."

"I suppose," said Sam in deep thought, "that there'll be another examination when they all get home to verify their virginity?"

"The fathers swore that they'd see to that," said Dawgleish. "And they said that if even one of the girls has had her. . . .uh, thingumabob broken, they'll go right to the top."

"You mean. . . .MacArthur?"

"None other, and he's already promised that if harm—of *any* kind—had come to the girls, he'll have the culprits—Japanese *or* American—in jail from now on."

The lieutenants' prospects sank to unplumbed depths.

— 174 —

Chauncey felt that all he could now reasonably hope for was simple survival.

After a minute of silence, he evoked the strength to ask, "When will headquarters permit the news about the girls' disappearance and the search for them to be published, Colonel?"

"Probably any day now. The Censorship Detachment has just about convinced them that it would be better to tell the public the truth—at least, a diluted version of it—than let these vile rumors keep circulating. Why, only yesterday a wild story filtered through to me that *one hundred and twenty* girls are missing."

"Maybe the Gyrenes are eating them," Sam conjectured deadpan. "You know, like dining at the Y."

The colonel pierced him with a glare. "Your levity's out of place, Bruce." Then to Chauncey he said, "My boy, our reputations are at stake. All I ask is that you do your best. Because the best for a MacArthur is the best there is."

On that note they took their leave of the C.O., as despondent and long-faced as they'd ever been.

Ruby Whacker, ebullient, busty, and raucous as usual, greeted them from her desk.

"Hey there, stallions! You slipped by me, didn't you? Where's True?"

"On special duty, Captain," Chauncey said, not wanting to explain anything. He was almost too depressed to speak.

"That devil! When will I get to see him?"

"When our mission's accomplished, Captain," Sam said.

Rudy Whacker smirked. "I don't know if I can wait much longer."

"We'll find them soon, Ruby," said Chauncey.

"Virgins!" she sniffed. "All that fuss about a little thing a girl doesn't need anyway. The Japanese are sure as hell primitive. Don't they know that virginity's no prize any longer? Why, we Americans are proving that everywhere. One of these days somebody's going to invent a pill that'll liberate women. Hey, won't *that* be the day!"

Leaving Ruby to her roseate dreams of the future, they slunk out of the Team headquarters and climbed aboard their jeep. The silence was heavy and morose.

The girls would soon be discovered, Chauncey reflected, and if their bad luck held, it would be by General Vandel's troops. Their immoral liaison would be exposed, and this news would produce an explosion audible in Tokyo seven hundred miles away.

Finally Sam said in a despondent voice, "Well, I guess that cuts it. Whether we or the Gyrenes bring in the girls, the doctor who examines them will report that twelve of them aren't virgins any longer. Then the shit will *really* hit the fan."

"And my illustrious uncle will appear on the scene—with gold-braided cap, corncob pipe, and cat-o'-nine tails," said Chauncey, foreseeing the tragic results all too vividly.

"Wait'll he finds out that the three men responsible for the deflorations are not only American officers but that one of them has been parading around Kyushu posing as his nephew."

"It will mean the end of civilization as we know it," Chauncey nodded grimly.

CHAPTER TWENTY-SIX

Although its external aspect remained largely unchanged, the interior of the old "haunted" temple in Oguni became the scene of intense feminine activity as the new occupants strove to convert their rooms into something approaching what the female mind could regard as livable. The three American lieutenants were kept equally occupied in their continuing endeavors to minimize the chances of anyone in Oguni becoming aware of their presence. Sooner or later they feared that the two *kamikaze* pilots would reason—even as they had—that Oguni was a possible hiding place.

After some initial difficulty—and a few whacks on lovely rear-ends, the lieutenants succeeded in convincing the girls that they should not under any circumstances leave the temple without first getting permission from one of them. Loud noises of any kind were strictly forbidden, so the girls soon fell into the habit of speaking in low voices, almost whispers. A major problem was the cooking of rice, without which no true Japanese will allow even one day to pass. This was solved by arranging to have it prepared in the new temple and carried to the old temple by two acolytes in the large quartermaster can previously used for chilling canned beer. Trash and garbage were thrown into the hollow statue of Buddha, through a trapdoor in its back, just above the waist.

During the morning of the first day of their renewed residence, an acolyte from the new temple knocked on the Chauncey's door, slid it open, and bowed himself in, while bidding them a pleasant morning in Japanese. Another bow, a flourish of the hand—and Chauncey was holding a note. Then a silent retreat, and they were alone again.

Chauncey opened the note, which was from Correct Path, and read it aloud:

"'Honorable Sirs: Buddha preserve your Reverences. The

full moon tonight marks the beginning of the Oguni Eel Festival. I pray that you have not forgotten your promise to honor us with your presence. The wassail will commence at seven. I shall dispatch linkboys to light your way over the hill. Your obedient servant, etc. . . .' It's signed Seido. Good old C.P."

"Think you can cheer up enough to go?" Sam asked. "I'd sorta like to see an eel festival."

Chauncey sighed. "I guess so. Maybe it'll take my mind off the mess we've gotten ourselves into. But tomorrow," he said firmly, "we're going to sit down and try to figure a way out of it."

"Best thing to do is to stay right here. If we take the girls back to Fukuoka now, they'll hang us. You know that. Besides, we've still got some unfinished business."

"You mean Irene Dunne and Betty Grable?" Chauncey asked incredulously.

"Yep."

"I am a man of a sanity who has fallen among lunatics!" Chauncey cried. "Don't you see that they might just decide to give us a year in prison for each virgin deflowered? Is it worth it, Sam? A year in durance vile for the dubious privilege of breaking a flimsy piece of membranous tissue that had no business being there in the first place?"

"Don't forget," Sam said with quiet dignity, "masculine duty and honor."

"Go pound sand up your anal passage."

"Tush," Sam said with restraint. "Don't you recall that proverb we learned in school, *'Doku kuwaba sara made?'*"

"Only vaguely. What does it mean?"

"As well hanged for a sheep as a lamb."

The new temple's banquet room where Sam, Chauncey, and True were first dined by Correct Path opened out onto a spacious courtyard. Beyond this lay the winding Chikugo River, soft and pale in the twilight. In the rich candle-glow of the banquet room, the banqueters' chaste white Buddhist robes were stained a faint gold as they sat or half-reclined in genial nonchalance around the low lacquered tables, each of which was laden with food dishes, porcelain warming jugs of *sake,* and beer in brown and green bottles.

A constant procession of nuns paraded back and forth from banquet room to kitchen. Four more sat among the male diners keeping their *sake* cups and beer glasses filled.

Correct Path sat at the center of the master table with novices on his right and left. Directly opposite him were three unoccupied *zabuton.* Flanking these were men and women in dark civilian clothes. These, they learned, were neighbors who had contributed to the cost of the construction of the new temple.

Chauncey had never seen Sam so impressed; his manner could best be termed awestruck.

"I had no idea," Sam whispered. "The only religious group I've ever seen that was completely relaxed. Not a dishonest bone in the whole parochial body."

From deep in the temple they heard the throb and clamor of ancient rites: the irregular thudding of insistent drums, the deep booming of a brass gong when a new guest arrived, the shivering and tinkling of bells—like wind chimes, and knitting the whole audio-spectrum into one complete fabric, the chanting of sutras, soft as a summer breeze across a ripe, rippling meadow.

At a signal from Correct Path the nuns removed the tops of several covered dishes. Rising, he said in tones of great authority, "Acting on Lieutenant Bruce's kind advice, I have had our temple chef experiment with several of the eel dishes we hope to serve in our projected restaurant, all part of the plan to make our shrine to the Lord Buddha successful and worthy in his eyes. In other words, friends and honored quests, profitable! This, for example—" he pointed with a flourish to a dish in front of True "—is our own fantastic Eel Pan Dowdy!"

True recoiled from it, as if from a rudely-awakened green mamba. He managed, however, not to let his face reveal much of his heart-felt revulsion.

"And yonder," Correct Path continued, "is our glorious Eel Brown Betty, the succulent sight of which throws my salivary glands into a veritable frenzy. Later, as dessert and the culinary chef d'oeuvre of the evening, we will offer you Eel Melba, topped with crushed gingko nuts."

A murmur of genuine admiration rippled through the Japanese guests, who were quick to show gustatory appreciation.

Then Correct Path frowned and said dramatically, "Since not *all* men are as devoted to eel for its own sake as the folk indigenous to our archipelago and especially to this region, our chef has prepared for them several famous *non*-eel dishes from other localities in Kyushu."

With that pronouncement, he clapped his hands twice, a subdued hush settled over the banquet room, the kitchen door opened, and a nun emerged carrying a heavy candelabrum of brass with six large lighted candles. On her heels came a second nun proudly holding aloft a tray piled high with dishes.

"A gourmet delight from Kagoshima," Correct Path announced in cathedral tones. "The traditional dish of that fair city—Sweet and Sour Sexual Organs of Ox!"

True whispered urgently to Chauncey, "Ah think Ah'm gonna be sick."

Applause filled the room as the dishes were set down. The candle-carrying nun returned to the kitchen to herald and light the entrance of another nun with the next offering.

"Bat Wings in Tempura," cried Correct Path, "All the way from Beppu!"

Applause again, followed by Vinegared Shredded Pig's Ear Salad from now hard-to-find Nagasaki, Brandied Fishheads in Pipkin from Kokura, and Six Varieties of Raw Meat on a Rare Cloisonne Plate from Miyazaki, each announced in bell-like tones by their distinguished host and each meticulously applauded as it was brought in.

As these dishes were being served, Correct Path offered his three American guests a mixed drink of his own wizardry.

"It is made," he explained, "with *awamori,* a distillation of millet, and from *Calpis,* a sweetish, milky-white beverage."

"Cowpiss?" True hissed in a startled voice.

"This drink is named the 'Christian Missionary's Down-fall in a Buddhist Land' and seems to me to be appropriate to the occasion," said Correct Path. "I should hasten to explain, however, that our Western friends here have had the courtesy not to bring Christianity to us, offering it in place for our enlightened ways, but have brought us instead such wonders as Spam, Lucky Strikes, C and K-Rations, chocolate bars, and canned spaghetti with meatballs."

Correct Path then turned to Sam. "I have given much thought, Lieutenant Bruce, to your many fruitful ideas for promoting eel sales. These I have attempted to blend with several thoughts of my own, thus melding East and West in a happy marriage of ideas. Soon I hope to have these in full-scale operation. I've already surveyed billboard sites at five points and have begun designing a neon beauty for the temple roof. I have also ordered fresh registered eel breeding stock from Lake Hamana in Honshu. And all this is being done," Correct Path said with becoming modesty, "without great expense. Ingenuity is the keynote. For example, this banquet room will become our restaurant. At least until we make enough money to build something more suitable."

"C.P., you're a commercial genius!" Sam said enthusiastically.

"Our nuns will be the waitresses," Correct Path continued, beaming at Sam.

"In those—uh, same outfits?"

"Do you object?"

"Not provocative enough."

"What do you mean?"

"You got to work in some cleavage, C.P. As a matter of fact, you should get yourself a nice solid little combo and have the nuns come on topless, maybe with cherries on their mammaries and a string of bananas across their loins. Josephine Baker's been doing it for twenty years in Paris and nobody's ever complained."

"Forsooth, sir!.." Correct Path said happily. "That *is* a splendid thought! But of course there *are* certain religious considerations."

"You'll find a way around them, C.P.," said Sam. "And another thing to keep in mind is bucket-size cocktails. A come-on at home is double martinis and Manhattans from four to seven, a lure for diners at restaurant-bars. You mustn't overlook this point. You might even serve triple measure."

"But how can we clear an honest one-hundred percent profit if we serve double or triple drinks at regular prices?"

"Simple. Put a lot of cheap, salty cocktail snacks on the table first. Let the guests have all this guck free. Most of them won't stop nibbling. The more they nibble, the more they'll drink—and the less dinner they'll eat. Basic rule 2-B of the food business. And even when they finally do order dinner, don't bring it right away. Keep it warming in the kitchen an hour or so."

"An hour or so? Great Buddha!"

"Sure, because in the meantime the clowns'll order more drinks and put away more salty guck like potato chips, popcorn, and rice crackers, which will cost you only a few yen. Sure, sometimes you'll get a complaint, but you can pretend the guy made a pass at somebody's wife and have your bouncer toss him out on his ear."

"In other words," C.P. reflected slowly, "you cheat your guests. You don't give them what you've promised."

"No, that's backass-wards, C.P. I mean, like it's all there for the asking but you get the guests so hammered they don't give a tinker's damn about dinner, sometimes not even a bite. Then one of your topless nuns whisks the uneaten dishes back to the warming oven as the clients stagger home sloshed. Presto! A three-dollar dinner can be served all over again at one-hundred per cent profit!"

"Fabulous! Shrewd!" C.P. exulted. "How wonderfully American the whole swindle is!"

"Sure it is," Sam agreed complacently, "I knew a restaurant back home in Chicago that once served the same dinner thirty-seven times in three days and nobody ever ate it. Eventually it was bronzed and mounted in the local Chamber of Commerce."

Correct Path's eyes gleamed with religious avarice. "If only we can make it work, Lieutenant Bruce! Why, in a year or two I'd be able to finance my life-long dream of sending *our* missionaries to your spiritually insecure and troubled nation and. . . ."

"Have you ever been to the United Stares?" Chauncey asked tautly, this imputation against his native land raising his hackles.

"Buddha bless you!" Correct Path exclaimed. "How could I be so remiss as not to tell you, Lieutenant MacArthur? I once spent a very enlightening year in your cultural desert, the place you call Texas."

"Did you get to know many Texans?"

"Yes, I did. But it was strange about their women. The longer I was there, by Buddha, the yellower they became!

Just like anywhere else, I suppose. But I never did really have a chance to prove or disprove that *other* rumor I heard about. . . ."

"My own research suggests a boring uniformity in female anatomy throughout the world," Chauncey interjected, and at that moment Dr. Ino entered.

Correct Path made room for Dr. Ino at the central table. The doctor was in his usual somber mood, or perhaps it was merely the esoteric climate of the laboratory that he emanated, Chauncey decided, as if he had more important things to do than attend frivolous banquets.

"This might be a propitious moment for Dr. Ino to explain his fascinating new surgical technique," Correct Path suggested, serving the doctor a mound of food as one of the nuns attended to his *sake* and beer requirements.

"Never mix menu and medicine," Sam said, "one of the first rules of a restaurant. Might as well start obeying the rules right now. . . ."

"You may have a point," said Correct Path.

"C.P., I'd like your opinion on an ethnic question, or perhaps it's a religious one. I can't be sure which. Tell me, what's the typical Japanese attitude toward female virginity?"

"Do you mean as a freakish sexual aberration?"

"Heh, heh. I see what you mean," said Sam, "but I guess what I'm trying to say is that American girls consider virginity a very desirable condition. They think of it as a commodity, something to barter for a wedding vow. We Americans pay a large amount of lip service to this pre-marital condition. Does this apply in Japan? In short, is there a strong mystique built around cherry blossom time here? "

Correct Path appeared surprised. "Virginity has nothing to do with the flowering of trees in Japan, but it's a pleasant thought anyway. In one famous village the virginal maidens carry through the streets an enormous phallus, as big as a Chinese festival dragon. This ritual heralds the arrival of another fertile spring but also announces the chaste and thus unhappy condition of the girls to the general public. As far as I've been able to determine, the girls think it's rather fun and games."

"You lost me somewhere in the shrubbery," Sam

confessed.

"Don't worry. In Japan it's a very complicated subject. I can't explain it to you in detail now, Lieutenant Bruce. Perhaps later on? Suffice it to say, our girls listen to a different drummer."

"But tell me just one thing now, please. What's the age of consent in Kyushu?"

"The age of consent? Oh, I don't know," Correct Path responded casually. "Perhaps ten or twelve? Isn't it, Dr. Ino?" And he repeated the question in Japanese.

"A little older than that, I think," the saturnine doctor responded in one of his rare public statements, then returned to his food.

Half an hour later, Sam nudged Chauncey and nodded toward the courtyard. "Do you see what I see?"

Chauncey did indeed. The two arriving visitors were none other than the last two virgins from Hilda Ritter's stable of vivacious fillies.

"Oh God," Chauncey groaned. "It's Irene and Betty. If we just ignore them, maybe they'll go away."

"Not a chance," said Sam, for the girls were being welcomed by Correct Path and then seated among the civilian guests. Finding the men absent from the old temple, they had trailed them over the hill, following their ears to the beguiling sound of music and revelry.

Smiling briefly at the girls, Sam went on to address more questions to Correct Path.

"Buddhists don't seem to believe in cloisters," he began.

"Cloisters?"

"You know, secluded places of worship, sacred to the devout, shut off from all possibility of temptation . . . ."

"Yes, I understand now. And this is what always dismayed me so in your country: You separate the body from the soul, whereas we hold that one is a complement to the other. If you give peace to the soul, you must also give it to the body, not mortify or chastise it. In fact, we believe strongly that sexual release brings one closer to Buddha, if anything. Frankly, I spit on such nonsense as abstinence, chastity, fasting, and temperance."

"Hmmmmh. Does that apply to the nuns and novices

and everyone else around this temple?" Chauncey asked, somewhat incredulously but deeply interested.

"Ah yes, my son," Correct Path affirmed, pleased that he was finally getting through. "Most of them, I am proud to say, are devout voluptuaries. Now take that novice over there—" he pointed to a young man on True's left "—he is an appalling womanizer. He holds the Oguni record for religious seductions. And the one next to him, the jolly one, writes obscene *haiku,* much more sophisticated than your Western limericks."

"How about that nubile nun who just came out of the kitchen?" asked Sam in a tomcat voice.

"That one? " Correct Path leaned toward them confidentially. "To tell you the truth, I'm a bit worried about her. We may have to ease her out."

"What's her trouble?" Chauncey said.

"She simply cannot learn to associate sexual intercourse with conception, and she's fertile as a sardine."

"Tell me, C.P.," Sam said, "have you ever derobed a nun?"

"Why, yes, almost nightly," Correct Path answered with equanimity.

"Uh. . . .that's not what I mean, C.P. I'm talking about banishment. Have you ever had to derobe a nun the way you'd defrock a priest?"

"Oh, that! No, quite the opposite. While we do not, of course, countenance such crimes as thievery or murder, we are totally permissive about most other matters. That's why almost everybody wants to embrace our faith. That shall be our prime selling point when we send out missionaries to heathen lands such as yours."

The rising noise and commotion in the outer courtyard was occasioned by the arrival of more curious townsfolk. Their chatter and laughter grew in proportion with their numbers. It was evident that Correct Path was going to be hosting most of the Oguni valley if this kept up.

"Buddha damn these religious fanatics!" Correct Path said sourly, then asked, "Have you dined satisfactorily?"

The three American guests of honor kept their innner thoughts to themselves and agreed that they had.

"Then let's go some place where we can drink in peace. I am anxious to open a bottle of your Old Parr for our moral edification."

"That suits me right down to the ground," True said as they were rising from the tables.

"Wait!" said Correct Path. "I have an inspiration! I could show you how we catch our eels. Why not take a jug and go out on the river in boats to watch the novices bring up the eel traps?"

"Lead on, C.P.," said Sam, whereupon they were conducted out through the throng of merrymakers in the courtyard, Correct Path in the lead cradling a fifth of Old Parr tenderly in his arms.

CHAPTER TWENTY-SEVEN

A Japanese print done in deep blue twilight, thought Chauncey as he viewed the scene. A flock of novices, robes hoisted to their thighs, were wading through the reeds along the river's edge to bring three boats of extremely shallow draft closer to shore.

Chauncey turned to the reluctant True, still high on the river bank. "Come on, True, let's go!"

"You studs are plain simple if you think Ah'm goin' with you," he said with cool certainty. "Ah just came to watch."

Sam lent his urging, "Come on, get in here!"

"You couldn't no more get me into one of them flimsy-lookin' things than you could get an ole yellow tomcat to whistle Dixie."

"Don't be a spoil-sport," said Chauncey. "Do the fun thing."

"Ah done tole you that Ah ain't budgin'."

"Well then, see you later," said Chauncey, following Sam into one of the narrow, tipsy craft while Correct Path and his novices clambered into the other two. In each of the three boats was deposited a large jug of Superior-Grade Kiku-Masamune *sake*. Additionally, the head priest carried as the standard of his flagship the bottle of Old Parr. Guiding them on their Stygian voyage was an asphyxiating, rusty lantern hung on a hooked shaft from the prow of Correct Path's vessel.

"To light us into oblivion," Sam observed. "Happy thought."

From the lead craft, Correct Path explained the operation: "It's what i believe you Americans would call running a trotline. One end of the line is tied to a tree or a stake on the river bank. The other is attached to the eel-trap itself. The eel-traps we use are made of bamboo withes and wire, one meter long, about half a meter in diameter, and cylindrical in shape. The traps are set with the one-way gate facing the current. An eel pushes this gate open and swims in after the bait. Once inside, it is unable to get out. We set the traps where there is the heaviest eel traffic but where the current is not too strong, lest the one-way gate remain continuously open from the water pressure."

The method of retrieving the traps was simple enough. A novice aboard one of the craft picked up the line at a point near its shore anchor, and while another novice used the single stern oar, they followed the line as it was lifted from the bottom until they came to the trap, which was then hauled into the boat and the one-way gate opened. Frantic eels, wild to escape, slithered out of their confinement into a waiting wooden vat. The trap was then rebaited and lowered again into the stream.

What made this a slow and boring process, Chauncey noted, was that the novices had to return to shore after each trap opening in order to find the next line. It was a tedious, almost ritualistic method, however, and one not likely to change soon. In the dark with the eerie, undulating shadows from the lantern and boats dancing on the swift clear current, the robed novices partaking of *sake*, and the bizarre figure of Correct Path directing operations and swigging from his bottle at the same time, the scene could almost transport the viewer to another by-gone age.

During the trap retrieval operations, their boat had drifted nearly a hundred yards downstream before Sam got the knack of the stern-oar. Then it took them fifteen strenuous minutes to fight their way back upstream and join the others, where Sam was at last able to steer the craft back into calmer water. Sweaty and exhausted from his unaccustomed exertion, he plunked down in the boat, breathing hard.

"What you need," Chauncey said, holding out the jug, "is a belt of good rice wine."

"It's not my favorite brew," Sam whispered, not wanting Correct Path to hear him. "The old boy's got the real gold, but it won't last long at that pace."

It was a beautiful warm night with a full moon edging up over the hills. The ghostly-robed head priest and his novices looked like spectral dancers gyrating to the distant ryhthms of the throbbing temple music.

Before approaching the trap-emptying operation again, Sam and Chauncey passed the *sake* jug back and forth between them in a leisurely fashion, at length consuming more than half of its generous measure. When neither was feeling any pain, they decided to move closer.

"I'll take over the stern-oar," Chauncey said. "You've served your apprenticeship already."

"I feel like I've already done ten years as a galley slave," Sam groaned.

With difficulty, Chauncey maneuvered their craft out into the current toward the other two. In the nearest boat, the fisherman-novice was on the point of hauling in a trap of wriggling eels, some of them almost a yard long. The sight was unique to both the Americans, and Sam suddenly stood up in the unstable craft to get a better view. No one could ever figure out in retrospect exactly what happened after that. It may have been that he was dizzy from the unaccustomed exercise and the *sake*. Or the full moon might have enchanted him.

In any case, Sam began to wave his arms and reel about in an abandoned manner, his antics rocking the boat dangerously. Seeing this, a novice in the nearest boat held out his stern-oar in an effort to steady Sam, who, in reaching for the oar, over-extended himself and fell into the stream with the penetrating cry of a lost soul. Then, in rapid Keystone-comedy fashion, the novice dropped the eel-trap he had just opened into the water, Chauncey lunged for Sam, and the boat overturned.

When the two lieutenants finally came to the surface, they both started to swim toward shore, while Correct Path and the others shouted advice to them in Japanese too rapid for either to understand.

Then Sam started to lag behind and splutter, and it was evident that something was holding him back.

Chauncey turned and swam back to him.

Sam's face was white with fright. "I'm stuck, Chauncey! Help me. . . ."

"Hold on a minute," Chauncey said, then submerged and groped around Sam's feet, one of which was evidently caught in the mesh structure of the eel-trap. After a few seconds of tugging and tearing, Chauncey managed to rip the trap apart, releasing Sam. Simultaneously, however, he also set free half a dozen berserk eels.

While they were both treading water and trying to get their bearings, a monster eel darted into Chauncey's shirt via his open collar. The eel's slippery presence pumped instant adrenalin into his veins, and thrashing and squirming, he tried to swim and rip off his shirt at the same time.

"Jeeeeesusss!!" he wailed, and then, deciding by pure instinct that his only salvation lay landward, he struck out madly for the shore twenty yards distant.

Correct Path told him later that the Chikugo River had never been host to such high-speed swimming as on that night. Chauncey covered the twenty yards in a matter of seconds, bounded up the slimy bank, and ripped off his shirt, thus parting company at last with the equally frantic eel.

But if Chauncey was fast, Sam swam even faster. His speed was incredible; he became a human hydrofoil. The moonlit surface of the stream, it seemed to Chauncey, was clearly visible beneath Sam's belly. And if not fully airborne, at least part of his body was clear of the water, his arms gyrating like propellers.

Sam's record-breaking speed was inspired likewise by an eel—if anything, larger and more depraved than Chauncey's nemesis—that had slithered from the broken trap into a leg of his trousers.

Its slimy presence around the Chicagoan's calf provided enough impetus to start Sam on his way with considerable alacrity through—and later, *over*—the water, but it was not until the eel—apparently bent on sodomy—tried to nose its way into Sam's major lower aperture that he achieved his most memorable speed in the event.

As Sam came flying low across the river's surface, Chauncey stood crouched on the bank, ready to try to save him. Quickly he hauled his friend ashore, helped rip off his trousers and seized the slippery snake-like creature. Shuddering with revulsion, he flung it far out into the stream where it disappeared with a splash.

Sam lay sprawled out where he had fallen, glassy-eyed, and traumatic, gulping great hunks of air as if his life depended on it.

"Take it easy," said Chauncey, trying to calm him, "your anal maiden-head's still intact, isn't it?" At that moment True came running down the bank, scratching himself and laughing like a hyena, "Goddam!" he cried. "Don't that just beat anythin' you ever did see? Ah'm sure gonna tell mah grandchildren about this ole city-boy comin' mighty near being raped by an eel."

Correct Path took them to his private rooms in the new temple, where they cleaned up and slipped into borrowed *yukata* while the nuns washed, dried, and ironed their uniforms.

In the comparative comfort of the priest's quarters they drowned their chagrin in excellent *sake*, the Old Parr having been consumed. Dr. Ino, bored with the revelries, had joined them.

"I still can't believe it," Sam mused. "Why should an eel try to commit such an indecent act?"

"As Kyushu's leading eel expert," Correct Path said, "I think I know the answer."

"Please enlighten me. I'm entitled to know the reason."

"Well, sir," Correct Path said in a voice blurry around the edges from Old Parr, "eels seek out small, narrow openings to hide in whenever they're frightened. This is why your eel, Lieutenant MacArthur, sought your open shirt and then the second one Lieutenant Bruce's trouser-leg. Unable to go any farther, it then began to cast about for one more escape hatch."

True chortled.

Dr. Ino stirred and spoke in one of his rare contributions to group conversation. "Yes, indeed, safety apertures. . . . That's a well-known fact among eel-mongers and rural folk around Oguni. And even in scientific circles. As a matter of fact—and this is very confidential, gentlemen—my youngest daughter was actually *deflowered* by an eel."

Chauncey couldn't believe his ears; his first impulse was to crack wise, but then he glanced sharply at Sam, whose expression was wait-and-see, so neither said anything.

"You're greening me," True said with a mild guffaw.

Trust our True, thought Chauncey.

"No, gentlemen. It's literally true," the doctor said, divining the meaning of True's words in English. "When Kazu was somewhat younger, she went swimming in the

Chikugo one evening with some other girls, all naked. They were adolescents, and children often swim like that out here in the country. Anyway, a large eel—probably frightened by all the children splashing about—sought safety in one of her lower—er, openings."

"Go on," Chauncey urged.

"It was a very slight penetration, but unfortunately deep enough to rupture the delicate hymen, which was probably quite thin to begin with."

"The devil you say!" Sam exclaimed, showing his first interest in anything since his eel experience.

"Yes, it was a shocking encounter for a young girl, especially a sweet, gentle child like Kazu. The traumatic effects were severe," Dr. Ino continued, "and as the days passed Kazu grew listless and despondent. At one point I feared for her sanity. I felt so utterly helpless, being unable to make her whole again."

"Hole again?" queried True, and Sam jabbed him hard in the ribs to shut him up.

"My concern led eventually to research of a very special nature, and this in turn led to the discovery of a new surgical technique."

"Tell us about it," Chauncey said breathlessly, the embryo of an idea taking shape in his mind.

"I've tried to tell you about it several times before without success," Dr. Ino stated with a note of amused exasperation in his voice.

"We're listening now," said Sam.

"You'd better believe it," Chauncey added.

"Well, then, I am fully aware of the value that you Westerners place on the unbroken condition of that flimsy membranous tissue called the hymen or maidenhead." The doctor's eyes sparkled as he warmed to his dearest subject. "After Kazu's encounter with the eel, I began to speculate on whether or not a ruptured hymen could be restored by surgery and whether or not this technique could be, in effect, exported to the United States and Europe, where the premarital taboo against broken hymens is the strongest."

"Now you're beginning to talk like Madison Avenue, doc," Sam praised him.

"Although the absence of the hymen was of no great

consequence to my daughter Kazu, the shock of the eel assault was. And I judged that if I could restore her hymen, I might also restore her confidence in the proper fitness of things."

"What did she do when you told her about such an operation?" asked Chauncey.

"She balked. In fact, at one point she became quite hysterical. But by threatening to cut off her supply of movie magazines, I finally was able to bring her around to my point of view."

"Courageous little tyke," Sam observed.

"I believed that a *jinko shojomaku*—a man-made hymen, that is—could be constructed by two methods: One, by stretching and suturing the remnants of the original hymen, like darning a tear in a sweater. And, two, by the use of a plastic insert. The former method is preferable if the loss of the original hymen is quite recent: within a month of penetration, say. I still haven't experimented with the latter method, but I have the technique ready. And as far as I am able to determine, the operation will be perfectly feasible when I have access to the new plastics that I understand have been developed and tested in Germany."

"Mmmm," said Chauncey, "a choice between recap or retread, is that it?"

"I wish I'd said that," Sam laughed. "Now about the former method, dector. How long would the operation take?"

The excitement that claimed Chauncey was reflected in Sam's eager voice. There was no need to confer with Sam to know that they were both thinking the same thing.

"Not long at all," Dr. Ino said. "Ten or twelve minutes at the most, I would judge. It's relatively easy."

"Are you sure it would work, doctor?" Chauncey asked.

The doctor shrugged. "I must confess, gentlemen, I am not entirely confident. It worked for Kazu. . . .so successfully, in fact, that when she was married, her husband rather shyly told me—as their family doctor—that he experienced considerable difficulty in rupturing her maidenhead. This was not told to me in the smug Western sense of proud monopolistic possession, however. . . ."

"So you've only experimented on your daughter?" asked Sam.

"Unfortunately, she has been my only test case to date."

"But why?" Sam and Chauncey asked simultaneously.

"I simply cannot get any volunteers for more experimental operations," the doctor explained. "It's partly due to the war and because I can't offer sufficient remuneration. Mostly, however, it's because the girls around here see no point in having their hymens restored. One girl to whom I made the proposal summed up the reactions of all the others: 'Who wants it?' she scoffed. 'It's just a   bother, anyway!' And I suppose she was quite right."

At that moment, Betty Grable and Irene Dunne, having tired of dancing the *Tanko-bushi* in the other courtyard, were ushered into the room by a nun.

"We wanted to be with you," Irene purred, fixing Chauncey with urgent eyes.

At a signal from Chauncey, True led Irene and Betty across the room to the window and showed them the view, so that this vital conversation would not be interrupted.

"Is there any danger from the operation?" Chauncey was asking Dr. Ino.

"No danger of serious complications. The subject must be healthy, of course. But there is no guarantee that the operation will be successful."

"How long would it take to heal?" Sam asked.

"A girl could count on getting married—and, in the Western sense, deceiving her bridegroom—five or six days after the operation."

"What if a physician examined the—uh, area?" Chauncey queried, now scarcely able to keep the tremor of his excitement out of his voice.

"Well," said the doctor after a moment's deliberation, "that depends on the degree of thoroughness. If an M.D. made a close-range, visual examination, he should be able to detect scar tissue. And, in the case of a plastic membrane, he would see that, too. The scar would remain for many years after the operation, providing, of course, that the female retained her 'virginity.' But usually the examination to determine an intact hymen is made by touch only. And in that case it's highly unlikely a doctor would notice anything unusual, at least not if the examination were deferred until five or six days after the operation, as I said. By that time the patient would not show any painful reaction to the tactile probing such an examination requires."

"One final question," said Chauncey, pressing on. "Is there much pain connected with the operation itself?"

"Using a local anaesthetic, there would be none at all. After the hypodermic needle's initial sharp prick, of course."

"Very fascinating," said Sam brightly. "Downright engrossing. I see that sharp pricks can be critical."

"One of the most remarkable reports I've ever heard," Chauncey agreed, shooting Sam a silencing glance.

Dr. Ino shook his head in amazement. "Gentlemen, why are you so interested all of a sudden? Previously I could never get any of you to sit still long enough to listen to my story."

Sam and Chauncey exchanged triumphant smiles, nodding happily at each other.

"Shall we tell him now?" Sam said.

"Go ahead," said Chauncey.

"Dr. Ino," Sam said, squaring his shoulders, "how would you like to have twelve volunteers for your experiments: young, healthy specimens—all lovely girls, in fact—who've been deflowered during the past two weeks?"

The doctor's eyes flew wide open in astonishment, then grew hooded in wary disbelief. "Twelve?" he said tentatively. "Are you really serious? How much yen would they want? I'm not a rich man."

"None," Chauncey assured him, "none at all. In fact, if you'll perform all twelve of the operations tomorrow, you and Correct Path here will each receive a case of Old Parr Scotch as a token of our esteem."

"Great Buddha in the Himalayas!" the head priest ejaculated. "Yea, verily a gift from Nirvana."

"Young man," Dr. Ino addressed Chauncey in hushed reverence, "this is an unbelievable opportunity. I am entirely at your service. Do tell me more."

Chauncey darted a speculative glance at Betty and Irene who were having a quiet though animated conversation of their own over by the window. True had meanwhile rejoined the male group.

"Are those two of your—that is, *my*—prospective patients?" said Dr. Ino, turning to look at the two charming girls with the gentle gaze of a devout vivisectionist.

"Well, not exactly, doctor. You see. . . ."

"Mercy, they are *lovely!* They would make such excellent specimens."

"They would at that, wouldn't they?" agreed Sam, as if this had given him an idea. He rose to his feet, collected the two girls, and signalled to his friends. "We really must go. We have to be up early tomorrow to round up your patients, Dr. Ino."

"Many thanks for your hospitality, Correct Path," said Chauncey.

"It was our pleasure," said the priest, beaming. "And don't forget your uniforms."

Betty Grable took Chauncey's arm. "Will you please walk me home, Chauncey?"

"And," declared Irene, "I'm going with you, Sam."

The room churned with bows and farewells for a few moments.

At the door, Sam stopped to turn to Dr. Ino and say with his own special mask of bland innocence, "Doctor, do you think you could squeeze in two additional operations tomorrow if you started early enough?"

CHAPTER TWENTY-EIGHT

By eight the following morning, Sam and Chauncey had completed rounding up all of Hilda Ritter's pupils and had ushered them as a group into the main hall of the old temple, where the voting was to take place.

Chauncey looked up at the Gautama Buddha's image that towered benevolently above them all. Its serene face was heavy-lidded and enigmatic, tolerant, almost smiling. It was strikingly similar to Correct Path's sage and placid countenance, he thought.

"You want to tell them?" Chauncey asked. He certainly didn't; he felt he lacked Sam's deceptive tone of authority.

"Okay, I'll do it," Sam said. He stood up, cleared his throat importantly, bowed slightly to the assembled girls, and began to speak in Japanese. Chauncey stood by with his handy pocket dictionary in case Sam's Japanese rhetoric failed him.

"Lovely young ladies," Sam began slowly. "In America many of our best public speakers begin a serious talk with a joke, so that the audience may laugh before it has to consider grave issues. This is one such joke." The girls were sitting tense and hushed, their alert eyes vectored in on Sam's intent face.

"A dog walked into a New York City bar one day and ordered a dry martini with two drops of ketchup in it. When the bartender brought the martini, the dog drank it quickly, licked his chops, and asked for another." At this point several of girls glanced quizzically at one another, but no one made a sound. Sam continued: "When it came, he drank the second one just as quickly and ordered still another. When the third cocktail came and was placed before him, the dog finally said to the bartender, 'Don't you think it's kinda funny for me to walk in here, jump up on a barstool, and order a martini with two drops of ketchup in it?' Whereupon the bartender put both elbows on the bar, regarded the dog thoughtfully for a moment and replied, 'No, not at all. I drink 'em that way myself!"

Sam paused, a half-expectant smile on his face, waiting for the waves of laughter to roll over him. But while the girls continued to regard him with concentrated interest, none of them so much as cracked a smile.

Under his breath he muttered to Chauncey, "What the hell did I do wrong? That should have them in stitches."

Chauncey replied, sotto voce, "That's for Dr. Ino to do. Anyway, how the hell should I know? Maybe they don't dig the weird New York scene."

"That's got to be it." To the girls he said. "Okay. That little joke was just to illustrate that in some places unusual situations are taken for granted. But where they aren't, then all of us must adapt to the morality of the place where we happen to live. Right now it's Kyushu, and more specifically for all of you ladies, your home town of Fukuoka, where will have to undergo physical examinations to prove or disprove your virginity." He and Chauncey had already explained in detail what they had learned from Colonel Dawgleish recently in Fukuoka. "Should you fail to pass such the examinations. . . ."

Sam paused, letting his point sink in. There was a distinct reaction; the girls began whispering avidly among themselves. He sighed, relaxing a little.

Lana Turner jumped to her feet and raised her hand for the floor.

"Sam-*san*," she began respectfully, "we have all assumed that because Lieutenant MacArthur is the nephew of the revered General MacArthur himself, who is the protector and advisor of our Divine Emperor, no question of this sort would arise."

Rita Hayworth stood up to interject an opinion. "We thought our parents would be pleased that we had offered our virtue to such an honorable personage and his friends."

"That's right," affirmed Lana Turner. "We have believed all along that we would be congratulated for being the most patriotic women in Kyushu, thereby earning great merit and distinction."

"Mmmmmh, besides having a little fun?" Sam murmured beneath his avuncular smile.

"After all," said Rita Hayworth, "if General MacArthur has the power to make our Divine Emperor announce on the radio to the entire nation that he is not the god that we all know he really is, then it seems to me that the General should be able to solve this insignificant problem by merely signalling from heaven with his little finger!"

A burst of warm applause swept through the assembly.

"This isn't going to be easy, Sam," Chauncey warned. "Watch it!"

As the applause died away, Carole Landis stood up, glared suspiciously at Chauncey and demanded, "You really *are* General MacArthur's blood nephew, are you not?"

In answer, Chauncey produced his corncob pipe, stuck it in his teeth, and exhibited a noble profile for all the girls to admire.

"Of course he is," Sam declared in confirmation of what the girls ardently wished to believe, anyway. "The lieutenant and his uncle are extremely devoted to one another. However, the lieutenant does not like to presume upon the relationship." Sam waited for the low-keyed murmer of approval to die away. "And the general doesn't like to help Chauncey openly because of the bad blood that exists between him and Chauncey's father: the general's brother who went to the United States Naval Academy at Annapolis."

"So what can we do now?" demanded Katherine Hepburn.

Sam gave the girls his most beguiling, confident smile.

"The solution is very simple and painless. But first, I must tell you a fascinating story of medical research which concerns a distinguished Oguni doctor and his charming daughter Kazu. And the local eels."

The audience listened intently as Sam told the story as he heard it from Dr. Ino. At last, in summary, he capped his narrative with a word of comfort and assurance: "There's no pain to speak of," he explained. "I have the good doctor's oath on this. The operation will only take a few minutes, and in five or six days you'll be able to pass a physical examination back in Fukuoka. In short, you'll be as good as new again. Now, let's do this in the good old democratic American way and take a vote on it! Everyone in favor of the operation, please raise your right hand."

Instantly the fourteen girls turned from an attentive audience into a seething mass of tense muttering, arguments, protests, even groans of dismay.

Ann Blyth wailed, "But it'll only have to broken again!"

Lana Turner cried, "I didn't want the old thing to begin with!"

In a lower voice heard by only a few, Deborah Kerr made the point that more of them should have been acutely conscious of: "If Yoshikita-san and Nemoto-san catch up with us, it won't matter one way or the other, will it?"

"Silence, silence!" Sam shouted, and gradually the clamor subsided. When it was relatively quiet again, Veronica Lake said in a clear voice, "I'm just going to tell my father the truth. He never punishes me, anyway."

"Girls, girls, please. . . ." Sam was pleading now. "I beg you to vote in favor of the resolution. It's for *your* ultimate benefit."

There was another general murmur following this announcement, which Chauncey prayed was favorable. But with these girls you never knew.

"All right," Sam announced, "now we'll take a vote: All in favor raise your right hand."

Only three hands went up.

"Oh, Christ!" Chauncey moaned quietly to himself. "We've lost!"

"Opposed?"

A count of eleven hands: Three for the operation and eleven against it.

"I give up," said Sam. "Come on, boys, let's adjourn the meeting and accept our fate."

Through all this, True had been standing at the back of the hall. Now he strode forward.

"Hey, you all just hold on! Ah gotta whisper somethin' important to you."

Sam and Chauncey went into a huddle with him while the girls buzzed and speculated. It was over in a moment; Sam turned to the audience:

"Listen, sweethearts. There's one thing you're overlooking. If any of you fail to pass the physical exam, Miss Ritter will share—largely, I fear—in the blame. Although she had nothing to do with your original decision to run away, she did agree to accompany you as chaperone. Without any doubt your fathers will take the position that she should have lived up to the responsibility she was accepting and should have prevented you from being compromised. It is almost certain that your fathers will see to it that she loses her job and then, of course, she will have to leave Japan. She will lose face and honor. Her career as a teacher will be in shambles."

A concerted gasp of dismay rose from the audience. The girls shot to their feet. Bedlam ensued. Somebody screamed out, "No, no, not that!" Somebody else cried, "We love our teacher! We'll protect her!" Several others wailed in anguish, one shrieked and tore her hair, another fainted dead away.

Above the pandemonium Ann Blyth shrilled at Sam, "We'll do it, Sam!! We'll have the operation right now!!"

Exhausted from his forensic ordeal, Sam shook hands with Chauncey and True. "You hunk of Alabama cornpone!" Sam told True with genuine admiration in his emotion-blurred voice. "You finally came through!"

"You remembered what we'd forgotten," Chauncey said. "The Japanese reverence for their teachers. Parent-figure transference, second only to the Emperor."

"If I didn't know better," San said, "I'd call you a genius." Balance restored, he turned to the girls: "Okay, ladies. We'll take another vote: All in favor. . . ."

All hands shot up. The girls' faces were shining with radiant smiles, eager and approving.

After that, matters progressed with satisfying speed, except for the minor problem of transportation between the old temple and Dr. Ino's surgery and residence just beyond Correct Path's new House of Worship and Fried Eel. They decided against using their jeep, since it would involve transit through Oguni; instead, they opted for making the short trip on foot over the hill between the two temples, despite the slight hazard inherent in exercising the newly-stitched surgical areas.

As Chauncey was leaving with the first contingent of seven ex-virgins shortly before nine, Sam said, "I think I'll go along, too. I'd like to see how the doc does it."

Chauncey, however, turned him down: "You tend to your knitting, and let Dr. Ino tend to his."

As Chauncey sat chewing his nails in Dr. Ino's waiting room, Correct Path arrived to give him moral support.

Over tea Chauncey put a question to the head priest that had been bothering him for some time:

"I'm still puzzled over the Japanese indifference to virginity," Chauncey confessed. "Especially in view of the fact that it's considered immoral to kiss or to even hold hands in public. The morality's tight on inconsequentials but lax on the big issues. How do you reconcile fathers insisting so strongly on virgin daughters with the fact that virginity's a low-value commodity?"

"You have a fascinating and ambivalent subject there, Lieutenant MacArthur," the priest replied with a beatific smile. "Fundamentally, I'm sure that a broken hymen in itself is a trivial matter to them. It would depend more upon *who* broke it. A matter of class distinctions, so to speak."

"Oh?"

"You see, for a nice neighborhood boy in Fukuoka to have made off with one of these lovely creature's cherry blossoms, to use your phrase, would not be so serious a matter, but for a hairy foreign devil to have committed the act—and I use that opprobrious term *only* within the context of this analysis—that is quite another matter altogether."

Shortly before noon, Chauncey departed from Dr. Ino's residence with the seven freshly restored virgins, not much the worse for their experience, and returned to the old temple. At one o'clock he left with the second shift of seven hymen-less hussies and returned them to the temple at four-fifteen, completely revirginized.

By five o'clock Sam and Chauncey, slightly dizzy from the events of the day, were doling out encouragement to each other from a bottle of Old Parr in their temple rooms while the girls napped or talked about their operations.

"Now all we have to do is lie low for a few days until the girls' doodads are all healed over," said Sam, already mellow.

"And hope the goddam Gyrene MP's don't get here in the meantime," Chauncey replied. "Think we ought to burn a few joss sticks in the temple for good luck?"

"Don't forget to pray that those two maniacs don't find

us, either."

"Amen to that."

Mabel awoke, stretched her long hairy arms, and rubbed sleep from her eyes. When she couldn't find True, she leaped onto Sam's shoulders and tried to grab his drink. She was extremely fond of Scotch, even though it made her sneeze.

"Okay, old girl, you can have some," Sam said. "Just a sip now."

Mabel sipped, spluttered, sneezed, and romped away. She had heard True coming down the corridor whistling *Smile, Darn you, Smile.*

"I didn't think Dr. Ino looked exactly jubilant after that last batch," Chauncey said with a worried frown. "Do you think anything went wrong?"

"Don't even think about it," said Sam, pouring another drink. "That would be all we need now."

CHAPTER TWENTY-NINE

The hymen restorations took place on a Monday.

All was tranquil during the next three days. The men lay around their temple quarters drinking and yarning, but behind their apparent gaiety was an anxious concern for the immediate future.

The girls slept, recuperated, gossiped among themselves, and prepared to return to Fukuoka to family reunions.

Late Thursday night, however, the Marines arrived in Oguni. No one was aware of it except the sleepy innkeeper who took them in.

The scouting party consisted of two MP's in a patrol jeep, both men and vehicle being attached to the 2nd Marine Division.

True was the first to discover their presence early Friday morning when he climbed half-way up the hill behind the temple.

"Jeehosophat!" he groaned. "Gotta tell Sam and Chauncey!"

After tumbling down the hill, True tore through the inn to their rooms; Sam and Chauncey were still asleep. True shook them both awake, ignoring Mabel's frantic love cries.

"They got heah!" he gasped. "They come in the night."

"They, *they*?" asked Sam crossly, rubbing sleep from his eyes.

Chauncey yawned and sat up. "Who's they?"

"The MP's! Who else?"

"So? They're not going to find us this very minute, are they?" Sam said.

"Council of war," Chauncey ordered hastily. "Sit down, True, and compose yourself."

True sat, and the huddle began.

"As I see it," Sam stated, talking quickly. "Our problem is two-fold. One, we've got to lure the Gyrenes out of Oguni. Two, we've got to get the girls and Hilda on their way to Fukuoka. The latter part of the problem, however, is complicated by the fact that we mustn't get them there too fast. For example, if the girls are handed over to their families today, and if, God forbid, they happen to be examined by a doctor tonight, disaster becomes a distinct possibility."

"I know what you mean," Chauncey agreed. "Dr. Ino specifically cautioned me to allow for sufficient healing time. Otherwise, those precious little hymens might give way or the girls might yell when examined."

"Needless to say, with dire results for the three lieutenants involved," Sam said portentously. Individual assignments were decided, decisive action plotted. Then they all shook hands solemnly, dressed quickly without any more talk, and separated.

True headed for the inn across the river where the Marines were staying. Sam ran to get their own jeep, which was still parked by the new temple. And Chauncey hurried to the *samurai* museum where the antique armor and weaponry were on musty display.

In fifteen minutes True returned to the temple with two five-gallon cans of gasoline, stolen from the backside of the Marines' jeep.

"Ah ripped out all the wires Ah could see on the two-way radio and Ah siphoned out most of the gas in the tank," he told Chauncey when he found him. "Ain't sure how much was left, but it can't be more'n a gallon, maybe only half that."

"Good show, laddie," said Chauncey. "Come on, let's find Sam and get into our special gear. We leave in five minutes."

When they were ready, they rushed out into the courtyard and climbed into their jeep, now devoid of all standard identification. (Sam had slapped wet newspapers over the hood serial numbers and wrapped rags around the bumper codes.) After finishing his chores in the museum room of the temple, Chauncey had tied one of Correct Path's donated sheets to a bamboo pole found lying in the courtyard and with a scrounged writing set—brush and India ink—had hastily printed in bold, brave, black letters the trio's clarion call of defiance. This war banner was secured to the jeep so that it would fly and flutter in the wind of their departure.

"Forward, ho!" Chauncey sang out, elongating the second word in cavalry fashion, then started the jeep and drove out past the inn and into the road that paralleled the river. At the approach to the bridge on the old temple's side of the Chikugo, Chauncey brought the vehicle to a stop but left the motor idling.

At this point, no more than fifty yards separated them from the Marine jeep on the far bank, with no obstructions between the two vehicles. The plan was that when the two Marine MP's emerged from their lodging, they could hardly help but see the Army trio in their jeep just across the river.

"I hope they don't take too long," Chauncey said.

"Yeah, the peasants are gathering," Sam observed, for while they sat burning gasoline, a small knot of curious villagers had collected to stare at them from a discreet distance. It was still early and the town was quiet, except for the insistent purring of their jeep engine.

Five minutes passed, then ten. . . .

"I'm getting nervous," Sam growled. Fourteen minutes slipped by, and then it happened so suddenly they were almost taken by surprise.

The two Marines strolled out of the inn's front door, both husky giants. One was nonchalantly picking his teeth, the other hitching up his pistol belt.

"Man, they're sure huge duck-lovers," Sam said, awed.

"Common damned hoodlums," Chauncey grated between clenched teeth.

"Piss on 'em!" True said.

The Marines stopped a few feet from their jeep and with an air of self-satisfaction, began a leisurely survey of the river, the town, and its environs.

The Marine closer to them saw the idling Army jeep first. Even across the river they could read his astonishment as he stared at them, glued to the spot where he stood for a moment. Then he half-turned and spoke urgently to his partner, pointing vigorously in their direction.

"Okay, men, here we go!" said Chauncey, slamming the jeep into gear but moving slowly at first along the road that would eventually lead them out of Oguni in the opposite direction from Correct Path's new temple.

What had undoubtedly stunned the Marines more than

the Army jeep itself was the bizarre appearance of the trio. Chauncey had chosen a rusty suit of sixteenth century *samurai* armor for True, who looked magnificently formidable in it, except that his helmet guard kept flopping down over his eyes in low comedy style. Sam lolled grandly back in a Highland costume of MacGregor tartan: kilt, tam-o'shanter, sporran, vest, and bagpipe. This bit of exotic masquerade Chauncey had dug up from an ancient wardrobe chest at the rear of the museum. He had also found a moth-eaten French Legionnaire's uniform, with kepi and neck-curtain, right out of *Beau Geste*, and chose this for himself. Where these items had come from, he could only guess. But they achieved the desired effect: these two costumes with the *samurai* armor. They were a sightful trio, ill-matched and war-like. The Marines simply couldn't believe their eyes, nor could they identify the vehicle. And to top it all off, Mabel was in full view, bouncing around the jeep's rear seat attired in a child's version of True's *samurai* armor, completely unrecognizable as a simian.

"Okay!" Sam ordered, "let 'er rip!"

As the jeep gathered momentum, their war banner unfurled and streamed out for all Oguni to see. The black, foot-high letters were plainly legible to the startled Marines, and the friendly message read:

"GO HOME, GYRENE RAPE-ARTISTS!!!!"

This message triggered the two giants. As if shot from cannon, they sprinted for their jeep. One took the wheel as the other unflapped his pistol-holster and shook a large angry fist at the departing masqueraders.

The Marine jeep churned dust and spewed gravel as it frantically rocked back and forth U-turning in the narrow roadway. In seconds it was catapulting toward their end of the bridge. The passenger Marine had turned on the siren and was leaning half-way out of the jeep with his .45 Colt automatic in the ready-to-fire postion.

"Hot damn!" Sam yelled. "Watch our smoke!"

As soon as Chauncey was certain that the Marines knew which road the Army jeep was taking, he stamped on the gas pedal and flew along the narrow, bumpy track southeast out of Oguni. By the time the Marines reached the end of the bridge and the opposite bank, the fleeing

Army jeep was out of sight beyond the crest of the hill, a plume of white dust punctuating its departure like a fat exclamation mark.

Before Chauncey had travelled a full quarter of a mile, however, he pulled up to a sharp stop so that he and Sam could pile out and scramble off the road into a handy grove of trees before the Marine jeep came into view.

True jumped into the driver's seat and roared away, laying down a heavy smoke screen of fine white dust.

"Christ," said Sam, peering after True, "Mabel's waving goodbye to us!"

Their hopeful conjecture was that the Marines would run out of gas about five or ten miles out of Oguni, stranded without a functioning radio or extra fuel and far from a functioning telephone or source of gasoline. Any Japanese cars—of which there were very few—that might happen along would be burning charcoal as fuel in oven-like tanks ingeniously fitted into the luggage trunks. All the Marines could hope for would be a lift, and even this was not likely. With the extra bonus of fuel stolen from the Marine jeep, True would be safe in making a very wide geographical circle north, then west, and eventually rejoining the main east-west highway between Fukuoka and Beppu somewhere near Fukuoka itself.

"Very smooth so far," Chauncey said with satisfaction as the Marines' jeep, hell-bent on vengeance, roared past their cover in the grove of trees.

"Bon voyage, you cruddy bastards!" shouted Sam, knowing his voice would be drowned by the roar of the pursuing jeep. When the vehicle was out of sight, they emerged from the grove and headed back toward Oguni on foot.

"I sure wish I could shuck this Scotch drag outfit," grated Sam.

"Never mind, you got beautiful hairy kness," said Chauncey, chuckling. "You don't exactly look *comme il faut* yourself," Sam retorted, "and that's French for go stick your head in a honey-tank."

A farmer at work in his rice-paddy gaped impolitely at them as they trudged by, then dropped his scythe, turned, and ran.

"What the hell's wrong with him?" Chauncey wondered.

Sam stopped short a moment later. "Goddam!" he growled.

"Now what? "

"I wonder if True forgot to tell Hilda to wake the girls up and start them packing?"

"I heard him say he did—from the depths of his armor."

"We're in a fucking mess if he didn't."

"That's exactly the kind of mess we're in, anyway," Chauncey reminded him.

"First we change out of these idiotic costumes into our uniforms," said Sam, his mood improving at the thought. "Then we herd our fourteen little virgins. . . ."

". . . .all retreads, no original rubber. . . ."

". . . .off to Fukuoka."

But as they approached the center of the small resort town, they sighted a *yakata-bune*—a larger craft than the one that had brought them upriver from Kurume—tied up to the dock near the front of the Inn of the Playful Hermit. And Hilda Ritter and the fourteen resurrected virgins were all aboard with their luggage.

"What the hell's going on?" asked Sam. "They've never been on time before, much less ahead of time."

"Look, they've seen us!"

As soon as she sighted the Americans, the Swiss teacher jumped back onto the dock and went running to meet them.

"They're here, right here in Oguni! Hurry, hurry!" She grabbed them by one arm each and tried to propel them over the few remaining yards to the side of the waiting *yakata-bune*. "I thought we were going to have to leave without you. *Please* hurry! Go on, jump aboard!"

"Who's here, Hilda?" asked Sam, doing nevertheless as he was told.

"Why, those two fanatics, of course. They've found us again," Hilda said, turning to the boatman and telling him in Japanese to push off immediately.

"Oh, dear, dear God," she prayed, looking around fearfully in all directions. "Not now, not after all this! It's just not fair!" she added, as if in rebuke to the Almighty.

"*Sensei*, I see them!" cried Sujiko Honekawa (Katherine Hepburn) from the stern of the craft. "See? Over there, coming out of that inn! Oh, they've seen us, too!"

CHAPTER THIRTY

As the *yakata-bune* pushed its maddeningly slow way out of the still water beside the dock and into the swift current of midstream, the two Japanese ensigns—now more tattered and gaunt than ever—started to run toward the bridge across the Chikugo. Before they reached it, however, first the shorter one, Nemoto, and then the other, Yoshikita, came to a reluctant stop as if realizing that their prey had again slipped from their prehensile grasp. Immediately the taller of the two appeared to propose something to his companion and then began to expostulate with military-like gestures when it seemed that Nemoto was not entirely willing or enthusiastic.

In a moment Yoshikita gave Nemoto a sharp shove, as if in exasperation, and the pair began to trot back along the line of inns on the far bank. At the fourth inn they found what they had apparently been seeking: two bicycles. As they started to mount, however, one or the other must have noticed that both vehicles were locked, for they threw them aside and ran on. On the boat, Sam grinned in private enjoyment; he could almost hear them cursing from here.

Two doors farther on, Yoshikita succeeding in finding an unlocked bicycle, which he instantly mounted and pedalled wildly off in the direction of the western exit from the valley. Hands on hips, Nemoto stood and watched him go for a long moment, then shrugged his shoulders rnd walked more slowly on in the same direction, apparently still looking for an unlocked bicycle for himself.

"Where are they now?" asked Hilda Ritter faintly from her prone position on the boat's *tatami.*

"One of them got on a bicycle and rode off," said Chauncey. "The other acts like as if he's looking for one, too."

"Oh, God, will those monsters *never* leave us alone?" wailed Hilda, weakly rising to a sitting posture. "Are we going to spend the rest of our lives running from. . . ." Her voice broke, then she added, "and just when we thought there was a chance everything might turn out to be all right yet!"

The fright passed quickly, however, for the fourteen girls, who had begun to take belated note of Sam's and Chauncey's new fall ensembles. In a minute, Claudette Colbert giggled and said in a stage whisper, "I think they're cute."

"Chauncey looks just like *Beau Geste*," proclaimed Ann proudly.

"Why doesn't Sam shave his knees?" mused Deborah.

"What's that bag hanging down in front of Sam's skirt?" asked Shirley with a titter.

"Why, that's his ball-warmer, silly!" cried Carole. "The Scots don't wear anything under their skirts and when the weather gets down to freezing, they have to. . . ."

"All right, all *right!*" interrupted Sam in the nick of time. "You ladies have had your fun now, so let me and Chauncey talk to your teacher for a minute."

Arraying themselves in their gay *kimonos* in the stern of the boat as if on display in a department store window, the Fukuoka maidens chattered, preened, and practiced amorous facial expressions in the cool air of the beautiful fall morning.

"All right, Hilda," said Sam as he and Chauncey sat down on each side of the still-frightened Swiss woman. "Tell us what happened."

"Well, Sujiko—I mean, Katherine—came into my room a little while ago. ." Hilda took a deep breath to steady her voice ". . .and told me they were here. Nemoto and Yoshikita, I mean. Lucky for us, we were all packed, so I had them take their luggage down to the dock while I hired this boat and. . . ."

"But how did Katherine know?"

"That's the strange part of the story," said Hilda, almost in control of herself again. "She. . . .but wait a minute, I'll have them make us some tea." In Japanese, she instructed Veronica and Ida to boil water on the charcoal brazier and set out the tea things. "Anyway, when we were all aboard, I wanted to start immediately, but the girls became so upset that I had to promise to wait ten minutes—but no more—for you, and you got there just in time. Oh, I forgot! What about True? Is he all right?"

"I'm sure he is," Chauncey said placatingly. "He and Mabel got a good headstart on the Marines, who should run out of gas in a few miles, anyway. You don't need to concern yourself about him," he added with more confidence than he felt.

Hilda looked relieved, then worried again. "I wonder where those two fanatics were going on the bicycles?"

"Who knows?" said Sam. "Besides, when we get back to Fukuoka, I'm going. . . .or rather Lieutenant *MacArthur* here is going to see to it that the MP's put those nuts out to permanent pasture on the funny farm."

"But what if they can't *find* them?" Hilda's voice was all a-tremble again.

"Now, now," soothed Sam. "You're not to worry."

Privately both Sam and Chauncey were just as concerned as Hilda, but they tried not to show it. Until this morning the Marines hadn't had much success in finding a much more obvious quarry: fourteen beautiful girls and their pretty Swiss chaperone. Nor were they doing much good in another search Sam and Chauncey had heard about on their previous trip to Fukuoka: the hunt for Tokyo Rose. She was Number Two on the list—right after Hideki Tojo—of persons wanted for questioning by Tokyo headquarters, and she had last been seen right here in Kyushu, in the small town of Yoshii.

"Say," asked Chauncey to change the subject, "where are *we* going?"

"Gracious, I haven't even thought about that," replied Hilda. "I just wanted to get the girls out of Oguni as fast as possible, and this was the only way I could think of. . . ."

"Well, let's go as far as Hida, anyway. We could get off there and spend the night and then think about how to get to Fukuoka."

"We don't want to get there too soon," Chauncey pointed out.

"Right," Sam agreed, standing up. "I'll go tell the boatman where we're going, anyway."

When he came back, Hilda took up the thread of her account about what had happened to Katherine Hepburn.

"Katherine told me about it briefly while we were waiting for you back there at the dock. Those two fanatics *kidnapped* her last night!" She paused to let that penetrate. "They laid in wait for her in the darkness just inside the temple and grabbed her as she came down the corridor."

"By the way," said Sam, "wasn't Katherine the one who was supposed to marry Nemoto?"

Hilda nodded.

"What happened next?" Sam urged.

"They dragged Katherine over to one of those inns across the river, where they had taken two rooms, and questioned her closely for more than an hour. Poor dear, she had to tell them everything, of course, and she says that it looks as if they intend to go through with what they have been planning all along."

"You mean, kill all the girls?"

Hilda nodded with a shudder.

"Then what happened?"

"Nemoto took Katherine to his room and then this morning she escaped." Hilda paused, then added, "But it was funny, she said. . .she got the impression that Nemoto deliberately left the room so that she *could* get away."

"Oh, God!" Sam exclaimed, "you mean she spent *all night* in the room with him?"

"Yes, but. . ."

"Don't you see," Sam grated in an sudden anger, "she may not be a virgin anymore!"

"Oh, no. . . ." Hilda paled and turned to call Katherine from the stern of the smoothly-moving *yakata-bune.*

"Yes, *Sensei?*" Katherine knelt gracefully by Hilda's side and bowed slightly.

"Katherine," began Hilda, speaking now in Japanese, "I have just been telling Sam and Chauncey what happened to you last night. . . .and how you were alone with Nemoto-san most of the time. Now, dear, I don't want to embarrass you, but this is important: What went on. . . .I mean, did anything *happen* between you and that. . . .man?"

"Oh, yes," replied Katherine brightly.

"Just what *did* happen, Katherine?" Hilda pursued. "Take your time now. Don't be nervous."

"Oh, all sorts of things," the warm-eyed girl stated happily.

Repressing a sharp reprimand, Hilda said patiently, "Now, dear, I don't like to ask you these questions, but we *must* know exactly what took place between you two last night."

"Well, you know that book we were all reading last summer?" Katherine began eagerly. "The pillow book? Anyway, first we tried the position described in. . . .hmm, I *think* it was Chapter Eight. Or was it Nine? That's the one where the girl gets down on her hands and knees and then lifts her left leg up in the air behind her while the man gets under. . . . It's a little hard to describe, but. . . .oh, you should remember, Chauncey! That night in Kurume. . . . when you and I showed the other girls how to. . . ."

"No, no, dear," said Hilda, wondering to herself why she ever left Switzerland. "Not *that* exactly. You see, what we're trying to find out is whether or not. . . .well, if you need another operation!"

"She's already answered that question," Sam said sourly.

"In letters a foot high," added Chauncey.

"It was just a *darned nuisance*, anyway," Katherine said, pouting.

"Oh, God," said Chauncey, taking off his Legionaire's cap and wiping his brow. "What an unfortunate choice of words that was!"

"I don't see what is so wrong with what I did," muttered the girl, her head bowed defensively.

"Don't you see," Sam cried in open exasperation, "that *one* non-virgin will be just as bad as *fourteen* non-virgins? They'll hang us—I mean, they'll hang your *teacher*—just as high for one as for fourteen!"

"The darned old thing, anyway," said Katherine, in a pet.

"Well, you've neatly *un*darned it again," said Chauncey in a voice replete with reproach.

"Oh, Katherine," cried Hilda, "how could you do this to us! And with that fanatic at that!"

"He's not so bad, *Sensei,*" protested Katherine. "It's the other one, Yoshikita-san, who's always egging him on. If it were up to Nemoto-san alone, why, I'm sure he'd just forget all about. . . .their plan." Then she added irrelevantly with the sudden smile of a deviant imp, "Besides, I think he's kind of cute."

"Virgin, non-virgin, virgin, non-virgin," Sam was chanting half to himself in English and looking wistfully off into the distance.

"I know it's only of academic interest now," said Chauncey in Japanese to Katherine, "but how did they find us?"

"They weren't fooled at all by Miss Ritter's trick back there in Bochu," she explained. "At least, not at the station. I guess the description of the maids from the inn didn't match ours closely enough. . . .or something."

"But Ann and I didn't see them coming down from Mt. Aso."

"They were on foot, and the rickshaws were just too fast for them." Then she added with a winning smile, "Especially coming *down* the mountain."

"And after that?"

"They lost the trail for a while in Kurume, when we changed from rickshaws to river boats, but finally they figured it out. It was probably Nemoto-san. You know, I think he's quite intelligent. You should get to know him better, Chauncey."

"Hmpf," Chauncey sniffed, not knowing just how soon he would be presented with that very opportunity.

In the middle of the afternoon, when they were still more than an hour away from Hida, the boatman blew the boat whistle as he sighted another craft approaching them from downriver. It being the only other vessel of any size they had seen all day, Sam borrowed the binoculars that were part of Chauncey's Foreign Legion outfit and casually focussed them on the other boat, which was still more than a hundred yards away but was shortening the distance rapidly.

As he looked through the glasses, his body stiffened. He turned and called Hilda in an urgent voice. "Here," he said. "Look through these at that boat."

"Yes? What is. . . . Oh my God, It's those fiends again!"

Chauncey came running up. "How in hell did they get *ahead* of us?"

"The river winds back and forth all the way to Hida,"

Sam said tersely, "but the road is straight. . Look closely at the boat itself, Chauncey "

Chauncey took the glasses. "Yes? What do you . . . Say, what *is* that thing sticking out of this end of the boat?"

"That's what I mean."

The ensigns' boat, which looked like a police launch propelled by a one-lung Diesel, was now only fifty yards away.

"Why, it looks like a. . . .bomb?"

The two boats were now less than thirty yards apart.

"That's what I thought, too,"

Only twenty yards.

"But why would they mount a bomb like that in the bow. . . ."

Ten yards.

"I   don't   know. . . .unless. . . .unless. . . .THEY'RE GOING TO RAM US!"

CHAPTER THIRTY-ONE

Understandably it didn't occur to Chauncey at the moment, but when he reflected on it later, at a less unsettling time, there was something decidedly magnificent about the last *kamikaze* attack of the war. And, seaborne though it was, it would be remembered, in all likelihood, as the last *kamikaze* attack in all history's pages.

Yoshikita stood in the bow of the old police launch (it had *Hida Keisatsusho*—or Hida Police Department—written in *kanji* on the port side of the prow) with one foot braced against the bomb itself and a wild light in his eyes. Nemoto stood at the wheel in the stern, guiding the launch as it chugged stoutly on toward mass destruction.

Aboard the *yakata-bune* chaos was doing a dervish dance. Fifteen females screamed in chorus, two Americans yelled for them to leap overboard, and one Oguni boatman blew a long blast on his whistle and frantically turned his craft to the starboard, which maneuver succeeded only in presenting the onrushing police launch with a broader target.

Five yards away.

At the last possible instant, however, Nemoto spun the wheel and the launch veered sharply starboard. Its side scraped the *yakata-bune* in passing, but the aerial bomb mounted in the bow touched only air. Then, as the stern of the launch came alongside, Nemoto leaped into the larger boat and shouted for Yoshikita to jump, too.

But Yoshikita was bent on doom. He stood his ground, unmoving, head high, arms folded across his chest, eyes fixed on a point in the distant sky. The launch was now headed straight for the bank, which was high and rocky along this stretch of river, and although Nemoto shouted again and again for him to abandon ship, Yoshikita stood unheeding and apparently indifferent. The passengers aboard the *yakata-bune* watched in transfixed horror as history's last *kamikaze* attack charged the rocky embankment. When only a few yards away, Yoshikita straightened—with unhurried dignity—to stiff attention and saluted.

At the last instant Nemoto shouted from the *yakata-bune*, "*Yoshikita-kun, gokigen yo! Minna ni yoroshiku!*" (Goodbye, Yoshikita! Give all of them my regards!)

The explosion that followed blasted the police launch into smithereens and made a hole of honorable dimensions in the rocky bank of the Chikugo. Even though it was by then sixty or seventy yards away, debris rained down on the roof of the *yakata-bune* and a series of diminishing waves rocked the boat with enough force to knock three of the girls off their feet.

Still unable to fathom Nemoto's intentions, Chauncey and Sam had seized the surviving pilot from behind, but when they saw that he was crying, they let him go. He sank to his knees on the *tatami* flooring, bowed his head in silence, and let the tears flow unashamedly down his cheeks.

They reached the town of Hida in the late afternoon, disembarked, and paid off the boatman, who was muttering to himself something about selling his *yakata-bune* and going into the safer and saner business of raising eels. Hilda herded the girls into a tea-room while she went to find an inn for the night. Chauncey went alone to the Hida Police Station to report seeing from a distance an explosion that sank a police launch under mysterious circumstances. (The police chief was profoundly grateful, apologized to Chauncey.... "You did say your name was MacArthur, didn't you?"....for the inconvenience caused him, and bowed seventeen times during the ten-minute visit.) Since they were undecided about what to do with Nemoto, Sam stood uncertain guard over him at the tea-room, awaiting Chauncey's return.

Hilda found lodging for all in the Inn of Ecstatic Welcome only two blocks from the tea-room. She and the fourteen girls went on ahead, while Sam and Chauncey with Nemoto in tow located the Hida Telegraph Office. Finding that service between Hida and Fukuoka had been restored, they collaborated on the following telegram to Colonel Dawgleish:

"SIR: HAVE LOCATED THE FOURTEEN MISSING PROPERTIES AND OVERSEER STOP ALL SAFE AND WELL STOP RETURNING ITEMS TO FUKUOKA BY BEST AVAILABLE TRANSPORTATION STOP ESTIMATED TIME OF ARRIVAL IN FUKUOKA LATE SATURDAY AFTERNOON STOP STAND BY STOP RESPECTFULLY BRUCE FOOTE MACARTHUR"

"I'm impressed that we can send the goddam thing in English." said Sam as they paid for the message. "Like sending a telegram from Dallas to Chicago in Japanese."

"Imagine what the Dallas telegraph office would say," Chauncey laughed, "if you handed them a message written in Japanese."

"Those omissions were smart, if I do say so. Like not saying where we found the girls or where we all are now."

"The C.O. could find us after he gets the telegram, Sam, but it went out as a night letter, so we bought ourselves some time."

"Yeah," Sam said without noticeable enthusiasm.

"It takes two hours of normal driving to get to Fukuoka from here," Chauncey calculated as the three of them walked to the Inn of Ecstatic Welcome in the gathering dusk, "but the slowest way would be to go by rickshaw. . . ."

"You mean *aboard* and not in front of, I hope."

"Correct. . . .and we need those extra hours for mending time, don't we?"

"All this talk of mending and stitching and darning makes it sound like a. . . .a garment factory. But say, what're we going to do about Katherine? There's not enough time for another operation and. . . ."

"I've got an idea," said Chauncey slowly as they approached their inn, "and it just might work."

Sam shook his head dubiously, then raised his eyes to the evening skies of over Kyushu in mute appeal.

CHAPTER THIRTY-TWO

By mid-morning of the next day, Sam and Chauncey had contracted for the services of seven rickshaws and two pedicabs, the latter being merely bicycles with rickshaw bodies attached.

The exodus from Hida drew record crowds. Everyone who sighted the spectacle stopped to stare at the bizarrely-costumed foreigners and the young girls. Sam and Deborah Kerr headed the procession in the first rickshaw, Hilda Ritter and Dorothy Lamour rode in the second, Ann Blyth and Chauncey in the third, and so fourth. Being faster, the two pedicabs were assigned the last positions in the parade and charged to watch out of stragglers.

With the exception of Hilda, who seemed genuinely worried about True and totally depressed about her own future, the female passengers were exceedingly gay and garrulous. Augmenting the rakish eccentricity of Sam's and Chauncey's costumes, the flock were dressed in their finest, most colorful *kimonos*? Perhaps this, Chauncey decided, was what made them so full of holiday spirits and determined to regard whatever happened as wildly hilarious.

True caught up with the party at four o'clock in the afternoon near Futsukaichi.

First in order was a tearful, highly charged reunion with Hilda, who broke down completely and had to be calmed by Sam and Chauncey as well as True.

"For God's sake, Hilda," Sam had to say, "think of your pupils."

The girls had gathered in a circle and were watching Hilda's display wide-eyed. Hilda grasped the situation immediately.

"I—I'm sorry," she murmured. "Let us go on. . . ."

But then their progress was delayed a few minutes longer while True told them about his trip around the northern perimeter of the island, including a set-to with still another pair of churlish Marine MP's. "They'd a' caught me sure but the sight of me and Mabel dressed up like this must've stunned 'em. They just sat theah an' gaped at us, so Ah got a good head start. And then Ah got mahself lost twice and had to spend the night in the back seat of the jeep on a spooky ole road ovah near—uh, Bungo-Takada or some such heathenish place. And say, Ah woke up next mornin' right plumb alongside the biggest, deepest-lookin' honey-tank in all Kyushu!"

"Never mind about that now," Sam said, distractedly. "We gotta get to Fukuoka before dark and deliver the goods."

With Hilda, Sam, and Chauncey as passengers in the jeep and True driving, they reached the outskirts of the city about six o'clock. At this point it seemed expedient to consider appearances. Making True stop, Sam got out, dressed up the line, and made sure that all fourteen girls were still present and accounted for. Since Hilda's reunion with True, Mabel had become wildly obstreperous and was now in a rickshaw by herself, following the jeep. From time to time she would jump up and down in a frenzy, screeching what presumably were simian obscenities at Hilda, the target of her jealous wrath.

When everything seemed satisfactory to Sam, he climbed back into the jeep and they started up again. As the procession moved slowly through the residential sections of the city, some passersby stopped to stare curiously while others fled down side-streets as if fearful of becoming involved with anything that looked so much like a visitation from outer space.

Soon the parade turned into the main thoroughfare that led to the railway station, in front of which was milling a huge throng of people. Even as they drew closer, the trio could not decide whether it was an angry mob or a crowd of celebrators. There was considerable noise and movement, but these did not appear to be directed at anything in particular. It was almost as if the several thousand people were waiting for something spectacular to happen.

"We may be walking right into a riot, "Chauncey said. "Maybe we ought to turn back."

"That's all we need at this point," Sam groused. "If anybody hurts the girls, we'll be responsible."

The throng, upon closer inspection, seemed to be a mixture of American GI's and Japanese civilians, mostly milling about and waving things in the air. Then suddenly the mob spotted them. Shouts and yells went up, and, to a man, a solid line of apparent maniacs began rushing pell-mell toward them.

"Oh God," Sam moaned, "they're after us! Do something, True!"

"What *can* Ah do, except keep on drivin'?" True demanded, practically enough.

"He's right," said Chauncey. "There's no place to go now. We can't even turn around."

And so it was: the crowd was on both sides of their small procession. They could make out faces; Chauncey recognized men from the Team office. Some of the Japanese civilians waved American flags over their heads as they danced about. Several of the GIs, obviously gassed, held Japanese flags aloft and were waving them as they closed in.

"What the hell *is* this?" Sam said. By then they were completely surrounded, almost crushed. The cheering, shouting, and waving became more frantic. Hands reached out to touch them. Chauncey could hear the girls behind them squealing with delight at so much attention. The crowd's mood was friendly enough, but not knowing what had begun it, Chauncey was afraid of how it might end.

"It's incredible," he shouted over the tumult. "At first I thought they were going to kill us."

"I'm beginning to get a funny feeling that they like us," Sam said.

A face swam up out of the crowd. "Shit a'mighty!" True cried and would have gunned the jeep for all it was worth had they not been surrounded by a living, seething wall of wildly exuberant human beings. "It's Ruby Whacker!"

And there she loomed: big, buxom Ruby, pelting them with red and pink carnations and crying, "Welcome, the conquering heroes!" in her foghorn rasp.

Ruby smashed her way past several people and grabbed True, almost yanking him out of the driver's seat.

"Lover!" she bellowed, squeezing him and covering his face with smeary kisses. "You brought 'em back alive!"

Hilda turned to Chauncey and asked coldly, "What's

that?"

"His senior officer," Sam said, "and that's as far as it's ever gone. Don't worry, Hilda, we'll rescue him for you!"

"What's the crowd all about, Captain?" Chauncey yelled at the ecstatic Ruby.

"For all of you, of course! Who else? Didn't you guys bring 'em back alive? Fourteen gorgeous little cherry blossoms!" Ruby cried. "Hey, you're already famous all over Japan! Heard all about you on Radio Tokyo a couple of hours ago. You're news, boys, *news*!"

But the biggest crowd thriller was yet to come. As the last pedicab in the caravan slowly made its way through the shouting, milling multitude, the sign emblazoned on the back of its cab became apparent to more and more of the delirious well-wishers. In Japanese and English it announced boldly but simply,

"JUST MARRIED"

Multi-colored streamers flowed behind and strings of empty tin cans trailed along, setting up a somehow appropriate clatter. Inside proudly rode Ensign Nemoto and a shyly smiling Katherine. . .no, *Mrs*. Sujiko Nemoto.

It did not matter to the thousands of Japanese and Americans in Fukuoka's broadest thoroughfare that they knew nothing about the groom of one of the long-missing girls or that they did not understand the significance of the affair. They knew only that the event was congratulatory, that the wedded pair were obviously happy, and that the mood of the day was joyful. Against a background of recent defeat and present privation, these factors only served to heighten their delirium.

Ensign and Mrs. Nemoto were pulled from their bedecked pedicab and carried on eager shoulders to the side of the street where her family stood in attitudes of obvious welcome. The tumult reached crescendo. The crowd was shouting "*Banzai* for the American Army!" and "*Banzai* for the Flowers of Japanese Maidenhood!" and other incoherent cheers.

The throng was now dividing its ardent attention between the newly-weds and the thirteen other girls, who were climbing down from their rickshaws with all the grace and aplomb of movie stars, so the three lieutenants took advantage of the moment to turn the corner by the

Kyoshintei Building and, with a mutually-suspicious Hilda and Mabel in tow, to hurry to their quarters in the Inn of Ultimate Delights.

Colonel Dawgleish awaited them in Chauncey's room beneath the picture of General MacArthur. Rosy-cheeked and reeking of Bourbon and Old Spice, the colonel was warmly congratulatory.

"I knew it!" he said, shaking each of them heartily by the hand. "I knew you'd succeed. You got 'em back, safe and sound." He noticed Hilda for the first time and smiled broadly. "Well, well, and here's the prize of them all! Peaches and cream! My stars, I wish I was twenty years younger myself!"

"Thanks, sir," Sam said humbly, "we did our best for you and the Army."

"A magnificent performance! Your best, Bruce, and Foote's best—along with the superlative best of Chauncey MacArthur—have made this a red letter day in the history of our Occupation of Japan. I don't need to say, do I, that word of our success has filtered through to the inner sanctum in Tokyo? With all the details. How's that, hmmmm?"

"Great, sir," said Chauncey, smiling mechanically, as the old fear returned. The masquerade still wasn't over, dammit!

"You're heroes, men, that's what you are! You've earned the respect of a conquered nation and its great leader. You've even earned the admiration of the folks back home!"

Heroes, eh? thought Chauncey. Maybe so, maybe not. The girls still had to pass their virginity exams, and Dr. Ino had given them no guarantees. Moreover, they had all been pretty frisky for the past several days. . . .

"Don't forget," reminded Colonel Dawgleish, consulting his watch, "I'm giving a champagne testimonial for you at the officers' club in exactly one hour. Come one, come all—except that damned monkey of yours, Foote."

"Mabel's all tuckered out, anyway, sir."

"Sick with jealousy is more like it," noted Sam.

"And boys," said the colonel with a half-pleading smile as he was leaving. "I don't want to be stuffy about this, but you will—heh, heh—change uniforms, won't you?"

CHAPTER THIRTY-THREE

True returned to the Inn of Ultimate Delights the next morning whistling Dixie in pure, dulcet notes, but his long face belied his cheery tones.

Sam was shaving; Chauncey was sloshing down two APC tablets with some hot tea.

"You sound okay," Sam said to True's image in the mirror, "but you look as gloomy as we feel. What gives?"

"All th' gals 'cept Katherine are gonna be examined this mawnin' at ten."

"We figured as much," Sam said.

"It's quarter to eleven," Chauncey said. "We should know soon. Anyway, I think we've got at least a fifty-fifty chance."

"Maybe," said Sam fretfully. "This is the sixth day since the operation. Timewise we might be safe, but what worries me is that Dr. Ino has performed the operation just *once* before. If only he had a successful record of, say, forty or fifty darning jobs behind him, I wouldn't be so damned nervous!"

"You've got a point," Chauncey conceded.

"If you all ask me," True said, "the gals was bouncin' up and down somethin' awful yesterday. Guys were liftin' 'em outta the rickshaws, tossin' 'em up in the air an' everythin'. . . . And the gals was actin' like they was *tryin'* to undo their—uh, 'darned nuisances' again."

"Oh, Christ! I cut myself," complained Sam. "Change the subject, won't you?"

"Sure," said True. "Ah tell you what the gals' daddies had to say 'bout how we looked yesterday. Hilda says they told her th' way we looked was an insult to their daughters' social positions."

"Hmpf," Sam sniffed. "They ought to see some of the positions their little darlings know."

"By the way," began True, "you guys might as well clear

up a couple of things Ah still don't rightly understand."

"Only a couple?"

"Fer instance," True went on unperturbed, "wheah did ole Nemoto and Yoshikita get the bomb?"

"Hell-fire!" Sam exclaimed, "you're supposed to be Arms Disposal Officer, aren't you? You should know better than us that there're still arsenals and dumps of live ammo and bombs and everything else all over this damned island. And mostly unguarded, at that. Why, we haven't even scratched the surface of destroying the stuff!"

"Yeah, Ah guess you're right at that," True nodded slowly. "But how 'bout gettin' Katherine and Nemoto married?"

"Chauncey gets credit for that," said Sam with a slight bow to Fresno's Finest.

"Really no credit due," said Chauncey modestly, privately thinking that it was nothing less than a stroke of genius. "I saw that Katherine had developed a sudden fondness for her previous fiance, after their night of depravity together, and then Nemoto admitted to me that he had the hots for her, too. Besides, her. . .uh. . .nuisance had come undarned again and there wasn't time to fix it, so marriage was the only answer."

"And how could Katherine's parents object, since this was what they had wanted her to do in the first place," Sam said, hitting another nail on the head.

"But what," True wanted to know, "made Nemoto turn that ole police launch aside at the last cotton-picking minute like that?"

"I asked him about that," Chauncey explained. "At first, he was a little shy and didn't want to talk about it but finally he told me that he got to thinking about things in general while they were riding their bikes to Hida and then coming upriver toward us. . . ." Chauncey stopped to take a breath ". . .and he decided that if he and Katherine. . . .he calls her Sujiko, of course. . . .committed suicide together, he didn't think he'd be able to get any more on what Yoshikita kept calling 'the other side'. And he sure as hell didn't want to do without what Sujiko had to offer very long. He kept thinking about that. . . .and about all the positions Sujiko had told him they didn't have time to try that night—and so when the launch was on the point of ramming us, he just couldn't help himself. He spun the wheel and jumped."

"He's not such a bad guy, you know," said Sam. "He was very apologetic about all the trouble he and Yoshikita had caused."

"Too bad about that," murmured Chauncey, thinking of the dead pilot.

"I'm not so sure," said Sam. "Nemoto believes that Yoshikita is really happier this way. If he had jumped off the launch while he still could, this thing he had about a glorious *samurai* death would have eaten away at his insides for the rest of his life."

After a long moment of silence, Chauncey intoned softly, "A tale of intrigue, tragedy, and mad romance in the far-off, mysterious Orient!"

"Yeah," Sam added morosely, "and with a sordid ending: the three red-blooded heroes locked up forever in a pokey with no key."

Sumiko knocked on the door, then bowed herself into their presence with a tray of food. "Something very special Aso-san prepared to honor your success," she said happily, rattling off the name of it in Japanese.

"Look it up," Sam said, towelling his battered face. "Once burned, twice shy."

Chauncey thumbed through the dictionary. "You won't believe this one," he said, "so get ready to run. It translates as 'unripe gonads of sea urchins'."

"Why don't you mix us a Bombardier, True," Chauncey requested. "Suddenly I'm terribly depressed."

True blended Scotch, pineapple juice, bitters, and maraschino cherries in three canteen cups, then handed the drinks around.

"Cheers!" Chauncey toasted.

"Luck!" from Sam.

"Heah's to Swiss nooky," muttered True.

They had no more than taken the first gulp when the telephone rang. All three of them jumped to their feet and rushed for it. True won. It was Hilda.

"All the girls passed!" she said tremulously, trying hard to control the excitement in her voice.

True whooped and hollered: "They made it!" he cried to Sam and Chauncey. "Flyin' colors, one and all!"

Chauncey cheered, Sam chug-a-lugged his drink, and Mabel ran shrieking around the room like a demented ape.

True promised Hilda he would call her back and then cut the connection.

"We're free, safe, and clear!" Sam exulted, mixing another drink for himself.

"Not quite," Chauncey said, staring moodily into his canteen cup. "I've still got this impersonation-of-MacArthur's-nephew thing on my conscience. Maybe I ought to go see Dawgleish and make a clean breast of it. . . ."

Just then the phone jangled again.

Chauncey answered it. The voice was a young girl's, speaking soft, meticulous Japanese.

"Is this Lieutenant Chauncey MacArthur?"

"It is. Who's this?"

A low, provocative laugh was heard against a background of other soft feminine sounds.

"Tsutako Sugimura," the voice answered. "Better known to you as Ann Blyth of Oguni."

"Ann! Where are you?"

"At Carole's house. Oh, Chauncey, we have wonderful news! All of us passed the exams!"

"I know. Hilda Ritter just called us. We're going out of our minds over here."

"I also wanted to tell you that I've just been elected president of the F.Y.L.S.C."

"Congratulations, but what does that stand for?"

"The Fukuoka Young Ladies' Sewing Circle."

"The Fukuoka Young. . . .? You've *got* to be putting me on."

"Don't let the name deceive you, Chauncey dear. It's really a kind of weekend.....hmmm, pleasure club, I guess you could call it."

"What's the club motto," asked Chauncey, "A stitch in time saves nine?"

"Heh, heh. Very good, dear. Anyway, every weekend until the weather gets too cold, we're going to have a party at my father's beach cottage near Karatsu. He never uses it anyway. And, of course, you three will be the guests of honor."

"Well, that's very nice of you," Chauncey managed to

— 228 —

say, suppressing certain misgivings. "Oh, by the way, True probably won't be able to go. He and your teacher, you know. . . .well, they sorta have a thing going. . . ."

"Hmmmm, I see. Well, just the two of you then. We'll try not to outnumber you too much."

"Thanks a lot."

"And Chauncey. . . ."

"Yes?"

"We've got a new book."

"A new book?" Chauncey asked weakly. "That's swell, Ann."

"All about how they do it in China and India."

Chauncey could not think of anything appropriate to say to that.

"I'll send you a map to the beach cottage with the invitation," she said. "And by the way, Chauncey, do you think you could persuade Dr. Ino to set up practice here in Fukuoka?"

"Why?"

"Well. . . .heh, heh. . . .we might need his services again if our fathers ever get suspicious. And we have some school chums who say they'd like to pay him a visit, too."

"We'll see," said Chauncey, uneasy at the prospect. "And Ann. . . ."

"Yes, dear?"

"Ann, I've got a. . . .well, I've got a confession to make. . ."

Sam leaped across the room and covered the mouthpiece of the telephone with his hand. "Don't be a fool, Chauncey," he hissed. "If you tell her about the MacArthur hoax, she'll spill all of it to someone else, and we'll be in the stockade inside a week."

Chauncey looked at Sam coldly and pushed him away from the phone. "Ann?"

"Yes?"

"I just wanted to say that I'm. . . .very fond of you. No, believe me, I'm serious. I don't really care that much about seeing any of the other girls."

Sam collapsed in a chair in obvious relief.

"That's very nice of you to say, Chauncey," Ann told him, "but let's talk about it this weekend, shall we? You must remember that as president of the F.Y.L.S.C., I have a responsibility to the other club members. No matter what my personal preferences might be, I can't be entirely selfish in this matter." She laughed suggestively, then murmured, "Until the weekend then. . . ."

Chauncey hung up and turned to his friends. "True, mix us another round, will you? And brace yourself, Sam. We're going to be the first men in history to deflower the same virgins twice!"

CHAPTER THIRTY-FOUR

The Officers' Club blowout that Sam, True, and Chauncey gave to celebrate the verification of the thirteen virgins and True's engagement to Hilda may not have been the largest gathering that the club was ever to see but it would surely qualify as one of the wildest and wettest.

It started as an intimate drinking brawl in the Inn of Ultimate Delights, then moved on to the club, picking up in the process most of the officers assigned to the Fukuoka Military Government Team—except Colonel Dawgleish, who was staying late in his office awaiting an important message from Tokyo.

The liquor flowed unstintingly, the juke box blared out a selection of new records from stateside, the dancing was inventive and even acrobatic, and sobriety did not raise its ugly head all evening.

As a private joke that they could not share with the others, the three heroes made Mabel a white cape from a clean bar towel, sat her on the bar, and let her wreak havoc on a bowl of pretzels. On her head they placed a crown made of beer bottle labels pasted together and at her feet they propped a cardboard sign that read "Virgin of the Month."

Mountainous Ruby Whacker was there, too, belting down straight Bourbon, dividing her stare-and-glare time between True, whom she now knew had been playing free and loose with her affections, and Mabel, whom she suspected of having an unnatural interest in True. (Hilda was late in arriving at her own engagement party.)

At the very summit of the festivities, the door burst open and Colonel Dawgleish marched in, his face stern and forbidding. Ignoring words of welcome, he strode up to the heroes' table.

"I want to talk to you three," he said tersely, and then Chauncey saw the official message form he held half-crumpled in one hand.

"Death knell," Sam whispered sidewise.

Chauncey could only nod in mute affirmation.

"Come into the club office," the colonel ordered briskly. "This has to be private."

They followed Dawgleish into the club manager's empty office. The colonel draped himself over the manager's desk. He didn't remove his cap; his mouth was set in a stern, uncompromising line. All three of them now expected the worst.

Colonel Dawgleish dangled the message sheet by thumb and forefinger, but it was too far off for Chauncey to read.

Then suddenly the colonel smiled. And it wasn't his smile of grim irony or his smile of justice vindicated. It was a new kind of smile. It might even be called a smile of pride, thought Chauncey uncertainly.

"My boy," Dawgleish said gently, looking directly at Chauncey, "you and your men really came through for me. Now that the girls have passed their official—uh, examinations, we can dismiss that aspect of the matter. Even though I could be picayunish and find fault with your unorthodox methods, I certainly can't find fault with your results. Nor, I might add, can a *certain* party in Tokyo, heh, heh. . . ."

"Did you get a message from him, sir?" Chauncey prodded.

"Did *I* get a message from him?" Dawgleish echoed. "We *all* got a message from him. Here's what it says:"

He held up the sheet and read:

"CONGRATULATIONS TO YOUR TEAM FOR A JOB WELL DONE STOP YOU ARE ORDERED TO ADVISE FIRST LIEUTENANTS CHAUNCEY MAC-ARTHUR COMMA TRUMAN FOOTE COMMA SAMUEL BRUCE OF THEIR IMMEDIATE PRO-MOTIONS TO RANK OF CAPTAIN STOP WRITTEN ORDERS FOLLOW"

The colonel lowered the paper and regarded the three stunned faces ranged before him.

"Well, gentlemen, what do you think of that? Chauncey, I knew your unc. . . . I mean, General MacArthur. . . .would know how to reward the successful accomplishment of such a mission."

"Sir, I. . . ." Chauncey began, but then thought better of it. No need now, he realized at last, to make a fool of himself. After all, he'd never actually confirmed that he was a blood relative of the great man in Tokyo, had he? At least, no more than once or twice.

"There's just one other little matter," Colonel Dawgleish was saying. "I feel free now to ask this of you, Chauncey, because I know you won't mind and you'll do the job of a perfectionist, coming as you do from a long, distinguished line."

"What is it, sir?" asked Chauncey.

"I'm a little embarrassed," the colonel hesitated, and Chauncey was surprised to see a blush mounting to his cheeks. "In fact, I'm *more* than a little embarrassed."

The colonel waved his hands helplessly and was momentarily silent.

"What's the tactical problem, sir?" Sam asked intuitively. "Does it have anything to do with. . . .finding something?"

The colonel nodded vigorously. "Yes, it does. And I know you boys won't refuse me. After all, it's something very near and dear to my heart."

"I'm listening, sir," said Chauncey.

The colonel gulped, redder than ever. "Well," he said, "I want you to find. . . .Tokyo Rose for me."

"Tokyo Rose?" echoed Chauncey.

"Sir," Sam interjected, "I wonder if you would care to settle for Rita Hayworth or Ann Blyth or maybe. . .Shirley Temple?"

"I'm warning you, Bruce," Colonel Dawgleish thundered, "Any more of your impertinent nonsense and I'll cancel your Tokyo leave! Is that clear?"

"Yes, sir!" said Sam, coming to attention.

"All right! Now all three of you get on your way to Tokyo. Get your leaves over with. . . .and hurry back here."

Sam, True, and Chauncey saluted and turned to go.

"I'll have your new orders ready when you get back," the colonel said.

"New orders, sir?"

"Of course. I wouldn't want you captains wandering all over Japan looking for Rose without proper orders, would I?"

BOOKS ABOUT JAPAN BY JACK SEWARD

<u>Title</u>	Price in Japan	Price outside Japan
Non-fiction in Hard-cover		
JAPANESE IN ACTION	¥1,500	U.S.$5.75
(The classic commentary on the Japanese language—and those who speak it. Humorous, yet invaluable to the student.)		
HARA-KIRI	¥900	$3.00
(A historical review of Japan's unique method of self-destruction. Numerous graphic examples. The only book in English devoted to this subject.)		
HOW GOODS ARE DISTRIBUTED IN JAPAN	¥1,600	$4.90
(Translated by Jack Seward. Written by Prof. Y. Tajima, a leading authority on distribution economics. Now in its 13th edition.)		
Non-fiction in soft-cover		
THE JAPANESE	¥900	
(Vivid, down-to-earth chapters about the humor, women, crime, language, sex life, drink, food, religions, suicides, democracy, etc. of the people of Japan.)		
MORE ABOUT THE JAPANESE	¥900	
(Sequel to above book. Chapters about the love life, manners, violence, geisha, night life, business ethics, men, home life, capital city, etc. of Japan.)		
Fiction		
THE CAVE OF THE CHINESE SKELETONS (hard-cover)	¥1,000	$3.50
(American private eye unearths a fabulous fortune—guarded by skeletons—in the Amagi Mountains of Japan.)		
THE DARNED NUISANCES (soft-cover) Co-Author=Charles Beardsley	¥800	$2.40
(The hilarious adventures of three young Americans who go into hiding in the hills of post-war Japan with fifteen sexually-frolicsome young girls.)		
THE DIPLOMAT (soft-cover)	¥800	$2.40
(A serious novel about an American diplomat's affair with a lovely Eurasian girl in Tokyo, with a highly unusual twist.)		

* * * * * * * * * * * * * * * * * * *

If these are not available at your favorite book store, please write to:

LOTUS PRESS
Chofu P.O. Box 15
Chofu-shi,
Tokyo, Japan 182-91

(Add ¥100 per book for mailing and handling charges within Japan; 30c per book for foreign shipment by sea-mail.

* *

ORDER FORM

Title	Price in Japan	Price Outside Japan	Number of Copies	Total
JAPANESE IN ACTION	¥1,500	U.S. \$5.75		
HARA-KIRI	¥ 900	\$3.00		
HOW GOODS ARE DISTRIBUTED IN JAPAN	¥1,600	\$4.90		
THE JAPANESE	¥ 900			
MORE ABOUT THE JAPANESE	¥ 900			
CAVE OF THE CHINESE SKELETONS	¥1,000	\$3.50		
DARNED NUISANCES	¥ 800	\$2.40		
THE DIPLOMAT	¥ 800	\$2.40		

Total_____

NAME: _____

ADDRESS: _____

Amount Enclosed_____